The Naked Corpse

By the same author

The Naked Corpse

Bill Jackman

Jackman Publications

ISBN: 978-0-9927588-0-6

Printed and bound in Great Britain by
Lightning Source UK Ltd,
Chapter House, Pitfield, Kiln Farm,
Milton Keynes MK11 3LW

Chapter 1

THE WINTER RAIN beat fiercely against Joyce Brooks' office windows. She glanced at her watch again; it was the fourth time in ten minutes. At last the clock on the wall showed 5 pm. Feeling relieved at last, she closed and locked her drawer. Some of the others had left the office already. She picked up her bag and was just about to leave when her team mate interrupted her train of thoughts.

'You're in a hurry tonight, Joyce, what's the rush – are you on a promise?' laughed Sally Meadows, the 25-year-old blonde who worked on the computer alongside her.

'No, it's nothing like that, Sally. Remember, I told you that Friday nights were my girls' night out? Well, tonight is Friday, and it means I am meeting some mates for an evening of drinking and dancing, with out our fellas.'

'Hey! That's really great. You mean like a hen night, it sounds real cool. Hell! I wish I had something like that lined up for me,' replied Sally.

'I must dash. I don't have much time to get home and have my tea. I'm picking them up at 7.30. Have a nice weekend, Sally. See you Monday,' said Joyce, as she hurried away.

This girls' night out every Friday had proved to be popular, and having just recovered from a genuine case of Swine 'Flu, which had left her bedded down at home for eight weeks, she was very anxious to restart their weekly revelry. The other members of her trio had kept up the Friday night out, using alternative transport.

Joyce popped into the ladies before leaving the office. Everyone was wishing each other a good weekend. She looked in the mirror and applied a bit of lippy and a dash of powder before running a comb through her nut brown hair. She had no children to worry about. There was just Joyce and her husband Frank, and he spent all his leisure time playing with his model trains. It was really boring to sit there all evening watching him or the telly, so she was glad of Friday nights. She was five foot four and had retained her slim youthful figure. She smiled at herself in the mirror. *Not bad for forty-five*, she said, quietly to herself.

Frank would have her tea ready. As he worked from home as an accountant, he had plenty of time. In fact it was Frank who ran the house for her, doing the cooking and cleaning. The only thing he hated was ironing and even Joyce didn't like that very much. Frank was a year younger than Joyce. He was a tubby man with brown hair and matching eyes. His skin was sunburnt from being in Egypt for three years before she met him. Both she and Frank were very compatible most of the time, but he much preferred playing with his train sets than going out drinking and dancing.

She ran downstairs, pulling her coat close round her and made a brave dash to where her blue Mini Cooper was parked in the company car park.

'Hello love,' she called as she undid her front door and let herself in. 'What a night. It's pouring with rain.'

'Are you still going out in this weather, just as you planned?' asked Frank, placing a cup of tea on the table for her.

'Of course I am, silly; I have been looking forward to this Friday all week.'

'Rather you than me,' he replied. Joyce took a few sips of her tea, and then went upstairs, showered and changed.

As she was the one who did the driving, she knew how little time there was to get home, get ready and pick her pals up at 7.30. There were three girls in their party, herself and two others. They had been going out like this on a Friday night for at least three months, though it seemed like it was forever. The other two girls were also married; not that it mattered. They just wanted a night of fun like she did. As Joyce did the driving she was content with drinking fruit juice, whilst the others enjoyed their favourite tipple. They didn't do anything thing wrong – at least they didn't let on if they did. It gave them a break away from their menfolk, some of whom were working at night, some out boozing and skittles, and others stayed at home babysitting and watching telly; or in the case of Frank playing with his trains. They all patiently waited for their wives to come home at about eleven.

Joyce's two regular pals were Fiona Walters and Debbie Carter. They both lived in North Worrel. In fact all three of them lived only a mile or two apart from each other. All three of them loved the freedom of their Friday nights out.

One of their regular haunts was the Wicked Elf public house in Barlham. The reason that they chose to go there was firstly it was free, that is to say it cost nothing to go in. Plus, there was a skittle alley where the landlord put on a disco every Friday. Plus it was off the beaten track, and if the landlord stayed open selling drinks – well nobody seemed to mind, as long as there was no trouble. Plus, as it was out in the country, one could take a short cut in their cars down the country lanes thereby missing the police patrols out to catch the driver who was over the limit. Not that anyone was condoning this sort of thing, but that was how it was. And last but not least, there were plenty of men there for dancing with.

It was a very popular and cheap nightspot. Most of the women were in their late thirties early forties, and were out for a night of fun, a few drinks and a laugh. With most of them that was as far as it went, but sometimes a relationship built up between the regular male dancers and the female ones.

'Right! I'm off now, love. I think the rain has stopped,' she said, bending down and giving Frank a peck on the cheek.

'Have fun,' he called, not looking up from his railway track.

The reasons she drove every time were firstly because she was the only one with a car, and secondly she controlled what time they came home. The rain had stopped now, though the ground was still wet. As she entered the market place of North Wirrel she saw her two friends standing outside the Silver Spoon café, which was their agreed meeting place.

As Joyce approached them she noticed Fiona having a last puff on a cigarette. She knew that one wasn't allowed to smoke in the car and put her foot on the stub as Joyce pulled up.

'I thought you were going to give up that dirty habit,' Joyce called to her friend as she entered the car. 'Good God, Fiona you stink like an overfilled ashtray.'

'Oh don't go on, you know I keep trying,' said Fiona, as she sulked in the back seat. When all were seated and belted up Joyce set off to the Wicked Elf for an evening of fun.

Fiona was the youngest of the three, and the prettiest. She was married with two boys. Fiona was twenty-eight and blonde. She had a small slim figure and was a pretty, blue-eyed girl who liked to wear clothes that flattered her figure, most of which left little to the imagination.

The Wicked Elf was already busy. It was a pub with a big car park, lots of dark corners for the lovers. The three girls got their drinks and sat down together at their usual table.

'It's busy tonight,' said Debbie, sipping her half pint of lager. She didn't drink a lot. She was quite content to enjoy the atmosphere of the place, as long as she had a few dances in the evening. After all it was only a disco. It was not really intended for young teenagers, but for the 30–50 age groups. They played a good cross-section of music, catering for most tastes.

Fiona Waters had been coming here two months now; she always looked forward to Fridays nights with her mates .Her two boys Darren and Clive were aged ten and eight, and weren't old enough to be left on their own so her mum came round and babysat.

Debbie Carter, on the other hand, desperately wanted to be a model. But what she wanted, and fate bestowed on her, were entirely different things, because apart from giving her a massive pair of boobs and a large bum, both of which defied her constant attempts at slimming, her black hair was of a lank, greasy nature which seldom kept its intended shape for very long. This was one of the main reasons Debbie loved coming to the Wicked Elf; it added some variety and excitement to life.

Debbie was nineteen when she met Sidney at a local nightclub. He was a tall, good-looking guy, with tattoos up both arms. His hobby was weightlifting and his muscular physique appealed to Debbie. Sidney worked at a car plant, making spare parts for cars, and he was very busy earning good money. So when he suggested they get married after a short engagement Debbie was pleased to find a willing father for her child, who was only too keen to take the pair of them on. They managed to get a council house of their own and started by adding a baby brother they named Clive. Once the boys were at school she began work herself.

It was here at her place of work that she teamed up with Joyce Brooks and Fiona Walters. They were a happy trio, and their Friday night was an event they all looked forward to. Although she enjoyed her work at the factory she found she could get better pay as a beauty therapist assistant in the local hairdresser. So she packed her job in and moved into the town.

Fiona had an assortment of dancing partners when she started at the Wicked Elf, until one evening Wayne took her in his arms and taught her how to smooch. The combination of being in his firm but tender embrace and close to his warm body, together with his Boss aftershave, just made her head swim.

They danced every dance together. She loved the slow foxtrots. They danced as if glued together, their bodies swaying, and their feet hardly moving. She reckoned they didn't move more than two feet in the whole dance number. When she came off the floor she felt as though she had spent a night on the tiles. Boy, it was fantastic.

'Those two are getting too much attached,' said Joyce, sipping her fruit juice. Although she loved the atmosphere at the Elf she didn't mind too much if she danced or not; she enjoyed the atmosphere and watching the others.

'Who?' asked Debbie, looking round the dance floor.

'Fiona and that chap she keeps dancing with. Did you see them kissing just now. She'd better be careful.'

Two weeks ago Fiona had kissed Wayne goodnight. The following week they were kissing even more on the dance floor. There was no doubt she had a big crush on him and she fancied him. The dance over, she went back to her table where her mates were sitting, keeping her seat.

'You're enjoying yourself, Fiona,' said Debbie

'Yes he's really dishy,' Fiona replied.

'Don't be silly and get carried away,' Debbie warned her friend. 'That's your third gin and tonic, you know you can't take drink, don't do anything silly.'

'Mind your own bloody business, Debbie, you two get on my tits keeping on about what I do. Leave me alone and let me lead my own life. I'm not a little girl,' she snapped, very irritated at the wisdom her friend was offering.

'Is he married, Fiona?' asked Joyce.

'I don't know I never asked him,' she replied.

'Here he comes again,' said Joyce, as Fiona stood up, ready for the inevitable invitation. He held out his hand, inviting her to join him on the dance floor. There was a soft Sinatra number she found irresistible. After one revolution of the dance floor, Wayne whispered to her.

'Do you want to come out for a breath of air, Fiona?' he asked. 'It's stuffy in here.'

'It's cold outside,' she replied with a laugh.

'It won't be in my car. How about it? I'll soon warm you up.'

She giggled at the implication of his words.

'Alright, I'll just tell my mates.' She nipped back to the table where her friends were sitting. She went up to Joyce and tugged her sleeve.

'We are going out for a smoke in his car. I'll get him to take me home.'

'Don't be silly,' shouted Joyce, above the sound of the disco.

If Fiona heard, she didn't acknowledge her friend's advice. Fiona linked arms with Wayne and together, without a backward glance, went out into the cold night air.

The interior of the car was soon warmed up as they cuddled together. Fiona knew what to expect and she was quite prepared for it, despite the fact that this was the first time outside of her married life she had allowed anyone to touch her. The gin and tonics were making her head spin. She felt suddenly warm and relaxed. She felt slightly aware what was going on but didn't try and stop it. It was lovely. They kissed and caressed. Wayne was tearing at her clothes in his amateur impatience to get on with it.

'Are you on the pill?' he asked.

'Yes,' she replied. No other words were needed before action took place.

*

'They have been gone a long time, go and see what they're up to,' commanded Joyce to her friend.

Debbie went out into the car park. She didn't want to call her friend's name out loud, but she was concerned as to what she was up to, especially as she had been drinking so much. She didn't trust that man she was with. He looked a right smarmy type.

There was one car with the windows steamed up and rocking to a regular rhythm. She went in to report to Joyce what she had seen.

'The silly fool. What's got into her?' asked Joyce.

'He has,' said Debbie, with a chuckle.

'It's no laughing matter, we should look after each other. I won't come again if it's going to be like this,' said Joyce, very annoyed at her friend.

The lovers in the car didn't last long. Once Wayne had got his satisfaction, he got off and zipped up leaving Fiona unsatisfied and frustrated. He stood outside the car and lit a cigarette while she adjusted her dress and combed her hair. Having satisfied himself with his conquest of the night he wanted to get back to his beer. They both walked back into the bar; him in front. He left her to rejoin her friends while he went to the bar to enjoy his beer. He didn't invite her to dance for half an hour; in fact he hardly looked in her direction, but stood at the bar with his mates. She sat at the table with her friends, not saying a word, knowing that they knew she had been up to something stupid.

'What's up, Fiona. Have you and lover boy fallen out?' asked Debbie.

'No, nothing like that. I told him I wanted a rest, that's all,' which she knew very well was a lie. Her friends looked at each other. The last dance was called, he came over and taking her arm, swung her gently onto the floor and started smooching again.

'Wayne, will you take me home?' she pleaded.

'I thought you went home with your friends.'

'Not tonight, Wayne. I want you to take me,' she replied, cuddling up to him.

'Yes, OK, it's on my way. Eleven o'clock sharp. I want to get home for the match on telly late tonight.'

The dance floor soon became empty after the last dance as the crowds hurried to get their cars. Despite the fact that Wayne was suppose to be in a hurry, the two of them were nearly the last to leave.

'Will you be there next week, Wayne?' she asked him, as they entered North Wirrel.

'I expect so, and you?'

'Yes I'll be there. I enjoyed tonight, did you?'

'Yes of course I did, it was great.'

'Drop me off here, Wayne, I can walk the rest, there is a short cut down the lane. Besides, Roger will be out walking the dog at this time. I don't want to bump into him. He knows I usually come home with Joyce.'

'Are you sure?'

'Yes, it's only half a mile or less, I'll be alright.'

He kissed her goodnight as he unlocked the car door. A white van was about to overtake them and he waited until it had passed.

'Bye Fiona, see you,' he said.

Then he drove off while Fiona set off home via the short cut

*

1.00 am, next day

'Where's Fiona? She's never this late. It's one o'clock,' said Mrs Elsie Freebury. She was Fiona's mother and had babysat, looking after her two grandsons while she went dancing and Roger went for a night out with the boys. He had only just come in the house himself.

'Where the bloody hell is she? Christ, she is two hours late. She's usually home by eleven. What could have happened to her? Have we got Joyce Brooks's telephone number? Give her a ring, Elsie. See if she's home,' said Roger.

Elsie looked up the number and phoned it.

'Here, give it to me I'll speak to them,' said Roger.

There was a long pause before the phone was answered.

'Hello, Frank Brooks,' said a grumpy voice.

'Hello, Mr Brooks. Is my Fiona there?'

'There's no one here except me and my misses and we are trying to sleep. What's wrong?'

'My wife Fiona ain't home yet. It's gone one. She's been out with your wife dancing?'

'I don't know. I'll ask her,' he replied.

'Who is it?' asked Joyce.

'Fiona's husband. He says she hasn't come home yet.'

'Give me the phone… Hello, is that Roger? Hello, Roger. It's me, Joyce. I don't know where Fiona is…. No, she didn't come home with us.'

'Who the bleedin' hell did she come with?' demanded Roger.

'Her dancing partner. We tried to persuade her not to.'

'Who's he. I assume it's a he?' shouted Roger.

'I just know him as Wayne, that's all. Sorry I can't be of more help, Roger,' said Joyce.

'Alright, thanks,' he said, hanging up the phone.

'What shall we do now?' asked Elsie.

'What more can we do? We will phone the police,' said Roger, picking up the phone again.

Chapter 2

THERE WAS AN AIR of tranquillity about Minehead Bay in Somerset, especially at seven in the morning. It would have remained that way had not Mr Jenkinson's terrier Ralph, who was walking on the beach, suddenly let forth a loud series of excited barks. It was as if he were trying to draw his master's attention to something he had spotted, which he knew should not be there.

'What are you barking at, Ralph?' he shouted, as he strode out to where his dog stood yapping at something in the water. He couldn't see anything at first. Then putting his hand to shield his sight from the morning sunlight, he made out the figure in the water.

'Good God, it's a woman,' he gasped, as he bent down to tell Ralph to stop barking.

He looked around but there was nobody else in sight.

The serene calmness of the bay was broken by screeching gulls as they hovered over the naked body of the young woman who lay face down in the water. She gently nudged the rocks on each swell of the incoming tide. The lazy surf sought to jettison the pretty maiden it had carried along for days at sea. Her long blonde hair was splayed out like that of a mermaid, over the calm dark green sea. Her slender arms were outstretched as if welcoming some unseen friend or lover.

The only downside to this picturesque scene was the fact that the naked blond beauty was dead. Her vacant unseeing eyes were staring down into the dark water of the bay.

Frantically he got his mobile out and dialled 999 and contacted the local police.

'Good morning, sir. How can I help you?' said the police woman constable on night duty.

'There's a dead woman in the bay,' he shouted, excitedly.

'How do you know she is dead, sir?'

'She's naked and lying face down. She's dead alright.'

'What's your name sir?' asked the police woman, calmly.

'Malcolm Jenkinson.'

'Alright Mr Jenkinson. Just stay there don't touch anything, and don't let anyone near the body till the police arrive,' she instructed him.

'Right miss,' he said taking on the air of a man with responsible duties to perform – just like he had done in the war. The police car with sirens screeching turned up less than ten minutes later.

*

Horace Herbert Solomon hated his Christian names. He wasn't too enamoured with his surname either, but at least that had a history dating back many centuries. It was his father who was to blame for the unpopular choice of Christian names.

Mr Solomon senior badly wanted a daughter and because he was blessed with a son instead he insisted he be burdened with these forenames; as if it was his fault he was born a boy.

His mother called him Bert, and his school friends, once they got the message (usually, via a punch on the nose) that he didn't like his Christian names, called him Solly; an abbreviated version of his name he found quite acceptable. He carried the name of Solly into his adult life and it was in regular use by friends, colleagues and girlfriends.

His father insisted on calling call him Horace; right up to the age he left home, by which time his father had died.

Solly was tall, slim and good looking. He could have been a model or a film star if he hadn't chosen the police force. Six foot two inches tall, he sported a neat officer's moustache, and his light brown hair and blue eyes drew the attention of the ladies who met him. The only problem with Solly was that he was a diabetic. He wasn't on injections, at least not yet, he had been born with the horrible complaint.. Apart from that he was fine, and for a man of forty-five he looked in the best of health. He had completed a course at Sheffield University on Philosophy and had gained a Bachelor of Arts in it.

Solly was married to Colein. He had met her in Canada while over there on a course on Skeleton Recognition, appertaining to those found belonging to murdered persons. Colein was twenty- four, had just finished her degree in history, and had taken a diploma in teaching infants and juniors. She was nearly six foot, and had black hair and eyes that fired like live hot coals. This, together with her sun-brown features, made her a girl that turned men's eyes in her direction.

Colein liked sports and was willing to try her hand at any new challenge. She also had a great sense of humour. She liked eating out, the theatre, and shows. She read a lot and made a very good conversationalist. Solly was taken with her straight away. He found her challenging and great fun to be with, so it was inevitable that when the time came for him to return to England they wanted to be together. This meant a quick marriage, in Canada, with just a few friends and relatives.

They found a three-bedroomed cottage in a village just outside Taunton and although the cottage was old, it had been recently rebuilt and decorated. There was a large garage, front lawns and flowerbeds. Behind the house were a patio and a small garden full of exciting fruit and vegetables. They were fortunate in that they had an uninterrupted view of the Blackdown Hills from their lounge window.

The little cottage suited them fine. They furnished it with local pieces of antique furniture which they found at fleamarkets and sales. Within eighteen months they were weaning their first child, whom they had christened Charles. Although the name had gone out of fashion, they knew it would return and they both liked it. When Charles was two they completed their family with a blue-eyed, fair-haired little boy they christened Philip.

It was fortunate that the village boasted its own junior and infants school which was only four hundred yards away. Colein decided to take a refresher course to update her to English methods of teaching and applied for a vacant post in the school, which she was successful in getting.

It was Monday morning. Solly stretched out his long legs. Still feeling sleepy from Saturday night's dinner party, he checked the time. It was 7.50 am, ten minutes before his governor Superintendent Josh Roberts, OBE, was due in; plenty of time. He slid out of the comfortable cream leather seat of his blue Rover 75. It was the car his mother had given him when he was awarded his MBE three years ago.

He looked skywards. Overhead the low wheezing sound of an Easyjet Airbus seemed to be showing its reluctance to land at the nearby Bristol International Airport, having just arrived from sunnier climes. He picked up his laptop from the boot of his car and walked into Channel View police station.

Having passed through the swing doors of the station he stopped to glance at the notice board, and this reminded him that he had no detective sergeant as from today; his previous one had left the force on Friday. The lad had left early to earn a decent wage and get married. That left a vacancy and he hadn't a clue who would be selected to fill it. The office of detective sergeant was a great help to the job of solving murders and other crimes. It was someone you could air your views with, a companion – though not necessarily a friend. Someone you could chew the problems over with. He or she could be an invaluable aid to crime detection. Besides, two heads were better than one. Detective Chief Inspector Solomon's greatest hope was that he too might be promoted when his own boss Chief Superintendent Joss Roberts retired next year.

Solly headed towards his office and as he approached he saw that Josh was already in his office as his lights were on; he hoped to pass unnoticed but the sound of his footsteps gave him away. The fact that Josh was early usually meant that something very important had cropped up requiring his immediate attention. Solly was nearly past his door when he heard the familiar bark of his chief's voice.

'Solly! Come in. I need to talk to you,' he called.

Solly stopped in his tracks. The fact that he had been summoned so quickly by his superior, without giving him time to settle in and get a coffee, meant that the important item of news he had for him could not wait. Josh Roberts, when in the privacy of his own home and walking the streets, enjoyed his pipe full of tobacco. But because smoking was no longer permissible in the police station Josh sucked on an empty pipe. There was no law against that, and being a creature of habit he insisted on wearing his tweed tobacco-spot burnt waistcoat to work.

Solly obeyed his instructions and entered a room he knew well. The office was furnished with a desk and cupboards of matching light oak modern furniture. On the walls hung a mirror and several diplomas awarded for police work over the years that he had been in office. A dark fitted carpet added warmth to the large office space. In the corner stood a bright steel coatstand supporting Josh's raincoat and trilby. Several radiators were spaced around the room and the large main window overlooked the car park and entrance. A large glass window was fitted conveniently so that Josh was able to keep an eye on what was going on in the main incident room; the room where all the CID staff worked at their desks. On each desk could be seen a computer. The officers each had their own offices, which were suitably fitted out in a businesslike fashion.

Last year there was a special occasion for a party when Josh went to Buckingham Palace to receive a CBE from the Queen for his services to the force. It was pleasing for everyone at the station, that one of their senior officers had been justly rewarded.

He won a police medal for bravery for rescuing a young lady from a factory fire. He had made a rescue by emptying fire buckets of water on himself and running up a flight of burning stairs to recover the woman. Josh was five foot four in height and part bald. He suffered very badly with arthritis. He had one more year to go before he could retire to his cottage, where he and his fifty-five- year-old wife Sylvia could retire, keep bees and pursue their other mutual interests such as archaeology and joining the U3A.

'Good morning, sir. What's new?' asked Solomon. He had known Josh fifteen years, back to the days when he himself had first joined the Met and Josh was his Detective Inspector.

'A dead, naked blond woman is floating face down in Bridgwater Bay. I want you to be the Senior Crime Officer on this case. A SOCO is already on site, as are the forensic team. Give this priority, Solly. I have a funny feeling it could be the first of many.'

'I hope and pray you are wrong sir,' replied Solly.

'Well it is very similar to an unsolved murder which happened two years ago. Remember the naked nude at the Wicked Elf?'

'Yes I do sir. There were no clues to follow up, if I remember rightly.'

'The file is still open, Solly. Take it with you.'

'Yes sir,' he replied, and left the office.

*

Solly could see his office door was open, and that Detective Sergeant Wendy Morrison was looking at a file on the desk and was already sorting through its contents. She looked up as he entered and welcomed him with the smile she reserved for special friends and colleagues.

Wendy Morrison was a pretty girl. She was five foot ten inches tall, though her figure was a little on the buxom side. She kept her auburn hair short and her bright blue eyes sparkled with vitality. She was fun to work with, very clever, and painstakingly meticulous in all her undertakings. He enjoyed working with her and together they had successfully solved numerous cases. They made a very efficient team, and although she was only twenty-eight, she was already studying for her Inspector exams, which she stood a good chance of passing.

'Hello Sergeant. Have a good holiday in Spain?' he enquired, as he leaned over the open file on his desk regarding the dead girl found murdered at the pub.

'Yes thank you, sir,' she beamed.

'You didn't get married then?'

'No, I had a bust up with my boyfriend though. I caught him kissing my best mate, and they were both enjoying it.'

'Never mind, Sergeant. Plenty more fish ...'

'I don't want a fish, sir, I want a man,' she said, taking out her hanky and wiping her eyes. 'Sorry about that, sir. I'm alright now,' she said, as she picked up the old file.

His eyes returned to the file as he took it from her. He was quiet for a while as he scanned what little details there were.

'Have you looked at this case?' he asked, pulling a chair up for her, next to his.

'Yes, I started on it just before you came in.'

'Have you opened a file on the girl found this morning in Bridgwater Bay?'

'Yes sir, The file doesn't give us much to go on. Mind you, sir, she wasn't found till early this morning.'

'I see, who found her?' he asked.

'A man walking his dog, sir. His name is Mr Jenkinson. He contacted the local police station on his mobile, and waited till they arrived. The forensic team is already there,' she said.

'Yes I know already, the Superintendent just told me.'

*

The Inspector went back to reading the file. He heard a discreet cough from someone behind him. He turned, and saw a young man in blue tweed sports jacket and grey flannel trousers standing there looking a trifle embarrassed.

'Hello, who are you?' asked Solly.

'I have been told to report to you, sir. I am your new Detective Sergeant, Nigel Mitchell.'

'Are you indeed! Where are you from, Mitch?' Hearing his surname abbreviated to Mitch did not please Nigel, but he said nothing, despite finding it degrading and belittling. After all, he had worked hard to attain the rank and status of detective sergeant, a rank he was proud of. However, he thought better than to make an issue of it at the moment, but would save that for later.

'Puxton, sir,' he replied. He glanced around the office, quickly taking in the significant points of his new surroundings: the large table and matching flexi-back chairs; the flipchart and large white photographic board where suspects were portrayed so that the CID could form a visual picture of the crime they were investigating; the two filing cabinets, the back-to-back computers and printers. He had seen these set-ups before, but this time it was his.

He would be making reports and discussing problems directly with his new detective chief inspector, and his decisions on the cases in hand, would be listened to and acted on accordingly. Becoming a detective sergeant was his next step up the ladder to his goal of inspector. He knew he had lots to learn, but he badly wanted the chance to prove himself.

Solomon leaned over and shook his hand. 'Welcome, Mitch, you're my second replacement sergeant in a week. Let's hope you stay with me because it's very important for teamwork and continuity.

'Yes, sir,' he replied.

'How long have you been a detective sergeant, Mitch?'

'Just over a month, sir.'

'Bloody hell! Why is it I always get the job of training the sprog sergeants is what I'd like to know,' moaned Solly. 'I just get them thinking the way I do and they move on.'

Mitch didn't say anything.

'Sorry for the outburst, Mitch. I had a bad night and have a lot on my mind.' Mitch realised how his superior must be feeling; Mitch was himself a young sergeant at twenty-six; he had mastered his exams already and had an exemplary character reference.

'You're very young for this job, Mitch. I've got a son about your age. I hope you are brighter and more obedient than he is.'

'David was only a youth when he killed Goliath, sir,' responded Mitch.

'Point taken …Are you married, Mitch?'

'No, sir, and I haven't got a girlfriend at the moment either. I live on my own in a flat about two miles from here. Also, I have recently acquired an old A35 and done it up,' he said, proudly.

'A what?' asked an astounded chief inspector. 'We won't catch many crooks in a bubble car like that.'

'It's a smashing little car. I found it in a farmyard.'

'What other hobbies have you got, Mitch?'

'Martial arts, in which I am mastering several forms of self-defence. And I am a Freemason.'

'Blimey. I thought you were supposed to keep that hush-hush, especially in the Force.'

'They don't encourage it, sir. But, there are so many of the top brass of the police who are in Freemasonry they tend not to make an issue of it today.'

'I see, well we have a dead mermaid in Bridgwater Bay who needs our immediate attention. Are you ready for work?'

'Yes sir, I am ready,' said Mitch, excited to be on his first murder case on his first day at work.

Chapter 3

IT WAS A GOOD HOUR and a half drive to Minehead on a very
dangerous twisty road with very few places to overtake.

'We will go in a police car as I expect we will need the siren
most of the way. Come on Mitch, let's go,' said Solomon, picking up
his raincoat.

'This is unusual isn't it, sir. A novice detective sergeant going out
on a murder case on his first day.'

'It is, Mitch. You're right. It's just that they were short-staffed
and as you are in my department it's a chance to get to know each
other.'

'I overheard your conversation with the WPS sir, was there a case
like this before.'

'Yes similar, in fact too similar. We still haven't solved the last
murder.'

'Sounds like it could be the same murderer, or some one copying
him.'

'We don't even know for sure whether this one in Minehead is a
murder. It may be suicide. Perhaps she jumped into the sea naked, and
drowned.'

'Yes, I suppose that is a possibility,' agreed Mitch.

The journey to Minehead was uneventful and Mitch and Solly
chatted away about Mitch's new job and what was expected of him.
Solly also explained how he worked, so that Mitch could work
independently of him when needed.

As they approached the road leading off to the incident a
policeman directed them.

'Take this road sir, and then there is a track leading down to the
beach.'

'Thank you, Constable,' said Solomon.

As they approached where the body was, they could see that
forensic had arrived well before them.

The area had been cordoned off and a white tent erected over the
body which had been taken from the sea. Men and women in white
suits were engrossed in their professional duties.

Solly and Mitch donned their white protective suits, hoods,
overshoes and masks, and were escorted under the tape to the tent,
from which came a man he didn't recognise.

'This is Dr Griggs, sir,' said the Scene of Crime Officer.

Solly, introduced himself, and his sergeant. They shook hands, and other introductions were made to the forensic team, many of whom he had worked with before. The detectives entered the tent where the woman lay, face up this time.

'When did she die, doctor?

'About four days ago as best I can tell, she has probably been in the water all that time.'

'She must have been dumped in the sea some way from here, don't you think, doctor?'

'That's for you to work out, Solly. I am only here to ensure she is dead – which she is.'

'Were there any other witnesses? Apart from that of the man who found her?' Solly asked the SOCO.

'No! Just him, sir.'

'How do you think she died, doctor?'

'I don't think it was drowning, Solly, the scull is crushed in a small spot suggesting a sharp blow to the head. It could have been a hammer blow,' he said, pointing out the spot where it was made.

'I see, then she was stripped naked, dumped in the sea and left to float here.'

'That's how it seems,' said the doctor.

Solomon bent over to look at the corpse close up .He took a good gasp of air before doing so. It was really beginning to stink now, and no one wanted to stay in the tent for long. The girl's eyes had been pecked out and she was terribly disfigured.

'She's not very old is she,' said Mitch.

'Late twenties, early thirties, I would think, I have finished with her, she's yours now.'

'Thanks, for nothing,' said Solly, smiling and waiving him off.

'No ID sir?' asked Mitch.

'Well, there no handbag, and she's been stripped naked. Whoever killed her removed any watches and rings she might have had. It's difficult to tell until the post mortem, but there doesn't appear to have been a struggle beforehand. She possibly never knew what hit her, or why. We must get her identified as priority one when we get back. Make sure we have photographs and statements.'

'They will already have been taken by forensic, sir,' said Mitch, cautiously.

'I know that, Sergeant. I want pictures of my own – now!'

'Yes sir.'

'Was there any evidence at all?' Solly asked the SOCO, who appeared to be standing around, just waiting to be asked a few relevant questions.

'Not a thing sir. She hadn't left the water, and we searched the ground carefully before you arrived. Here is the name and address of the person who found her. We have his statement. There is a copy here for you.'

'Thank you, Sergeant,' said Solly, taking the paperwork and handing it to Mitch.

'OK, fine ... Alright, the forensic team can have her now,' said Solly, after a final look round.

'Shall I take her picture sir with my mobile and send it through to the station? That way Wendy could probably get us a match on her from missing persons,' said Mitch.

'Good idea, I'm glad to see you have a brain, that comes in handy in this job,' said Solly, very impressed with his new sergeant.

They were about to leave the tent when Mitch noticed something.

'Wait sir,' he said, returning to the corpse. 'Look here, sir; it appears as if someone has cut a lock of hair from her head.'

Solly turned to see for himself. 'Yes, you're right. It may not be anything but it could be our killer. Was he also a trophy hunter, I wonder? Murderers do the strangest of things, you know. However, it's another clue and there aren't many of those. Well spotted, Sergeant.'

They left the tent, dumping all their white paper protective clothing in the contamination bin outside.

'Let's get back, we have a lot to do,' said the Chief Inspector.

'Where will she be taken, sir?'

'Taunton, that's the nearest.'

Just then Solly's mobile phone rang.

It was Wendy on the line, telling him that the corpse matched the description of a woman reported missing early Saturday morning.

'What's her name?' asked Solly.

'Fiona Walters, sir,' she replied. 'She was reported missing by her husband at 0110 hours Saturday morning. Here is her home address,' she repeated Fiona's address, which next appeared on the phone as a text.

'Thank you, Sergeant. We are on our way now to interview her husband.'

Solly briefed Mitch as to what he knew about the body and who she was. 'We have a missing woman from Friday night, Mitch, it could be her – a blonde by the name of Mrs Fiona Walters. She's on our books and is listed as a missing person.'

'Who reported her missing, sir?'

'Her husband, a Mr Roger Walters.'

*

The two of them got into the police patrol car and sped over to Slinkwell Crescent. It consisted of a row of 1930 terraced houses in red brick that opened straight onto the road. Cars were parked on the overcrowded kerb.

The Inspector knocked at the door and a woman appeared, dressed in a pink blouse and red skirt. She didn't appear to have washed or combed her hair. She had been crying a lot. Her eyes were very red, and she looked as though she hadn't slept a wink. Solly guessed this was the dead girl's mother.

'Hello! What do you want?' she demanded of the men, as if they were a pair of unwelcome Jehovah Witnesses.

'Is Mr Walters in please? I am Detective Chief Inspector Solomon and this is Detective Sergeant Nigel Mitchell of Updownside Police.'

On hearing this, her attitude towards the two detectives changed immediately.

'Have you found my daughter, my lovely Fiona? Something's happened to her, hasn't it? I can tell.' She started sobbing.

'Is Mr Walters in? We'd like to talk to him.'

'He's asleep. He has hardly slept a wink with worry these last four days. He's been worn out searching every day. He's taken a week off work because he can't concentrate, he is so upset.'

'We won't keep him long; we just have to ask him some questions.'

She nodded her consent. 'Come in. I'm Jean Crombie, Fiona's mother, have you got any news?'

The two of them entered the lounge which was tidy and clean, with well used furniture and a large flat screen television. They stood waiting while she called up the stairs.

'Roger, the police are here. It's about our Fiona, something's happened, hurry, please,' she cried, hysterically. 'They want to ask some questions. Can you hear me, Roger? Are you awake?'

'Alright, I'll be down in a minute,' he shouted down.

A few minutes later a very sleepy-looking man entered the lounge. Although a young man, Roger Walters was already going bald on top. He had brown hair and brown eyes. Apart from appearing sleepy and carrying a two-day stubble on his chin, he wore an earring in his left ear, and had LOVE and HATE tattooed across the fingers of his hands. On entering the lounge he slumped, without a word, into an armchair facing them.

'Have you found her then?' were his opening words.

'Are you Roger Walters?' Solomon asked, he had to make certain he was speaking to the right man; one couldn't assume anything in a suspected murder enquiry.

He nodded his head.

'Yes I am,' he replied.

'I am sorry to have to tell you that a woman answering your wife's description has been found dead in the sea near Minehead.'

'Minehead? What the bloody hell was she doing down there, I want to know?'

'So do all of us, Mr Walters, we think it's possible she had been in the sea some time, and was possibly carried there by sea currents,' said Solly.

'Oh no, my baby is dead,' screamed her mother. 'She was such a good girl. Who would want to kill her?' She sobbed.

'We don't know how she died, or where. Nor do we know why. We won't know anything until we get the autopsy report later today, Mrs Crombie.'

In fact Mrs Crombie, we cannot be certain it is your daughter until we have had the body identified by her husband. Have you a current picture of her I can see?'

'Here's one she had taken with the family last summer.' She handed it to Solomon, who having seen it passed it to Mitch.

'Yes, it appears to be the same girl, I'm sorry to say, Mrs Crombie. May I take this with me to have copied? I will bring it straight back, Mr Walters?'

'Yes of course,' said Roger. 'Make a brew, mother,' he said to his mother-in-law. 'Do you want one?' he asked the detectives, but they declined.' Please sit down,' said Roger wiping his eyes. 'My Fiona ... I can't believe that someone would kill her. Was there any sign of a struggle?'

'No Roger, there wasn't,' said the inspector.

'Why the hell would anyone want to kill Fiona? She wouldn't hurt a fly.'

Roger was very upset over his wife. Mrs Freebury ran to her son in law and together they hugged each other in their grief. 'What do you want to know, Inspector?' he asked, breaking away from her.

'When did you last see her?'

'About seven o'clock on Friday evening, just before I went to play skittles.'

'Have you got any children, Roger?' asked Mitch.

'Yes, two boys one ten, and on eight. That's them on the picture that you have'

'Did you know she was going out?'

'Yes, she usually went out on with her mates on a Friday. I didn't have any objection. She was a good wife and mother to our children. She always came home at a respectable hour, and she didn't mess about with any one else.'

'You had a happy marriage, Roger?'

'Yes, you know, same as most, better than a few I know.'

'What sort of girl was she?'

'She was a happy, fun-loving girl; a good wife and mother. She always took care of herself.'

Her mother butted in the questioning. 'She told me she was going dancing. She usually went on Fridays. I expected her home by eleven, but she didn't come home at all,' she said, crying and patting her eyes with her hanky. 'I was here watching over the boys. I got my own key, and I wanted to make sure they were asleep.'

'Did she say who the friends were she was going dancing with?'

'No, not exactly, but it was the same ones every time. Joyce and Debbie, I don't know their surnames.'

'I think one of them is named Brooks. She does the driving. Her numbers in your phonebook,' said Elsie.

'Were they workmates?' asked Mitch.

'They used to be, but Fiona found another job last month.'

'Where do her friends work?'

'Langston Woollies in Codmore, about ten miles from here,' replied Roger. 'I just remembered, she said once that the girl who did the driving was Joyce Brooks, that's all I know about her friends.'

'Did you phone her last night?'

'Yes, she said Fiona didn't come with them. Apparently she was brought home by her dancing partner.'

'Who's that, do we know?'

'Only that his name is Wayne.'

'No surname, no address?'

'Sorry no. That's all we could get from Joyce.'

'That's fine, Roger, you have been very helpful,' the Inspector replied.

'Did she say where the venue was?'

'It was some pub. I know they went by car to it. Joyce did the driving. They picked her up in the town.'

'Can you tell me what she was wearing on the night she disappeared, sir?'

'Yes, she was wearing a blues and white dress I had bought for her birthday, with black shoes. Oh, and she had a sequined jacket on as well.'

'Did she have a handbag?'

'Yes, a small silver one.'

'Was she wearing any jewellery?'

'Yes, she wore a watch and a plain white necklace.'

'Did she have a mobile?'

'Why are you asking all these questions? You must know how she looked if you have found her,' said Roger.

'Normally we would, but she was found in the sea, naked, with no possessions at all on her.'

'Oh my God no,' screamed her mother.

Roger turned, and took her into his arms to console her.

'That's unusual isn't it, Inspector?'

'Yes, it is a very unusual case,' he replied. 'Do you mind if we look around?'

Roger looked at his mother in law for confirmation.

'Yes I suppose so, you won't find much of interest.'

'We're not looking for anything in particular. It's just that often we see something which helps us solve the case much easier. We are not conducting a full search, just a look around her room.'

'That's alright, help yourself.' Mitch and a PC went looking around the house.

'Which way does she normally come home?' asked Solomon.

'Well, normally she is brought right to the door, but of course that night she didn't arrive,' said her mother.

'That means she came home with someone else – possibly the killer, or she walked the last part and was abducted. Or she didn't set off home at all. We will get the answers.'

Solomon stood up when the other two policemen returned.

'Did she have any enemies, someone she didn't get along with?'

'Not really, no one I can think of.' Roger sat there with his head in his hands. 'What will the boys say? They will be devastated,' he said. 'Poor Fiona. You've got to find her killer.'

'Mr Walters, we will be leaving a FLO here, that's a family liaison officer. He is the link between you and us, he is here to help and advice. There will also be a constable on duty outside, and the immediate area will be taped off. We will be searching the whole area diligently for clues.'

'Yes alright. I can't get over it,' said Roger. 'It's just unbelievable, my Fiona.' He started sobbing again.

'What time did you get in, Roger?' asked Mitch.

'About quarter to one, I think it was. When I found she wasn't home, I phoned the police.'

'What time did you finish your skittles?'

'About ten thirty.'

'Then what did you do?'

'I went with some of my mates to one of their houses and played poker at his house till I was broke, then I came home.'

'What time did you leave the game?' continued Mitch.

'I don't know,' he said, scratching his head to try and remember. 'Must have been about half twelve, then I walked home; it's not far from here.'

'Surely you don't think it was Roger, do you inspector?' asked Mrs Crombie.

'No Mrs Crombie, but we have to account for his movements on the Friday night,' said Mitch.

'Yes of course,' she said, sort of understandingly.

'You will have to come and identify the body, sir,' said Solly.

'Of course, just tell me when and where.'

'We are sorry about the loss of your daughter, sir, and will do our utmost to solve this foul crime. We will leave now. Please contact us if you come across any information which will help us.'

The two detectives left the house and returned to the station.

'I think you handled yourself very well, Mitch, on your first murder inquiry. You asked the right questions.'

'Thank you, sir,' said Mitch, inwardly glowing with pride and satisfaction.

Chapter 4

THE POLICE CAR sped back to the station where Wendy and Detective Inspector Simon Collins were getting an incident room prepared for the murder investigation. It was complete with a computerised illuminated incident board on which Wendy was already attaching copies of the corpse that Mitch had mobiled to her. As Solly and Mitch entered the room, the crowd of detectives, both male and female sat down at their desks, waiting for the latest news from their Detective Chief Inspector.

Solly stopped to blow his nose. He suffered terribly with hay fever.

'Right, where was I? Ah yes! We have found the body of a young woman in the sea. She was naked and it appears she had been hit on the head.'

Just then Superintendent Josh Roberts entered the room. Solly was going to stop, but his boss signalled for him to continue. He was content to listen.

Solly continued, 'It's probable this caused her death. Here are some pictures we took at the scene with Sergeant Mitchell's mobile phone. They will do till the official ones come through.'

'Do we know who she is, sir?'

'Yes! Though we can't be certain until the body has been identified; which is going to be done this afternoon. But we have a missing person we have been investigating and we think this could be her.'

'How long had she been in the water sir?' asked the DS.

'It was estimated about four days. Her husband reported her missing at 1 am Saturday morning, so that's four days today,' Solly replied.

'We could find out where the currents run round that area, sir. It might give us a clue as to where she was placed in the sea,' called out Wendy.

'Good point, Sergeant. I leave that to you. Now we have a name for the woman. It is Fiona Walters. Her husband reported her missing. His name is Roger Walters. They live at ...' He looked at Wendy for the information.'

'It's 45 Slinkwell Crescent, Weston super mare, sir,' she called out.

'Thank you, Sergeant. We have no suspects or motive for the killing but the fact she had been stripped of everything, clothes and jewellery, proves that her killer didn't want to leave any clues. Plus the fact she had been at sea all that time means there is very little chance of finding external DNA to help us. I want to know where she had been, who she had been with, her place of work and friends and contacts. Sergeant Mitchell, our new detective sergeant, who has been a sergeant for a whole month.' This statement was washed down with cheers and boos, and various comments such 'Get some in.' From which Mitch knew he had been accepted by his colleagues.

Solly smiled and waved for silence.

'We have interviewed her husband, but he had little to offer, except he did give us the name of the driver of the car in which Fiona and her pals went out that night on a hen party. I want her, the driver, interviewed and anyone else involved that night.'

'Meet back here at 4 pm sharp. Right get to it,' he said, closing the meeting.

Josh came over to speak to Solly. 'I'm glad to see you are making some progress on this case Solly. Do you think it's a one-off?'

'Can't be certain sir, could be a copy of the Wicked Elf pub murder.'

'Yes, without a motive it's difficult to get very far, sir.'

'You're right,' said Josh, turning away. 'Keep me informed, won't you.'

'Yes sir, of course.'

Solly, returned to his office to handle a pile of paperwork that had manifested itself into a mountain in a very short space of time. He was filling in his timesheet when Detective Inspector Simon Collins tapped on his door.

'Come in, Simon,' he called.

Simon Collins was a tall, thin man. He was a graduate from Sheffield University, married with two baby girls. He had light brown hair and blue eyes and was a devout Methodist. Sometimes he wondered himself how he chose the police force to the church as he was very attached to both.

'I am going to interview this Joyce Brooks who drove the car and the other girl when I find out who she is.'

'Good Simon, take Sergeant Mitchell with you. He seems to have a knack at interviewing.'

'Right sir, I will,' said Simon, leaving the office.

'Send Sergeant Morrison in please,' said Solly. He had just got the words out when she appeared. Mitch was sitting at his table in Solly's office. She smiled at Mitch as she passed.

'Ah! Wendy. I want all CCTV to be checked around the area she lived in. From 10 pm till 1 am. Find out the name of the pub she went to, and I want all CCTV of that area up till an hour after the pub closed on the day she went missing. I want a search done along the banks of the Severn for any clothing or anything likely to be a clue as to where she was put in the water. Find out who this fellow Wayne is and bring him in for questioning .It appears he was the last one to see her alive.'

Wendy was writing all this down.

'I want a search done in the area of her house. There is a good chance she was snatched using a short cut near her house. We know that she was brought home in this fellow Wayne's car and it is reasonable to assume he dropped her off some distance from home and she walked the rest of the way. It seems likely it was on this walk that she was snatched. So don't bother too much with clues round the pub itself. Get cracking right away.'

'Yes sir,' she replied. She certainly had a lot on her plate to sort out. When she was in the incident room she allocated the various jobs Solly had given her to do. Her teams would report back to her and she would consolidate the facts before presenting them to the Chief Inspector.

It was late afternoon when a report was made available from the forensic officer. Josh was given the report to read and having done so he passed it to Solly. He read the contents with interest. The facts were that the diseased had not drowned. She had received a blow to the head which it was believed was used to knock her unconscious. However, the blow killed her. There was a distinct circular indentation to the skull which would not have been obtained whilst in the water. There was no other damage which was attributable to a third person.

There was DNA evidence available from the sperm found inside her, showing she had sex some time before she was placed in the water. The water in her lungs was consistent with that found in the Severn Estuary so it is probable that was where she was dumped. There was no evidence of rape or sexual abuse. There was some saliva DNA which matched the sperm and it was obtained from inside her mouth which was consistent with her engaging in passionate kissing. The rest of the report detailed statistics that were not important at this stage of the investigation. Solly passed the report to Wendy, who would be responsible for ensuring that all the detectives involved in solving this murder were kept up to date.

*

DI Simon Collins and Mitch went to Langston Woollies to interview the two girls. Joyce knew of Fiona's disappearance. He wondered whether she was aware of her friend's murder. They arrived at the factory, parked up and went to reception. Simon introduced themselves and told of their need to interview the two girls. They further explained they wanted to interview two women but not together, and asked that a room be made available where they could interview them. The production manager offered his office, after he was assured that the whole thing wouldn't take more than forty minutes.

'Joyce, you are wanted in the manager's office,' called Richard Dock, who was laughingly nicknamed 'Dick Dock' by his colleagues. He was a junior production manager, a bit of a wimp the girls thought.

'What for? What's it about?' she called, rising from her desk. She padded along the corridors and tapped lightly on the frosted glass door. The invitation to enter was not that of her manager but seated at his desk were two smartly dressed people men who she immediately twigged were police officers, and it had something to do with Fiona – she just knew it.

'Hello Joyce,' Simon introduced himself and Mitch. 'Sit down please. I am sorry to tell you but your friend Fiona Walters is dead, we believe she has been murdered,' said Simon.

'Oh no, how terrible.' She started sobbing. The detectives gave her a moment to come round. 'I bet it was that chap she was dancing with – Wayne something or other. I didn't like him, a slimy bit. He appeared to be a real womaniser. He was all over her. They were snogging on the dance floor. I think he fancied her. How did she die?'

'We're not certain till the autopsy which is being held today,' Mitch replied, picking up some notes to assist his questioning. 'And you say she said she was being driven home by her friend Wayne. Do you know his surname, or where he lives?'

'No nothing. As I said I didn't like the chap,' said Joyce.

'Can you describe what he looks like?' asked Mitch.

'Tall, about six foot and slim with brown hair, and he had a dragon tattooed on the front of each arm.'

'Thank you, Joyce, that could be useful. What was he wearing?' Simon asked.

'Jeans and a sweat shirt, most of them were dressed like that.' she said.

'What was the name of the place you were dancing at?'

'It's a pub called the Wicked Elf out at Barlaston,' she replied. 'Oh this is terrible, just terrible, poor Fiona,' she sobbed

'I would like you to call into the station as soon as you can and write and sign a statement. Here is my card,' said Mitch. 'Will you ask Debbie Carter to come in. She was the other lady in your group wasn't she?'

'Yes, she was, but she doesn't work here any more. She moved into town when she changer her job.'

'Oh, I see My records aren't up to date, have you got her new address?'

'Yes, it's Barnwell Fashions.'

'Thank you Joyce, we will trace her from there.'

'We will pick up their addresses at reception on the way out,' said Simon.

'Where to now, guv?' asked Mitch.

'We will go to the pub and see what they can tell us.'

They arrived at the Wicked Elf half an hour later. The car park was very large but empty except for a white transit van and a green Mondeo. Simon noted there were security cameras on each corner of the park. The landlord's name was above the door. It read Mr Jerry Long. The front door was locked so they went round to the back. The door was partly open. No one was in sight. Simon rapped on the door. Then he did it again calling this time, 'Hello, is there anyone at home?'

Eventually a woman appeared. 'Hello! What do you fine fellows want? We're not open yet, though looking at you I would guess you were the police, am I right?'

'Indeed you are right ma'am.' DI Collins went on to introduce himself and Mitch.

'What can I do for you?' she asked. 'I am Elsie Long, the land landlord's wife.'

'May we come in?'

'Of course, come through to the bar'.

They followed her into the pub.'

'Sit down. What is it you want to know?'

'One of your customers who was here last Friday night has been found murdered. She was last seen in the company of a man from here who it appears was her regular dancing partner.'

'Oh! Who could that be?'

'We were hoping you could tell us. We only know his first name is Wayne.'

'Oh you must mean Wayne Coldcrow. Yes I know him.'

'Can you describe him?'

'He's about six foot brown hair. I don't know what colour his eyes are. I have never looked into them,' she laughed.

'Any distinguishing marks,' asked Mitch.

'Yes, he has two dragons like figures on his arms. He's a nice fellow. I can't see him hurting anyone. Was it that pretty little blonde thing that he was always dancing with that got murdered?'

'It sounds like the same person. Here is a picture of her,' said Mitch handing over his copy.

'Have you a CCTV of the interior and the car park?' asked the Inspector.

'Yes, but we don't keep them,' she said.

'Don't you, not even for a week?'

'No! If nothing of importance has happened, we record over them.'

'That's not going to be much help is it,' said Simon.

'Did you know Wayne took her home?' asked Mitch.

'I thought he might have done. They were the last to leave. Her two pals had already left,' she said.

'We will need to interview all the staff,' said Simon. 'How many have you?'

'Well, there are myself and Jerry. Then there's Justin and my youngest son Johnny. He works in the kitchen mostly. Then we have extra staff to help in the bar at weekends.'

'You sound a very busy pub, Mrs Long.'

'Yes we are very popular with the locals.'

'I would like to speak to the staff tomorrow. Will you arrange it here for say 10.30 in the morning?' said Simon.

This was agreed and the two detectives said their goodbyes.

'We'd better get back. The boss said he wants us all there for an update as to how we have got on this today. I have a post-mortem tomorrow afternoon on Fiona's body,' said Simon.

The two detectives arrived back at the station just on time as the team were already taking their seats ready to hear from Solly.

The inspector came into the room, glanced at the assembled members present, then at the activity board to see if it had been updated.

'Right, I want to hear from you what progress you have made today on Fiona Walters's murder. We will start with Detective Inspector Simon Collins.'

Simon stood up, but Solly indicated he should remain seated. Simon told of his interviews with the two friends who were with Fiona the night she was murdered. Then he went on to tell of their visit to the Wicked Elf, and the results of that. Solly thanked him and Mitch for their good work.

Sergeant Wendy Morrison was next. 'My team have been working on the tides in the Bristol Channel and have tried to find a point on the Severn Estuary where she might have been dumped in the sea so that she could catch the outgoing tide which the murderer must have known would keep her at sea for at least four days.'

'Did you find a spot suitable?'

'We think so, sir. We intend to visit the area and hope to find traces of it being used recently.'

'Alright, fine, Sergeant Morrison. Have you handed the items of clothes and other items you found to Forensic?'

'Yes, I have, sir.'

'Sir,' said DI Collins standing up. 'She was stripped naked, so her clothes must be somewhere. I think it would be a good idea to search all charity shops and jumble sales in the area.'

'Excellent idea, get a team together and get started on it first thing tomorrow Simon,' said Solly, gathering up the paperwork for his file.

'Simon,. I will do the post-mortem call with Mitch tomorrow. You take Wendy with you and carry out the interviews at the pub.'

Solly wanted Mitch to attend the autopsy of Fiona. It was the first one he would have attended, outside of his training.

*

Early next morning Solly took Mitch out, intending to head for where the autopsy was to be held only to find they were too early.

'Let's go and have a sandwich and coffee while we pass the time,' suggested Solly. He was a devil for his tea and coffee breaks. It was part of his fascinating character that made Mitch take to him, not only a good cop, but the sort of guy he liked to know. They chatted amiably about their investigations, exchanging views and ideas.

'Can I ask you a question that's been bothering me from the moment we met, sir?'

'Feel free, what is it?'

'Why do you refer to me as Mitch, and not by my rank and title?'

Solly was taken back by his sergeant's question. He hadn't meant to insult the young man.

'I'll tell you why. Do you remember the crime writer Colin Dexter who wrote stories about Inspector Morse?'

'Yes sir.'

'Well he had a sergeant whom he called Lewis. That was his surname – no rank, nothing. We are in a similar position. The reason why I do it is because I don't want to keep calling you by your rank and name because it's too long. I won't call you by your Christian name because it undermines authority and is not allowed, and yet calling you Mitch is kind of halfway, not too formal and yet not exactly familiar. Let's put it another way: if I didn't like working with you I wouldn't be calling you Mitch.'

'I see, thank you for explaining, sir. Feel better about it now and am proud to be called Mitch. Can I call you Guv, sir?' he said with a big grin.

'No you bloody well can't,' he replied good humouredly. 'Any other problems?'

'No sir.'

'Right! Let's try and solve this bloody blonde murder,' said Solly, standing up ready to leave.

*

When the time drew near, they drove to the mortuary, passing through the heavy plastic curtains which led into the science department of the mortuary. Fiona lay on her back. Her head had been shaved and was ready for the skull to be cut open. Solly and Mitch waived their hands in front of their noses, because the smell from the body was so strong.

'There's tub of Vick over there, put a good dollop on your nostrils,' said Jerry Naptree, the pathologist. 'You get used to it in time,' he said smiling.

'You can see here a distinct circular indentation caused I think by a hammer blow. It has broken the skull and a piece has gone into the brain. There are no other marks of physical injury. We have found traces of sea water in her lungs but that is not what caused death. We are waiting for a match on the DNA match because she had sex the day she was killed; but we don't know who with.'

'Did she put up a struggle?' asked Mitch.

'If she did, Sergeant, she didn't receive any bruises and there is nothing under her fingernails other than what I expect to find, so she didn't scratch him, or her, whoever did this.'

They stayed and watched the autopsy. The top of the skull was removed, showing the indentation to the brain.

'It must have been quite a blow,' observed Solly, taking a close look at it.

'Yes the cracked skull has haemorrhaged the brain,' said Jerry.

Mitch had to run from the room when the stomach was opened. He couldn't stand it. He was only gone five minutes.

'Not much to go on is it sir,' said Mitch. 'Was the stomach alright?'

'Yes, there was some salad residue, and traces of an excess of gin in the bloodstream,' advised Solly. 'We will leave you to it, Jerry. I just wanted my sergeant to get acquainted as to what a proper post mortem involves.'

'That's alright Solly, any time. I'm going to investigate the vagina area, sure you don't want to stop, and watch?'

'No thanks,' said Mitch, heading for the door.

Chapter 5

THE PAIR OF THEM entered the incident room and there was an air of activity in the place, so much so that the Chief Inspector had to cough loudly and clap his hands to summon their attention.

'Right everyone. You have had six hours working on this murder case of Fiona Walters. Let's get together and consolidate our ideas.'

A reconstructed enlargement picture of the victim complete with eyes had been stuck on the incident board; it was the only one on there.

Solly opened the meeting. 'The mortician had concluded that the victim's cause of death was a blow to the head, and that she was dead before being put in the sea. What else have we got to report?'

'Sir, we have made enquires with the coastguard and they confirm that the currents from the Severn Estuary would float a body out into the Bristol Channel and that it might well end up in Minehead. Apparently this has happened many times before when people have drowned in these waters,' said Detective Sergeant Wendy Morrison.

'Thank you, Sergeant. So it appears she must have been put in the water within a few hours of being killed,' said Solly.

'What about the CCTV camera at the Wicked Elf and those in the town where she lived?'

DC Meadows stood up. 'Sir. DC Fable and I checked on the area she was picked up and supposedly dropped. We have pictures of her getting into the car with her two friends, and of her getting out of a car, just after a white van drives slowly past. We have the registration of the van and we have traced it to belonging to the owner of the Wicked Elf.'

'Interesting, but it proves nothing,' said Solly. 'Go on, anything else.'

'Yes sir, it seems quite likely that she may have taken a short cut to where she lived.'

'What do you mean?' asked Solly.

'We walked the area the two of us and there are lights on the short cut, in fact a vehicle can pass down it. One of the lights had been smashed and although there was a CTV camera it wasn't working.'

'So it seems likely that this is where she was snatched. You have done a good job, Constable.'

Josh was standing at the back of the hall taking it all in. He didn't interrupt the discussions at this point.

'It appears that the taking of Fiona was carefully planned. The killer knew she was going out and possibly where she was going. He knew the path she would take if she walked home, so he made sure the light was out. Her killer knew a lot about her comings and goings. There is a good chance she knew her killer. That's why there was no resistance,' said Solly.

A murmur of discussion at this conclusion revealed how the remainder of the detectives felt and agreed with Solly's perceptions.

'It still leaves the problem of a motive, sir,' said DI Collins.

'Yes I know. This is going to be a difficult case.'

'Do you think it is a one off, sir?' said Mitch.

'I bloody well hope so,' said Superintendent Josh Roberts from the back of the room. He came up to the front. 'You and your staff have done a good job up till now. We need the motive and the killer. What are your plans Solly?' he asked.

Solly thought for a moment.

'We need to find her clothes and where she was put in the water. Also we need a comprehensive list of everyone she knew, male friends, relatives, and acquaintances, workmates. We have a name and are trying to find him. We know where he lives, but he isn't at home.'

'Is he married?' asked Josh.

'No sir, that's what makes him so elusive. But we will get him.'

*

A short while later Wendy tapped on the door and entered Solly's office.

'Sir, there is a man downstairs who says he is Wayne Coldcrow and has called in because he was out with Fiona the night she went missing,' reported Mitch.

'Oh, that's quick, did he say how he heard of it so soon.'

'Yes sir, I asked him and he said he heard about her body being found on his car radio.'

'Alright Mitch, take him to an interview room and we will see what he has to say.'

'Right sir, I already have his name and address.'

Solly and Mitch entered the interview room together. A young man aged mid thirties dressed in a blue denim suit sat in a chair.

'Are you Wayne Coldcrow?' asked Solly, pulling up a chair and extending his hand to Wayne.

'Yes I am,' he replied.

Solly introduced himself and Mitch to Wayne. 'Thank you for coming in on your own accord. It saves us time. I understand you were out with Fiona the night she went missing.'

'So it appears,' he said.

'We have been trying to contact you. Where have you been?'

'I went to Monaco to watch the Grand Prix.'

'Oh, so you're into motor racing, are you, Wayne?'

'Yes, very much so. I got back last night. It was as I was driving home I heard about Fiona. What a horrible thing to happen to her.' He was leaning back in his chair very relaxed.

'And apart from whoever killed her you were the last person to see Fiona Walters alive,' said Solly.

'Yes, I am very sad at what has happened to her.'

'You knew her well?'

'Yes we were good friends.'

'Were you lovers?'

Wayne didn't answer right away. 'We did make love on the last night we met. Why is that important?'

Solly didn't answer his question but added his own.

'Where did you make love that night?'

Wayne looked embarrassed. 'In the back of my car.'

'Where?'

'In the car park of the Wicked Elf.'

'We will need DNA samples from you; they will be destroyed after six months if you are not guilty of an offence.'

Wayne said nothing.

'Why did she come home with you that night rather than return with her friends as she usually did?'

'She asked me. I said I would.'

'Did she ever ask you before?'

'No. I was surprised that she did.'

'Did you know she was married with a family?'

'Yes, but so were most of the women there that night. We know why they come along. It's easy to pick one up.' Mitch didn't like this chauvinistic cocky bastard.

'So you drove her home. What, right to the door?'

'No, she asked me to drop her off near the café in the town and she said she would take a short cut. She was worried about bumping into her husband who might be out walking the dog.'

'And that's the last you saw of her?'

'Yes, we arranged to meet again the following Friday.'

'Is there anything else you can tell us?'

'Like what?'

'Well, was there anybody hanging around the café who might have done this deed?'

'No, the only thing I might mention was I was followed from the pub by a white van which overtook me when I stopped to let Fiona out. I overtook it shortly after that.'

'What sort of van was it?'

'I didn't note the make or number, but it was moving annoyingly slow as if it was looking for something and wanted to be overtaken.'

'Did you get a good look at the driver?'

'No, I looked at him but he was wearing a woollen hat and was looking the other way.'

'Have you got a new girlfriend now, Wayne?'

'Not really, why do you ask?'

'Just a hunch. Are most of the women you go with married? We know you are single and out to enjoy yourself.'

'Yes that's true. No law against that is there. I find they are less resistant and we have no ties.'

'Thank you, Wayne. We need a sperm DNA from you, for which the desk officer will supply the bottle. Don't forget to keep us informed of your married dates.'

'Yes alright, can I go after that?'

'Of course.'

*

'Well I think we can rule him out, Sergeant, don't you?' said Solly, as they walked back to the incident room.

'I didn't like him, sir. He was too self-assured.'

'What's that? A posh word for a cocky bastard?'

Mitch didn't reply.

Chapter 6

BRENDA MARLOW was bored. She was bored with her husband and the same boring, lazy, spasmodic effort he called making love; or bonking as he preferred to call it. She was bored with the kids, on the want all the bloody time, and she was bored with the price of fags. It was just one bloody boring day after another. A girl shouldn't be subjected to a life like that; all work and no play.

She thought about her love life with her husband. One couldn't call five minutes in bed with Arthur lovemaking. A mongrel dog would show more attention and take longer than that. It was just drudgery, and besides she wasn't getting any younger. She was forty-three now. 'Who was it said life begins at forty? Well it bloody doesn't round here mate,' she said aloud to her self, as she unloaded the week's shopping from Sainsbury's.

The kids were at school, she had the rest of the day to herself and nowhere to go, no money, no fags. No wonder she was cheesed off. She slumped in a sagging upholstered armchair and found an unfinished 'dog end' in the grate and lit it, drawing in the remnants of nicotine the cigarette end contained.

'That's another bleeding nail in my coffin,' she said, as she indulged in one of her regular coffin fits; or fall of soot as Arfer called it.. She looked at the blue Smiths alarm clock on the mantelpiece, where yesterday's bills were being kept. Ten past eleven. Bloody hell! The morning hadn't long started. She went and made herself a coffee and wondered what she dare do to make life interesting.

This morning she had been with the girls all about her age, they nearly all had children. To hear them talk one got the impression that all of them felt the same about the drudgery of marriage and running a home.

The boring everyday routine of getting kids ready for school, the old man off to work and then housework and shopping. It wasn't fair. They all agreed that. They all wanted something interesting and fun, but there was nothing. They would take it if something came along to tempt them, try me and see, every one of the group agreed.

The lucky ones were those with their children at school had all day; especially if they didn't need to work.. Boredom and opportunity was a fatal mixture and there was always that old saying about while the cat's away. She knew for a fact that two women in her coffee group had had kids by another father. What did they call it – 'playing away'? And their husbands were none the wiser.

The menfolk don't go short, what with their skittles, football and pool and snooker. Then they have the darts matches and nights out with the boys. It's not fair, we got bingo if we're lucky, and we can afford it. Annual holidays mostly spent at Butlins or sometimes a week in Majorca; big deal.

*

Jim Macdonald was a big man, that's why he was nicknamed Big Mac by his friends and customers at the Silver Spoon café, of which he was the owner.

He was a Scotsman from Glasgow, weighing twenty stone with a mop of red hair.

He was married to Miriam, and they had a boy aged seven called Shaun and a daughter Agnes, a year younger. He never spoke of his time in Scotland and said he was a Scottish Englishman. Though he did let slip once that before he came to England and bought the café he was a junior school maths teacher. The walls of his café were adorned with framed poems. They were mostly humorous ones he wrote himself. People used to come in just to read them, though he usually managed to sell each of them a coffee at least. He was a very jovial soul. He was a school governor at Lakeside Primary and served on the town council. He was also an active member of the town's tug of war team.

Miriam by contrast was a small, slim, demure lady with horn-rimmed glasses and black hair retained by a Victorian tortoiseshell hair comb. They were an odd couple, but seemed happy enough running the café together.

The café was empty. Ten minutes ago it had been busy with the mums and their toddlers. They didn't spend much and up until last year the place was always full of smoke. Mac was pleased when that dirty habit was banned. It certainly made his life easier. He was always busy at lunchtime and the café had a good reputation for home-made cooking; especially Steak and Kidney pies. They always sold out. Miriam just couldn't keep up with demand. Mac knew all of his customers and they often came and told him of their family problems, and about their children, because as a school governor they often sought his advice.

'Hello Brenda, how are you today,' asked Mac, as she pushed the café door shut.

'Bloody cheesed off,' she said. She was never the most cheerful customer of his. She always had a moan and was dissatisfied with life. He always thought she should never have got married, but have said that she had always been a good mother and wife to her family.

'Where is everybody?' she asked.

'They were all here ten minutes ago. You missed them, Brenda. Do want coffee or tea.'

'Coffee please.' He took it over to her.

'Looks like rain,' he said, placing her coffee down.

'Go on cheer me up, that's all I bleedin' need. I got a line full of washing at home.'

He smiled to himself as he returned to the counter. Just then the door clicked open and a smart young man in a blue pin-striped suit came in and ordered coffee.

Brenda sat sipping her coffee and looking at the passers-by in the high street. Brenda was finishing off her coffee when this smart young man came in and ordered a coffee. He saw her on her own and no one else in the café so he went over.

'Hello, do you mind if I sit at this table. I know there are plenty of others but I am new in the town and thought you might help me.'

'No, help yourself,' she said, clearing away some of the debris.

'Thanks, I'm trying to find Wynchfield Close. Nobody seems to have heard of it.'

'Oh that's easy down here, second right, and go for a mile and it second on the left.'

'That's great, thanks,' he said, taking a sip of coffee. He wasn't that young, thirty or over, she guessed. He looked dishy, and very smart in his blue pin-striped suit, white shirt and blue tie. He certainly looked like a rep.

'Are you a rep?' she asked him.

'What made you think that? Actually I am an insurance consultant, you know, self-employed. I am my own boss with my own car,' he said.

'Very nice. I expect you get about, don't you?'

'Oh yes, never a dull moment. Trouble is when I am working in a place like this it gets lonely not knowing anyone, and staying at hotels on my own.'

'Poor old you,' she said, sarcastically. I wish I had that life. I'll swap with you. He held out his hand.

'My name is Jim Doulting.' She took his hand.

'Brenda Marlow, not the famous one,' she said, with a laugh. Jim liked her, she was cheeky and she had spirit. He liked a girl like that.

'You look prettier than she did,' he said, referring to the film star of that name.

'Flattery could get you into trouble,' she said, as a reply. He looked clean cool and dishy; he could leave his slippers under her bed any time. She never got the chance to talk to nice intelligent young men.

'Are you married, Jim?'

'Good heavens no. Why make one woman happy when I could make dozens happy by staying single.'

'I can see you're married,' he replied.

'Yes, I'm married alright, with three kids, two at school and the third starts next week.'

'You will have time on your hands then.'

'Yes that's true.'

'Do you go dancing?'

'You're a nosey bugger aren't you?' she said suddenly.

'Sorry, just trying to make conversation.'

'Chat me up, more like it.'

'I'm sorry I didn't mean . . .'

'No I should apologise for being tetchy, yes I like dancing, but haven't done any for years.'

'I understand.'

There was a distinct pause in the conversation; rather like a battle of wits. She wanted him to ask her out, and she thought he wanted to do it, but either he was shy or nervous.

'Do you want to ask me out dancing one night?' She boldly asked him. He was too stunned to reply for a moment.

'Would you like to go out one night Brenda?' he finally said.

'Yes, yes I would.' They looked at each other, both knowing what the other wanted: besides companionship.

'Right, when?'

'There's a dance over at Trimscombe village hall. Nobody I know goes there,' she said.

'When?'

'This Friday?' she said excitedly.

'No, I'm working that evening,' he replied, getting out his diary, and knowing he had a date already for that night.

'This Saturday?' she suggested, expecting him once again to make an excuse.

'Fine, this is my card, see it's got my name on and my mobile,' he said, as he handed it to her.

Brenda grabbed a napkin and wrote her mobile number on it, then handed it to him.

'I'll pick you up, where? Outside here at 7.30?'

'Yes that's fine, wait for me if I'm a bit late. Anything untoward we phone each other, OK?' she said.

He agreed. He squeezed her hand, smiled and left the café.

Brenda sat there, not believing what had happened in half an hour. Bloody romance had come into her life at last, she thought. With a spring in her step she made her way back home.

*

On the Saturday, Arthur, her husband, was on nights as usual. This generally meant an evening at home watching television, but tonight she managed to convince her mum to babysit as she told her she was going to Bingo with a friend and then on to her friends house for supper. When she arrived at the café the blue car was there waiting. Jim opened the door for her with a welcoming smile.

'Glad you could make it. You look very pretty.'

'Thank you, let's get going. There are too many nosy people round here.'

Jim glanced at Brenda's tall, slim figure appreciatively. Brenda had re-permed her brown hair for the occasion and was wearing her emerald blue necklace and earrings.

Jim moved the car along and out of the town. From the illuminated dashboard, soft orchestral music was playing.

'I was wondering if you would like to go to a pub for a meal and drinks as opposed to the village dance you mentioned.'

'Oh yes, definitely. I would much prefer that, only I've just had me tea.'

'Oh dear, what a shame, only I know a nice pub up in the hills where you can relax and enjoy the evening.' She leaned back and closed her eyes as the big motor purred its way into the country. This was just what she had in mind for relaxation.

The car stopped outside the Happy Chappie pub; the car park was comparatively empty, which was just what they both wanted.

'This pub has a reputation for very good home-cooked food, I'm sure you will enjoy it.'

'I've already had my tea,' she said again

'Don't worry, you don't have to eat a big meal.' They entered the three hundred year old pub and Jim had to bend low to avoid banging his head. The pub was illuminated with low wattage soft lighting. The yellowed smoke stained walls added to the aura of a place of comfort and age. They found a little nook and having got settled they perused the menu.

'Golly, look at the prices? You can't afford that. I will just have a ham sandwich, if you don't mind.'

'No that's OK, have what pleases you,' said Jim, who felt a little foolish as he was starving and looking forward to a good three-course meal, which he couldn't very well indulge in with a lady who just wanted a ham sandwich; so he chose a curry.

Brenda did agree, after some persuasion, to have a glass of wine. Jim sensed that this evening was going to be hard work. Unfortunately Brenda wasn't versed in literature or the arts, though she was up to date with the soaps.

'Where do you live, Jim?'

'My home is in Wiltshire in a small village just outside Devizes.'

'Have you got any brothers and sisters?'

'I have an older sister who lives in America.' said Jim, wishing he could find some way of getting this boring conversation going. He had only invited the girl out for one reason, and she must be stupid if she didn't realise it. He sensed Brenda had second thoughts about a night of fun together, though he could be wrong. Perhaps he should have chosen his evening's companion more carefully and taken his time. He tried to keep the conversation going, though it was difficult and there were many silent moments. Their food and wine came and it was good; even the ham sandwich looked appetising. His curry seemed to fire his desire for some sexual Saturday night play. He kept topping her glass up as well as his own.

'You're driving, don't forget,' she said.

'I will be alright I have only had three small glasses over the course of two hours.'

My, this girl really was fun, he thought. Eventually the time had come to make a move. He tried to make conversation as they drove leisurely back to town. The dashboard clock showed 9.38. He was trying to find a secluded spot where he might try his luck with her. There were, he remembered, some rifle ranges nearby. There would be no one on them to night.

'I know a shortcut,' he said, swinging his car off the main road onto a country lane. He drove along thinking to himself that the night wasn't over yet and it was worth a try to see if Brenda enjoyed kissing as a prelude to more exciting things.

Suddenly out of the darkness and approaching them at speed came a tractor. Jim pulled the car over onto the grass verge to let it pass.

Once it had done so he tried to move off. The wheels of his car just spun in the soft mud.

'Damn,' he said, realising they were bogged down.

'What's the matter?'

'We're stuck.'

'What?'

'We're stuck, the car is bogged down.'

'Oh dear. I have to get home, it's getting late.' Jim tried to keep his cool.

'There is nothing I can do, wait here.' He got a torch from the glove compartment and went to see how bad it was. The car was up to its axles in mud. It would need a tractor, or something to shift it. They were roughly six miles from town and it was starting to rain. *What a bloody waste of time tonight has been*, he thought.

'What's wrong? Can you shift the car? I need the toilet,' Brenda shouted from the open car window.

'Oh shut up, woman. I have to shift the car. I can't leave it here.'

'Why not? We could walk it.'

'Firstly, because it's not my car.'

'You said—'

'I know what I said, but it's not,' he replied sharply, showing his irritation at the predicament he found himself in.

'What we going to do?' she said, starting to cry.

'Get out the car and we will walk back down the lane. I saw a cottage with lights on. We will knock them up'.

'What about your mobile – phone the AA?'

'I have tried that and can't get a signal. We're surrounded by trees.'

Brenda got out the car and shut the door. 'It's pouring with rain – we'll get soaked. Hell! I have just cut my hand on some brambles. Have you got a hanky?' she asked.

'Yes, here,' he said, passing his clean one over. Having mopped up the small amount of blood she handed it back.

'Gosh that's sore,' she moaned.

'Oh come on, so we get wet, let's start walking,' said Jim.

Eventually they reached the little cottage, and Jim knocked on the door, which an elderly man eventually opened. Jim explained they were stuck.

The man's wife appeared. 'You poor dear, come on in and dry off. Billy, see if you can help move his car.'

'Wait in the house,' said Billy. 'I will get a jack and spade,' Jim was very grateful. Together they set off back to the car.

'What are you doing down here on this farm track? It only leads to the old ranges,' he said.

'Yes, I realise that now, I thought it was a short cut,' said Jim, lamely.

It took nearly two hours to get the car out; they were both tired and muddy.

'Come on, let's go back and pick your wife up,' said Billy. 'She is your wife isn't she?'

'What? Yes of course she is.'

'Where do you live?'

'In Clevedon.'

'That's some way from here.'

'Yes I took her out for an evening meal to celebrate our anniversary.'

He realised he was piling one lie on top of another. When Billy opened the door Brenda was waiting.

'Thank you both for your help, especially you, Billy,' said Jim.

'You keep to the main roads in future young man,' was Billy's parting reply. Once they were back in the car Brenda started on at him.

'I'm going to be in trouble. My mum's babysitting, she thinks I've been to bingo.'

They were back on the main road now and Jim found he could get a signal.

'Here, phone her up on my mobile, make some excuse for being a bit late.'

'Alright, pass me the phone,' she said. Having done that she felt more relaxed.

'Do you know, they think we're married,' said Jim.

'Did you tell them we were?'

'Yes, I had to think fast – why?'

'I told her we were just friends out for a drink and that you took a wrong turning.' They both laughed heartily at the situation they had been in.

'Can I see you again, Brenda?'

'Are you sure you want to. It hasn't been a lot of fun, has it?'

'I'm sure it will be better next time. Shall I drop you off at the café?'

'Yes that will be fine.' He stopped the car and she gave him a sisterly, non-passionate kiss before getting out and shutting the door. He would take her out again; he felt it was worth while.

Tonight had been a dead loss; even he didn't feel like making love to the girl after digging the car out of the mud. He had her number and she had his, so there was no reason why he shouldn't see her again. Besides he wouldn't let a muddy ditch ruin a conquest.

Chapter 7

THE PHONE RANG on the reception desk of the police station.
'Is that the police?'
'Yes sir, how may we help?'
'My misses didn't come home last night. I want to report her missing,' said Arthur Marlow.

*

Wendy was talking to Solly in the incident room, going over the evidence – well, the little they had.

'Right, that will do for tonight,' said the DCI.

The occupants of the incident room were just breaking up when the door burst open and the desk sergeant came in and announced loudly, 'Sir, a woman's body has been found by a fishing boat in the English Channel. It is being brought ashore tonight.'

'Thank you, Sergeant. I can't wait to see her,' said the Detective Chief Inspector. This could confirm his worse fears. A serial killer was active on their patch.

Chief Inspector Solomon did not want to hear the news that another body of a woman had been found at sea, because he feared he might have a serial killer on his patch. He didn't voice his opinion out loud but there was always a risk of this when an unreasonable murder has taken place. Somebody had gone to a lot of trouble to hit a woman on the head, then take her somewhere he could strip all her clothes off, and then dump her in the sea; but not before taking a snip of her hair as a trophy. It was a very difficult case to solve with no clues, no witnesses and no proper suspects or motives.

'Do you think the killer knew Fiona Walters, sir?' asked Mitch, when back in Solomon's office.

'An interesting question, Mitch, the answer to which could make a big difference to the motive,' said Solly.

'I thinks it's more likely he didn't know her, sir. Murderers with revenge on people they want to kill don't go to all that trouble, do they?'

'Not usually, if he didn't know her then did he choose her at random, was she in the wrong place at the wrong time; could it have been any girl who happened by?' suggested Solly, feeling very perplexed, and desperate for some answers. 'I would like to think it was a one off, but we will wait to see what the boat brings in tomorrow.'

*

DI Simon Collins and Wendy were at the Wicked Elf next day as arranged, to interview staff. Mitch was working with Solly that morning so she stood in for him.

Mrs Long greeted them at the door and brought them through to the dining room.

'Can we see the skittle alley, please?' asked Wendy.

'Yes, I'll get the key. There's not much to see,' she said, getting the key from under the bar. They entered the alley, which, when she turned the lights on, appeared as a proper skittle alley, with the pins standing up at one end, ready to play.

'Of course we clear all this away when the dancing is on.'

'Where was Fiona sitting that night, here?' asked Wendy.

'Yes, in the chair near you, she comes with two friends and they sit together. Oh dear, this is very sad that a girl has been murdered who was here dancing. Do you know who did it, or why?'

'No but there is a lot about it in the papers this morning,' offered Wendy. There was a noise from the public bar.

'That will be my husband. Do you want to speak to him?'

'Yes please,' said Simon.

Janet called him into the skittle alley; introduced the detectives and explained why they were there .Jerry Long showed genuine surprise and grief at the loss of one of his customers.

'This is bad, not only for the family of the deceased, but for trade,' sighed Jerry

'Did you know the woman?'

'Yes, very well, she often came to the bar and was chatty and happy. She was a very pretty girl, though she did wear clothes which tended to be on the revealing side.'

'Were you fully staffed a week last Friday?'

'Oh yes, I remember because there was a birthday party here for the regulars.'

'Did you notice any strangers here that night?'

'There are always strangers, this is a pub after all,' said Jerry.

'Did she make any statement which implied that evening was any different. Was she meeting anyone?'

'No nothing,' said Jerry.

'Apparently Wayne Coldcrow her dancing partner drove her home, so as far as we are concerned he is the last person to see her alive.'

'And you say Wayne and Fiona left together,' asked Wendy.

'Yes, they were some of the last to leave, they waved and shouted goodbye.'

'There is one last thing, Mrs Long, I would like the list of all your staff please, with addresses and telephone numbers. We need to speak to them all.'

'Certainly, Inspector. I will get a list for you.'

Five minutes later she was back. 'Here you are, Inspector. They should all be in soon as we have a busy lunch time usually on a Wednesday.'

'Thank you, Mrs Long. Please send them in one by one as they arrive.'

The first one to come in was their son, Justin. He entered the room giving a cheery smile and bidding good morning to the detectives.

'Good morning, Justin. You are the son of your father's first marriage, is that right?'

'Yes.' He sat there looking very confident. He was dressed in cord trousers, a flannel shirt and a windcheater. He had a thin face with a pale complexion, light brown hair and blue eyes.

'How old are you, Justin?'

'Forty-two,' he replied.

'And you work here full time?'

'Yes.'

'What, bar work?'

'Yes mainly, and I help in the kitchen.'

'Where do you live?'

'Here with my parents.'

'I see. Are you married?'

'No.'

'Never have been?'

He shook his head

'Courting?'

'No, not exactly but I have girlfriends.' Justin felt he ought to explain why he hadn't settled down by now. 'I have been abroad for many years, working on oil rigs.'

'Oh yes, what company?'

'Shell, in Iraq.'

'You have lost your tan, Justin.'

'Yes,' he laughed. 'That's through working here.'

'Do you remember seeing Fiona Walters here in the pub?'

'Yes, she was a pretty and cheerful girl. I liked her. I would like to get my hands on the man who killed her.'

'Did you leave the pub after Fiona had left to go home.'

'Yes, I took the van out to get it filled up as we were going to Cash and Carry next morning.'

'Where did you fill it up?'

'At Asda. It will show up on their CCTV,' he said, reassuringly

'Are you the only child, Justin?'

'No, I have a brother. He visits us quite often. His name is Johnny. He is a little retarded, but he is a good driver, so we let him drive the taxi for us. The ladies love him and think he's cute.'

'Where can we find him?'

'He should be in later; he normally calls in on a Wednesday.'

'Alright Justin, thank you, sign your statement here please. By the way, Justin, was your brother working the night Fiona died?' called Wendy, as he was leaving.

'Ask him yourself, he's just arrived,' replied Justin, going out of the door.

Johnny came into the room unannounced. He stood there looking round, unsure what he should do.

'Hello, are you Johnny?' asked Wendy.

He was a big lad and walked with a bit of a limp. He had long black hair a round podgy face and thick lips. He was also constantly smiling.

'Yes.'

'Can we have a talk to you, Johnny? We are police detectives trying to find out who killed Fiona who used to come here. Did you know her?'

He shook his head. 'Don't think so,' he replied.

'She was a pretty, blonde girl,' said Wendy, passing him a picture of her.

He took it and peered at it for a few moments. 'Oh yes. I remember her. Father said she was a tart,' he replied with a grin.

Wendy felt uneasy in Johnny's presence. 'Did you see her the night she went missing? It was two weeks last Friday.'

'No. I was out doing taxi runs, that's all I know.'

'Alright, Johnny, here is a copy of your statement, will you sign it at the bottom?'

Much to their surprise he signed his name with no trouble.

The two girl bar staff and waitresses could add nothing of any significance so having concluded their interviews the detectives returned to the station.

'That place gives me the creeps.'

'Yes, I admit I felt a little uneasy myself,' said Simon.

'That didn't reveal very much did it sir.'

'No, not a great deal. I wish she had kept her CCTV tapes. They might have been important.'

'If the killer had been there he would have known the cameras were in operation, he would be a fool to expose himself on CCTV,' observed Wendy.

Solly was called down to reception as a man had come in seeking assistance. The PC on duty addressed him as he came into reception

'Excuse me, sir. We have a man here who wants to report his wife is missing.'

Solly stopped and walked over to the reception desk.

'Can I be of help?' he asked

'This is Mr Marlow, sir, he is reporting his wife missing.'

Frank Marlow sat on a chair in reception, his head in his hands. He had been crying. He looked up at the detectives. Frank was of medium build, wearing denim jacket and trousers and trainers. He had brown hair in need of a wash and was sporting two days' growth of hair on his chin.

'When did she go missing, Mr Marlow?'

'Last night, she didn't come home; I just know something's happened to her,' he said tearfully.

'Come into the interview room, Mr Marlow,' said Solly, showing him the room.

The three of them entered, and sat down. Stan was very upset and tears rolled down his stubbly chin.

'Can we get you a drink, Mr Marlow? Would you like a tea, or coffee?'

'Yes please, tea,' he replied.

'Get him one, Sergeant, would you please.'

Mitch knew he was not the tea boy but he was doing his boss a favour so without comment he fetched three from the canteen.

'Constable,' said Solly to the uniformed man on the door. 'I want you to take down all Mr Marlow's details, including address, email and mobile numbers.'

This was done while drinking tea. When they were finished and Mr Marlow was once more settled, and ready to be interviewed, Solly started again.

'Right, Mr Marlow, tell me all about it from the beginning,' said Solly.

'There's not a lot to tell. Brenda went off to bingo at 7.30 last night.'

'Does she go regularly?'

'Yes most weeks on a Saturday. I had a snooker match on in the British Legion, which is my local, and usually we get home at the same time. But last night was different. She phoned her mum, who was babysitting, to say she would be a bit late as she was seeing a friend afterwards. She never said who this friend was, only that mum was not to worry. Well, when she never came home we didn't have a name to ring. I went out and searched the streets but there was no one around. We went to bed about three, and then I came here to report her missing.'

'How did she get to bingo?' asked Mitch.

'By bus,' Mr Marlow replied. 'Only ...'

He hesitated, as if he knew he should, but couldn't bring himself to continue.

'Go on, Mr Marlow. Is there something else we should know?' asked Solly.

'Yes there is. She never went to bingo that night. I spoke to one of her friends who she meets there, she phoned me this morning to ask where Brenda was, and was she ill. That's when I learnt she hadn't been to bingo. I don't know where she was.'

'I see. Do you think she was seeing anyone else, a man?'

'I don't know. She has never been unfaithful before.'

'I don't suppose you have a picture of her on you,' asked Mitch.

'As it happens I have, taken last Christmas. That's our two children, Doug and Penny.'

'Nice family,' said Solly. 'We will have this copied and return it to you.'

'What's going to happen now?' asked Mr Marlow.

'We will list her as a missing person and she will be broadcast to all the police stations on the Web. In the meantime we will carry out a search of your area and further afield. It is not going to be easy. We don't know if she is dead or gone off with someone. Are all her clothes intact at home?'

'Yes everything. Her credit cards and mobile are at home, which is unusual.'

'Yes, not the sort of things one would leave if they had no intention of returning,' said Solly. 'Alright leave it with us, we will get on to it right away. Here is my card if you have any new ideas or evidence that may help.'

Solly stood up and shook hands with the deflated man. 'Don't despair, Mr Marlow. Most missing persons turn up with a plausible excuse'.

He gave a week smile of acceptance, and said thank you.

Solly saw them out.

Chapter 8

'WHAT DO YOU think sir, could this be number two?' asked Mitch.

'It could be. Notify missing persons and get the police helicopter and coast guard to search the Severn estuary as soon as possible. If she is a victim we want to bring her in before the tide carries her right out to sea.'

'Yes sir. I will arrange that right away,' said Mitch.

*

'How did you get on Simon?' asked Solly when he appeared in his office after his visit to the Wicked Elf.

'There wasn't a lot to learn sir. Especially as we have already interviewed Wayne Coldcrow. They have CCTV but have recorded over it. We met and interviewed the landlord and his wife. They were very cooperative. One wonders if the killer was at the pub. He could have been as there were plenty of strangers there that night.'

'We have that other body found at sea last night. It should be in the morgue this afternoon .Find out what time we can call, if they don't know make sure they tell us when they do,' said Solly.

'Come on, Mitch, we will go and see the boat come in with her body on board. The details are in the incident room.'

Mitch followed obediently behind him as they made their way to the police car and their driver.

'The fishing boat is coming into Watchet harbour. I want to get there before they unload the body,' said Solly.

The area that the fishing boat was unloading on was taped off with police tape. There were already TV cameras there and some Press boys.

'Doesn't bad news travel fast,' observed Solly, as he ducked under the security tape. A uniformed policeman came over to intercept them, but having shown their cards they were granted access. They had to stand and wait thirty minutes before the boat came in with its grizzly cargo. A black zip-up body bag was unloaded first. Solly walked over and the bag was unzipped to show him the contents. The woman's face was clearly recognisable. She looked like the woman on the photograph her husband had loaned them. She was naked, just as

Fiona had been. He nodded that he had seen enough, and she was placed in an ambulance and driven away.

'That's her Mitch, that's Mrs Marlow.' He paused for a moment. 'Why, Mitch? Why?' he demanded. 'What the hell is the killer's motive?'

'Perhaps he just hates women, sir,' offered Mitch.

'No it's something more than that. These two girls are different. There is no link there. They're not prostitutes. No, this killer is more subtle. He takes more care and is more selective.'

'He's in a hurry, sir. That's two bodies in ten days. What's his rush?' asked Mitch.

'If he is on a roll. I think we can expect some more bodies very quickly, and then it will stop,' said Solly.

'I wonder if the women knew each other, visited the same clubs, or worked together.'

'That's a good point, Mitch, we will investigate along those lines,' said Solly. 'Come on let's go and have a cup of tea, your turn to pay,' he said with a smile.

Solly and Mitch arrived back at the police station to be greeted with the news that another body had been recovered from the sea off Lundy Island in the Bristol Channel. It was highly decomposed.

'This is unbelievable,' said the Detective Chief Inspector to his sergeant.

'Come on, Mitch, we will go and look at this one before our meeting this afternoon.'

'I have checked the missing persons list, sir. There is no woman listed,' said Mitch.

'We better check it out. Get the address of Mrs Marlow. We will call on the husband later.'

The pair of them was driven to the mortuary where the latest corpse had been taken.

'This is going to be a really smelly one, Mitch,' said Solly, as they entered the mortuary where the remnants of the female found by the other fishing boat lay. Luckily the pair of them only had a sandwich for lunch, otherwise they would not have kept it down. She had been at sea at least a week and the body had been trawled in the nets after feeding shoals of fish and crabs in the channel.

'We will have to get a dental recognition, Solly, as the body is so badly decomposed. I expect she was trapped in the rocks off Flatholm, or somewhere.' said the mortuary scientist.

'What can you tell us?' asked the Chief Inspector, holding a large Vick-covered handkerchief to his nose.

'Aged about thirty, height five foot six, medium build. Afro Caribbean nationality. She appears to have drowned; there are no marks to tell me otherwise.

'You mean it's not murder.'

'That's right, she was found fully dressed complete with wedding ring and earrings.'

'Thank goodness it's not one like Fiona Walters and Brenda Marlow. We don't want a run of them. So as far as you can see this one has drowned, fully dressed.'

'That's right, Solly.'

'I wish someone had told us these details. It would have saved us another journey, and the worry that we had another murder.'

'Sorry about that. I will speak to reception and tell her to be more descriptive if it happens again.'

'Alright, send me all the details and I will get someone to look into her death.'

Mitch and the Inspector drove back to the station, feeling very relieved that the corpse was not one of their murdered women, and hoping there would be no more.

'Look sir, there's that café, the Silver Spoon, where the girls got picked up from. Do you think it's worth a visit?'

'What an admirable idea, Mitch. I could do with a cuppa tea. Lead the way.'

The two detectives entered the café which was empty of customers. Big Mac was on counter duty and knew he had two special types of customers in his premises.

'I bet it's the law,' he said.

'You what?' said Mitch, surprised.

'I said I bet you two are the law,' repeated Big Mac.

'We are, as it so happens,' confirmed Solly. 'And like other members of Planet Earth we need sustenance. That is tea for two and two buttered teacakes.'

'I'm sorry I didn't mean to be rude. Only you see I always try and guess my customers job when they come in here; usually by the way they dress. You two look like typical coppers, detectives. Is that right?'

'As it happens, you're correct. Now, what about our teas?' asked Solly.

'Here you are a pot of tea with milk and sugar. If you like to sit down, I will bring it over to you.'

'Right, we'll sit over here,' said Mitch.

Once the two were seated and the tea tray delivered, Big Mac spoke again.

'I used to be in the force,' he said.

'What! The police force?'

'Yes, up in Scotland, in Glasgow.'

'Why did you leave?'

'I got too big, too heavy. I was medically discharged. They couldn't get my weight down,' said Big Mac.

'That's a pity,' said Solly,

'Sorry, my name is Jim MacDonald. It won't surprise you when I tell you the customers and friends refer to me as Big Mac.'

'Very appropriate,' said Solly, buttering his second slice of tea cake. Big Mac decided to leave the detectives to it and finish their tea; besides another couple had come into the café.

'Do you know I think our killer is very local? He knows the girls, where they go, who they go with, and where they live,' said Solly, licking the tips of his fingers.

'I agree, but it doesn't supply the motive,' said Mitch.

'Don't place too much importance on the motive, Mitch. I know it would simplify finding our killer but it won't stop him killing. We know he is after married women from this town.'

'I know sir, I checked and can find no other killings like we have anywhere in England. Somebody has a hate against certain women.'

The café had emptied again and Big Mac came over to where the detectives were sitting.

'I see in the press and on the local news that Brenda Marlow has gone missing.'

'That's right,' said Solly. 'Bad news travels fast.'

'She was in here the week she went missing.'

'On her own?' asked Mitch.

'Well yes to start with. Then this guy in a posh suit comes in and chats her up. I overheard the conversation that's how I know.'

'Go on,' said Mitch.

'There is naye more. That's all there is to tell,' said Big Mac walking back to his counter.

*

Wayne Coldcrow drove to his two bedroomed cottage in the suburbs of Bristol. It was a semi-detached, built in the 1950s. It was rather drab and had a quarter acre of land with scrub grass on it on the side and rear, that's where he kept his vehicles, a car and a white van he used for moving peoples things around at a price. He didn't make a lot but he managed.

He lived alone, having got divorced five years ago from Cindy for playing the field; her not him. Up till then he had always been a one woman man. How times had changed. Now he was earning a steady income from being an insurance agent. He liked the freedom and meeting people; especially some of the women. He thought back to Fiona; that was a shame. He had a good thing going there. He wondered why she was murdered. He knew he would be involved once the police found out he was possibly the last person to see her alive.

He thought back to his own married life to Cindy. He knew it was his fault she left him after six childless years, and all because he had a constant eye for other women. The press had kept the death of Fiona in the public eye, and yesterdays evening's paper reported the recovery of Brenda Marlow's body from the sea. Wayne was aware he would be implicated yet there had been no mention that he might be a suspect. He lay back in his chair and went over in his mind his past very traumatic love life.

His ex wife Cindy had gone off with a toy boy whom she found more interesting and who wanted her and no other; he was a university dropout, a dirty lazy slob, whose father used to be a customer of his. This lad Steve used the same football club as him and Cindy, that's how she got to know him. They were the most incompatible couple to know; but there's no accounting for taste. One day Cindy came up to him and said she was leaving him for Steve, and handed him back his credit and bank cards. It came as a shock to him, it was so sudden. He hadn't realised she was seeing so much of Steve; mainly because he was chasing spare skirt all the time himself. Because of the situation he found himself in, he decided to play the field; love 'em all and marry none – that was to be his new motto.

He had found from experience that it was not a good idea to bring every girlfriend home. It had got him into a few scrapes in the past. Once he was in bed with this woman in the afternoon. He was thinking of selling the cottage and was just in the middle of the most interesting and enjoyable bit when the female estate agent opens the front door with her key and yells up stairs she was bringing this couple round to view the place. He forgot what he shouted down to her, but it did the trick; they left.

He was always getting into marital scrapes, but he enjoyed it.

He lounged in a wicker work chair on the patio. It was a sunny day the morning haze had disappeared and warm sunshine was filtering through. He started to doze off and was rudely awakened by being surrounded by police and police dogs.

'Hey! What's the hell is going on,' he protested, as he was roughly pulled to his feet.

'You're Wayne Coldcrow?'

'Yes but…' He was roughly hauled off his chair and handcuffed. A policeman gave him his formal warning and he was bundled in a car and driven off. The whole operation must have taken no more than a minute. Wayne was expecting the police to call and interview him, but not like this. He felt he was already convicted by the way he was being handled; stuffed into a police car and driven to the police station.

Totally confused, and despite his protests, nobody would explain what he had done. He was booked in, made to change into a paper suit and placed in a cell, and there he stayed until once more he was brought and placed in an interview room to await CID investigation.

A man dressed in a suit came into the room and introduced himself as Mr Tony Roots. He explained that he had been nominated to act as defence lawyer for Wayne. He was allowed ten minutes to speak with him regarding the two missing women. Wayne was now plainly a suspect and needed all the help he could get.

*

The Detective Chief Inspector and his sergeant Nigel Mitchell entered the interview room and seated themselves on the opposite side of the table to Wayne and his counsel. The Inspector opened the proceedings in the formal manner, introducing those present.

'Is your name Wayne Coldcrow?'

'Yes you know that – I told you so on the first time I came here,' Solly ignored him.

'Do you live at 22 Afrington Villas, Nowle, in Bristol?'

'Yes,' answered Wayne.

'Do you know this lady in the picture?' asked Solly, passing the picture of Brenda Marlow over to him. Mitch recorded the fact on the tape that this had been done.

'Yes, I have been out with her,' said Wayne.

'When were you last out with her?'

'I suppose it was in the evening, a week this Saturday.'

'What did you do that evening?'

'We went for a meal.'

'Did you both eat a meal?'

'What relevance has this to the inquiry, Chief Inspector? My client has already said they ate a meal.'

'It will help determine the time of death, Mr Roots.'

'Answer the question please, Wayne,' said Mitch.

'Yes I had a curry and she said she had already had her tea, so she just had a ham sandwich,' Wayne replied.

'What happened after that?'

Wayne explained how their car was bogged down and about getting it free.

'Did you have sex with her.'

'No, neither of us felt like it after getting the car out.'

A little laughter came from those assembled in the room.

'Quite so,' said Solly. 'What happened after you got the car free.'

'I drove her home.'

'What time was that?'

'About 10.30.'

'Where exactly did you drop her off, Wayne?'

'Outside the Silver Spoon café, that's where I picked her up.'

'And she walked home from there, did she?' asked Solly.

'Did you make further contact with each other, for instance by mobile?'

'No, we said we would, but I think both of us knew we weren't compatible.'

'I see. We have searched the house and grounds of where you live. We had a warrant to do this and we found not only a hammer which matches the one used on killing those two girls you admit to have being out with, and both of whom have finished off being murdered.'

'That doesn't prove anything. Most people have hammers in their houses like that,' protested Wayne.

'This one was in the white van you own, Wayne, an ideal vehicle for transporting a body. We also found a man's handkerchief with blood on it. It is with forensics now for DNA testing.'

'Yes the blood is hers. She cut herself on some brambles as we got out of the car, so I lent her my handkerchief,' volunteered Wayne.

'How convenient,' said the Inspector.

'My client has answered all your questions satisfactorily. I see no reason why you need to detain him further,' said the solicitor.

'Did anyone see you that night?'

'Not that I know, but I can take you to the house where the man helped me dig the car out.'

'We will go there now, Wayne, and see if he verifies your story because at the moment you are our nearest suspect, having been the last person to see both women alive.

*

DI Simon Collins and Wendy were writing up their reports of the interviews they had carried out at the Wicked Elf.

I don't know about you sir, but I am not happy about those two brothers; especially the older one, Justin. I feel we ought to check both brothers out and see if they have any past we should know about.'

'Go ahead, sergeant,' said Simon. 'Let me know what you find. The boss wants a meeting of everyone at 4 pm and there is a press conference tomorrow. I don't want anyone to leek out any information on this case to the press. Do I make myself clear?' said Solly, looking around the room.

The room full of detectives returned to the various tasks they were undertaking in this double murder inquiry.

Mitch came and asked Solly to watch the CCTV tapes taken from the cameras in the centre of the town.

'OK, Sergeant, what have we got?' he asked.

I have been going through the CCTV cameras in the high street. We start with the pictures showing the two girls waiting on Friday night to be picked up and taken to the pub. Then there is nothing that concerns us until we see the blue car which is carrying Wayne and Fiona. Behind him we see a white van but the camera doesn't show the driver, but it does show part of the number plate. Fiona crosses the road and goes down a side street, presumably to walk home.'

'Does the part number plate match that of the van used by the Wicked Elf?'

'Yes it does sir,' said Mitch.

'That confirms what Justin told us when he said he took the van to get it filled up.'

'Yes but it was just after this that Fiona was abducted,' added Wendy.

'How long would it have taken Fiona to walk home?' asked Solly.

'Fifteen to twenty minutes.'

'Plenty of time if the scene of the crime had been prepared beforehand,' said Solly.

'That's right. Wayne had driven off and passed the van which gave the driver time to follow Fiona home, and then go for petrol.'

'How far is it from the drop-off point to her home?'

'About half a mile, sir.'

'Is the road lit and are there any cameras?' asked Solly.

'Two lights had been smashed and the only camera has been vandalised and is not working.'

'It looks as if that's where the girl was snatched. Someone had done their homework and knew she was being taken home by Wayne.'

'Wait sir!' said Mitch. 'How could the killer prepare the area to snatch Fiona when he didn't know that she was being driven home by Wayne, and not taken home by Joyce. And how would he know? Unless, he overheard her ask him, and knew where she lived. That means it must have been someone in the pub. Perhaps the lights on her short cut had been vandalised as well as the CCTV cameras by other people.'

'Alright we will discuss it more at 4 o'clock.'

The group broke up and Solly went with Mitch to the morgue to find out the results of the autopsy on Brenda. There was nobody on display in the theatre, though there were several scientists going about their forensic business. Solly looked around and spotted one he knew.

'Have you the results on Brenda Marlow?' he asked.

'Yes, wait. I will get them for you. Ah here we are. It's pretty well a copycat of the first girl hit on the same spot with a heavy hammer. The killer seems to know the exact spot to strike to ensure he kills his victim and it won't require a second blow. These crimes have been thought about carefully. The whole operation seems to have been practised like clockwork.'

'She's a big girl. I don't know whether this task could have been carried out by just one man,' said Solly.

Mitch looked at him. 'You think it might have been carried out by more than one man, sir?' asked Mitch.

'It's quite possibly. It would make the act of killing her and getting her quickly into the van that much easier,' said Solly.

'Two murderers. Well, that's an unusual angle. It should make it easier to catch them.'

'Yes, I agree with you. Is there anything revealing like stomach contents?' Solly asked the forensic scientist.

'Only the remnants of a ham sandwich and a glass of white wine, that's your lot.'

'Thanks Curly,' said Solly. 'Send me the ID from the dental records as soon as possible please.'

'OK, but it won't be today,' he said with a grin.

Chapter 9

THE SUN WAS starting to break through the cloudy sky and the pavements were drying out as the detectives motored back to their police station. They had both been quiet for ten minutes, each buried in their own thoughts regarding the unsolved murders.

'If we have a serial killer, we can expect a third body shortly,' said Solly. 'And then some more until we stop him, or her,' he said.

Mitch was driving the Rover.

'So now we have two bodies, no motive and no suspect,' said Mitch, a little despondently. 'A motive would be a good start. I've racked my brains trying to think of one. It's not sex, I can't see it being robbery. It seems he hates women.'

'What all women?' asked Solly.

'No, a certain type of woman,' replied Mitch.

'Well, I don't think they are prostitutes, we have no proof of that, besides they are a bit too old.'

'That's the point sir, they are ordinary housewives. He has a vendetta against ordinary housewives, sir.'

'I think it goes deeper than that, young man.'

'Have you any ideas sir?'

'I think we might get a better idea of a suspect and motive when Sergeant Morrison has finished her investigations.'

They made their way upstairs and walked into the incident room.

'Sir, we have taken Wayne over to speak to the man who he said helped dig him out of the mud the night he took Brenda Marlow out. The man and woman confirm what he told us,' said Simon.

'Thanks Simon, but I thought they would. It doesn't mean Wayne didn't do the killings. In both instances he was the last person we know to have seen them alive,' said Solomon.

*

Roger Walters didn't feel like work. He was all screwed up at the loss of his wife, Fiona. She was such a lively girl and fun to have around; he really missed her.

'Try and stop crying, Roger,' his mother said. 'Try and find something to interest you, to take your mind off of Fiona.'

'I can't, Mum. I can't get her out of my mind. Look at the boys, they're not interested. Clive just wants to lie on his bed, they don't even want to go out to play. I'm going down town, Mum. I need time to think.'

'Alright dear,' there was nothing she could say to take away the pain he was feeling. He got to the door and turned to face her.

'Why mum, why kill Fiona? They didn't want sex, or money, nothing, they just killed her; stripped her and dumped her in the just stood there unable to answer his simple question.

It was ten minutes to town he decided to walk; the exercise would do him good and give him time to think. He gazed into the shop windows without really seeing their contents or taking any interest in them. Suddenly he spotted something across the road which caught his eye. He became excited and curious, because there was a woman about the same size as Fiona and she was wearing the same top with sequins in that he had bought her for her birthday.The same top and she had worn the night she was murdered. He had bought it in a good class of ladies clothes shop as a special treat. It wasn't exactly a one off; but he didn't think there was many around like it. Dodging the busy main road he crossed over. She was standing at a bus stop. He went up to her.

'Excuse me. Would you tell me where you got that sequined top you're wearing?'

'Why do you want to buy one for yourself?' she said, with a laugh not stopping chewing her gum. She was about Fiona's height and physic, and she had long blond hair like Fiona. But she had a lot of bright silver studs dotted around all the exposed areas of her face; which he found repulsive.

'Here's my bus I got to go.'

'Wait, don't go I must know.'

'I'm not telling you where I buy my clothes you nosey git. Go away before I call the cops.' The bus came and she was about to get on. He gripped her arm

'My wife was wearing a top like that when she was murdered, please.'

'Let go of my arm or I'll scream.' Roger ignored her and hung on.

'I can't let you go. You are my only hope of finding her killer.' He pulled her out of the bus queue. She screamed.

'Help, I'm being attacked.' A man dressed in jeans and a sweat shirt pushed through the passengers and grabbed Roger

'Leave her alone you bastard,' he yelled

'No! I need her; she is wearing my wife's blouse. The one she died in.'

'You're hurting me,' shouted the girl. The bus drove off, leaving Roger with the girl and the man who had tried to release her. He threw Roger to the ground but Roger kept hold of the girl bringing her down with him.

'I've sent for the police,' says a woman who had overheard the conversation from the beginning.

'What you want to do that for. It's just this drunk molesting this young girl. What he needs is smack on the nose,' he said raising his fist. Roger and the girl were still trying to sort each other out so they could stand up. The shrill call of the police siren could be heard approaching.

'I'm going to sue you mister for assault,' the girl said, straightening out her scanty skirt. Sid got up and shook the big mans arm off. Two policemen got out of the car and asked what had happened. Both parties started to tell their stories at once. Neither policeman would take sides.

'I saw it all officer,' said the lady onlooker. 'I saw and heard it right from the start.'

The taller of the policemen phoned for another car.

'I think this is best sorted out at the police station .I want all of you to attend and give a statement, and we can get to the bottom of it.'

'I want him charged with assault, he's a fucking drunken bully' said the girl.

'You can make your charges down the station.' It was at that moment that another police car pulled up and took all those interested parties away.

They piled out of the police cars and into the station.

'Sit down on those chairs all of you and we will call you out and get your details.'

'Who is the plaintive?' Asked the sergeant at the desk.

'I am ,'said the girl, raising her arm in the air .

'First thing you can do young lady is put that chewing gum in the bin over there ,'she complied with the instruction from the desk sergeant.

'Name?'

'Cilla Peterson'

'Age?'

'Twenty one'

'Address?'

'76 Printon Rd, Exselley.'

'Tell me your side of the story.'

Cilla told truthfully the series of events leading up to policemen coming.

'Sign here Cilla,' said the sergeant . 'Next.'

Roger stood up

'I've seen you before haven't I?'

'Yes, it was my wife that was murdered, and it was you who took me to identify the body.'

'We have your details on record. What's your side of the story?'

'She is wearing a top identical to the one my wife wore the night she died.'

'So what? There must be possibly hundreds of tops like that.'

'No sergeant. I bought that from an exclusive shop .It cost me forty quid. It was a present for her. I asked her where she got it and she wouldn't tell me. I couldn't let her get away, could I?'

'Wait here,' he said . He made a phone call and two minutes later Detective Sergeant Mitchell came down stairs. The situation was quickly made clear to him as to what had happened.

'You're sure this is the same top?'

'As near as I can be.'

'Come into the interview room and you Miss Peterson.' All three of them and a WPC went to the room where an interview was to take place.

'Can you identify this top in any way that makes you sure it's your wife's.'

'It's not his bloody wife's, its mine,' Cilla shouted.

'One moment Cilla you will have chance to have your say,' said the WPC. Cilla leaned back in her chair and pouted.

'As near as I possibly can be.'

'Where did you get that top Cilla?' Asked Mitch

'From an Oxfam shop if you must know.'

'When did you buy it?'

'Two days ago.'

'Which shop?'

'The one in Jeremy Street.'

'I'm afraid were going to ask you to surrender it to us for DNA testing. Don't worry if it's clear we will return it strait away.'

'And if its not?'

'You will be compensated for it. We will take you home and WPC Clark sitting here will escort you while you change out of it into something else. Is that clear?' She nodded her agreement.

*

At 4pm a meeting was held in the incident room. Detective Chief Inspector Solomon and his Superintendant were there. Josh Roberts had been away on a course for two weeks and Solly had brought him up to date on the events since his departure. Josh was very disturbed at the news, particularly as there had been two murders and up to now no suspects or a sound motive for either.

The room was full of detectives talking together. The electronic incident board, which was the latest gadget they had to aid them was illuminated, and displayed the faces of the two women together with that of Wayne Coldcrow.

'Quiet and attention every one,' addressed Solly to the assembled crowd. 'We now have two bodies as shown on the board. Both of them were killed the same way within a week of each other. We have a suspect who we have not charged but could have carried out these murders. However, apart from opportunity there is nothing else to go on. I am desperate for a good motive and a confirmed suspect. What have you to offer me from your investigations?' Sergeant Wendy Morrison stood up.

'Yes Sergeant, what have you to say?'

'I have carried out investigations into the eldest son of Jerry and Elsie Long of the Wicked Elf sir, whose name is Justin.'

'Yes, Sergeant, and did you find out anything interesting?'

'Apparently they run a pizza business between them. Justin cooks them and Johnny delivers.'

'Nothing unusual in that Sergeant,' said Josh, from the back of the room.

'No sir, but I wondered why they didn't tell us at the interview.'

'Perhaps they overlooked it. I don't think there is any importance to be gained from that line of inquiry,' said Solly.

'There is more sir,' she added.

'Yes, what is that?' asked the Chief Inspector.

'When we interviewed them all at the Wicked Elf, we asked him had he gone out the night Fiona Walters was killed. He said he had taken the white van belonging to the pub into town to get it filled up for the following day. It is shown on the CCTV passing Wayne's car when he is dropping Fiona off.'

'Well done, sergeant,' he said, smiling in appreciation. 'I know it proves nothing, but if he had planned to snatch Fiona, he could easily have made sure the camera in the lane wasn't working and the lights were out. As I see it, it would depend on what time he filled the van up. If it was immediately after passing Wayne's car then I don't think he is our man as there would be insufficient time to do both. I want the CCTV at Asda to be checked for that evening to see how long Justin took to fill up and what time he went there. Are there any further reports we need to know?' said Solly, looking round the room.

A detective constable stood up.

'Sir, we had that sequined top checked at forensic but we could gather no evidence that it belonged to Fiona. However, we have checked and she was wearing one like it the night she disappeared. There were no other clothes or belongs found in the charity shops.'

'Thank you, Detective Constable Miles,' said Solly. I want to inform you all that Wayne Coldcrow is on remand for further investigation. His white van and car are in for forensic testing and he was using another name the day he chatted up Brenda and took her out. This I am sure you will agree is very suspicious.'

*

Detective Chief Inspector Solomon called a press conference for ten o'clock next morning .He had been pestered to give one all week but with no new evidence he felt it was fruitless. He sat next to Superintendent Josh Roberts, DSO, his immediate superior. It was Solly who would conduct and answer the inquiry.

'Have you got a suspect? You had someone in to help you with your enquiries. Are you going to charge him,' the reporter from the *Daily News Echo* called out.

'Hello Tom, Yes we have a man in for questioning. He has been involved with both women. We are carrying out forensic tests on various pieces of equipment of his.'

'Have you got a motive?' Tom shouted out.

'No! All we know is that both women were married and their husbands were unaware they were seeing another man.'

'So it could be that the motive is a hatred of women who are playing away from home; sexually I mean,' suggested a young girl reporter from the *Woman's Daily News*.

'That's an interesting theory,' said Solly. 'Perhaps he has been a victim of this act himself.'

There was a roar of laughter from the assembled reporters when one smart Alec at the back of the room suggested that nearly all the men in the area could be suspects. When the laughter had died down Solly made an observation.

'Because of that very fact you can see the difficulty we have in finding the right one.

'Do you think it is a serial killer?' called a young lady Solly had never met before. She introduced herself as being from *The Detective News Magazine*.

'It seems quite likely. We have two identical deaths.'

'The public want results, women are scared. When can you tell us something definite?'

'I hope to have some encouraging news at our meeting next week,' and with that Solly and Josh got up and left the room.

As they came out of the press conference Mitch was waiting for Solly.

'Sir, I want Justin Long brought in and I want his van to be given a good check over by forensic.'

That's no problem. I'll get a search warrant. First thing we must do is visit the relatives of Brenda Marlow.

Chapter 10

IT WAS A WEEK later that Detective Sergeant Nigel Mitchell plucked up courage and made a friendly invitation to Wendy. Their chief murder suspect Wayne Coldcrow had been released from custody, and warned to keep away from married women until this matter had been cleared up.

'Do you fancy coming to a dance tonight?' Nigel asked Wendy, who was busy sorting some papers. She turned round to face him.

'What, with you, Nigel? Yes, why not. I haven't been out since Gary left me and broke off our engagement. Where shall we go?'

'What do you want – pictures, a meal or a drink?' he asked.

'I think a drink would be enough for a starter,' she said, with a welcoming smile.

'Would you like to come to the Wicked Elf?' She looked surprised for a moment, then agreed that it might be interesting.

'It's Friday, so there should be a dance on there.'

'Good, I'm looking forward to it,' she said.

'I'll pick you up at eight,' he suggested.

'Yes that's fine, you have my address and mobile, haven't you, Nigel. I know I have yours,' she grinned.

Wendy and Mitch were already at the Wicked Elf pub having a drink of orange when the two ladies they had interviewed reference the first murder walked in. They didn't acknowledge recognising each other. It was the same when Wayne Coldcrow came in later alone. Mitch was interested to watch him perform tonight in finding a new partner to replace Fiona.

'There's a good film on at the Curzon next week. Will you come and see it with me?' asked Mitch, having had a good look around the bar.

'What's it called?'

'I forget, but I would like you to come.'

'Sounds a funny title, but yes, I would love to.'

'Good,' he said, with a big smile. 'Would you care to dance?'

'Oh we are posh,' she said. They stood there, gyrating on the floor, not making any physical contact but trying to gaze into each other's eyes. They were out for a night of fun. But it was difficult to resist the duty of the detective in their make-up, and search the room for something of interest which would help them solve their murder cases. Wayne was now dancing with a woman who looked older than he was. She was nearly as tall as Wayne and had shoulder-length brown hair. They were chatting away. Wayne wasted no time in finding a replacement girlfriend, showing no remorse for those he lost.

Suddenly the door burst open and a short, stubby man with a North Irish accent came into the room. He stood at the edge of the dance floor looking for someone. Mitch heard her say:

'That's my husband who has just come in. I didn't know he was coming here. Be careful as he has a temper,' she said, very agitated. They started to leave the dance floor when the husband shoved his way through the crowd towards them.

'Ah, there you are, you bitch! You didn't know I'd follow you did you. Out with your bloody fancy man again. By now the dance floor had cleared, leaving Wayne his partner and the irate husband on the dance floor. He looked up at Wayne who was at least a foot taller than the Irishman.

'So you're the lucky bastard who has been shagging my misses,' he roared.

The bar staff had come round to break up the disturbance. It looked as if it could develop into a fight.

'I didn't know she was your wife, I didn't even know she was married, she isn't wearing a ring.'

'Don't come that with me,' said the Irishman.

'He's right, I never seen him before tonight,' said his wife.

'Don't lie to me, you tramp,' and so saying, he drew a knife from under his jacket. 'I'm going to kill you, you lying bitch. It's not the first time you have done the dirty on me, having said that, without another word, lunges at her belly.

Wayne, seeing what was about to happen, jumped in between the husband and his wife. Mitch was on his feet and starting across the floor. The Irishman plunged the knife into Wayne's belly instead of his wife. Blood spurted everywhere and Wayne dropped to the floor.

The man made a dash for the door, leaving his wife behind. Mitch bent over Wayne while Wendy, pulling her police card from her bag, shouted, 'Stop! Police!' She made a grab at the killer as he passes her. The Irishman pushed his hand into her face which knocked her to the floor and he ran for the door. Mitch, who was bending over Wayne, saw Wendy falling and tried to help her. By now, the bar was in a screaming, shouting atmosphere. Mitch yelled at the bar staff to get an ambulance. Wendy had recovered from the blow which appeared not to have caused any facial injury, though her face was flushed by the blow of the man's hand.

'Are you alright, Wendy?' Mitch shouted, seeing her get to her feet. While this was going on, one could hear the revving up of a motor bike as it left the car park.

Mitch returned to where Wayne was laying. He checked his pulse. It appeared he was dead. He closed Wayne's eyes and one of the bar staff brought a towel which he used to cover Wayne's head.

Wendy looked across at Mitch questioningly; he shook his head, implying Wayne was dead. A crowd had gathered round the dead body. Wendy flashed her warrant card and told them all to disperse. They reluctantly withdrew, traumatised by what had gone on. The night of fun was over. The dance hall was closed down as it was now a crime scene. Mitch went over to where Wayne's dancing partner stood crying. Mrs Long, the publican's wife, was with her, trying to comfort her. Mitch took out his warrant card and introduced himself to the sobbing wife of the killer.

'Can I have your name and address please,' he asked her.

She gave him the details.

'Wayne appears to have died, murdered by the man who said he was your husband. What's his name? Does he live at the same address?'

'Yes.'

Mitch phoned the details of the killer and the number of his motorbike to police headquarters. When he had finished a policeman in uniform came in together with the ambulance crew who had just arrived.

'He got away and we haven't got a picture of him unless it's on the CCTV,' said Mitch.

'I got one,' said Wendy.

'You what?' asked Mitch, very surprised.

'I snapped him as soon as he came blustering in. I could see there might be trouble,' she said, smiling at Mitch's stunned look. 'I got two on my mobile when he came in.'

'My God, Wendy, you will make a good inspector one day,' said Mitch in admiration.

Police cars and an ambulance were at the pub within twenty minutes. The area was taped off and men and women in white paper suits took the place of the happy dancers there an hour ago. The incident had shocked all those who saw it.

'The Hall is shut, you can all go home. This is now the place of a crime and is off limits to you all until we have completed our investigation,' called Mitch; having introduced himself. The happy crowds of thirty minutes ago gradually drifted off. Mitch and Wendy were the last to leave.

'Well, that was a first date I shall always remember,' said Wendy, as she cuddled up to Mitch as he drove her home.

*

'I hear we lost our only suspect last night, he was stabbed to death,' said Solly.

'No! Who was that?' replied DI Simon Collins.

'Wayne Coldcrow, apparently he was seen with another man's wife, so the husband stabbed him.'

'In fairness it must be pointed out that Wayne purposely stood between the killer and his wife. The killer said he intended to kill his wife, not Wayne,' added Wendy, who overheard the conversation.

'Do we know the killer, sir?' asked Simon.

'Yes, Sergeant Morrison's got some pictures of him. We have his ID out on circulation.'

'Well, that is a blow sir. I have one piece of news that might help. We checked the CCTV at Asda the night Justin Long said he filled up his white van and he didn't go there till after midnight. Which leaves over an hour unaccounted for between passing Wayne's car and going to Asda?'

'Bring him for questioning, Simon.'

*

Mary Dagleash was a woman, who, although she had been married for seventeen years, was very lonely. Mary was a pretty woman. She had short light brown hair, blue eyes and a cream complexion. No one, except her husband, ever saw her with her face not made up with carefully selected cosmetics. She was seven stone ten in weight, and five foot two in height.

She would never admit to being lonely, but she was; and even stranger so was her husband. He was a loner. He could be found standing at the crossroads of town with his hands in his pockets doing nothing. He would pass the time of day with people he knew, but would stay on that spot for an hour or two. Meanwhile, his wife would be found at the other end of town strolling around the shops, just to pass the time. Often she would call on a friend or an acquaintance completely unannounced or invited; she just sought company to help her pass the lonely hours till sleep took over another boring day. Sleep at night she looked forward to, where she could enjoy the companionship of imaginary people in her dreams. It wasn't for the want of money; both of them had plenty.

The main reason that Mary and her husband Shaun weren't close was that they married each other as friends, not lovers. They were lonely even then. Mary had a boyfriend who was at sea in the navy, and Shaun, who was eight years older than Mary, was lonely because he had not long completed a divorce from his first wife who found him boring. Oh, they could pretend that what they enjoyed was love, but it really was only a substitute for it. He was a good man, very generous, smartly dressed and Mary wanted for nothing, except love and compassion.

People who knew Shaun well in both his marriages said, 'He never knew what real love was and pretended good friendship was love.' So he proposed marriage and acted the part, giving his wives children, but showing little warmth and affection which every married woman needs. So Mary hung on to anyone that showed her that affection whether male or female, and this inevitably led to her enjoying dances and parties where she could relax and have fun, while her understanding husband Shaun stayed home.

She often went into town and sat in the Silver Spoon café on her own, sipping and thinking. Big Mac often tried to make conversation with her but his wife could be seen in the background keeping an eye on him.

Mary's love of companionship and her need to be loved and have love, including physical love, led as one might suppose to her playing away from home and leaving the marriage bed. She was quite open about it to her friends that her husband took his pleasure and went to sleep, like many men do, but she needed more and she had so much more to give, and that when the opportunity came around she was a willing participant.

Mary had a long and successful relationship with a married man. His name was Justin Martin. She took every opportunity to be with him. She enjoyed his cuddles and kisses and she would make love at any convenient time. In the meantime, Shaun her husband did his own thing. He enjoyed work, reading, television, and travel.

He would go away on the Continent and visit the battlefields of World War I, nearly always on his own He loved to go to museums, anything to pass the time. He wasn't always on his own; sometimes he went out with his wife for a change. They went for a meal or a drink, but there was little conversation – they had very little in common.

They always danced together, and it was something they were both good at.

Neither of them smoked and their drinking was purely social. The children were grown up now: Peggy and Dorothy with only a year between them looked like twins with their straw-coloured hair and blue eyes. Mary dressed in simple clothes like skirts, blouses and dresses, but was never fashion-conscious or bought expensive clothes; most of her clothing came from Oxfam shops where she often found a bargain; and she loved swimming and sunbathing. She came up to the shoulder on her six foot six inch high husband. It is only fair to point out that although Mary looked a picture of innocence, she thrived on sex and could never get enough of it.

As one must expect, all good things come to an end and Mary's love relationship with Justin came to a rapid end when the two of them, herself and Justin Martin, were found in a compromising position in the greenhouse. As a result of this, the mere mention of his name in her house was forbidden, and she was told in no uncertain terms by Shaun, that if ever she cheated on him again he would kill her. This was quite possibly the main reason she used for not leaving him; he only demanded loyalty from her.

Mary, from then on had to be careful not to be caught again, and to make sure of that when she played away from home, that she was a long way away. It wasn't long before she found a replacement for Justin.

Brian Wilcox drove his car slowly towards the phone box on the A38 where he had promised to pick Mary up. They had been going together for four months, and what had begun as a one afternoon stand had now developed into a full-blown love session, with Brian begging Mary to leave her husband and start a new life with him. She had all the attributes he wanted in a wife or partner. She was a good cook, kept a clean house, and many other points including she had plenty of money.

'Hi sweetheart, hop in. We're going for a picnic,' he said.

She wore a short skirt today, showing off those long beautiful suntanned legs, and a summer blouse which when opened displayed her full bosom of a pair of firm, well developed breasts. Her face was also suntanned and her new, red, kissproof lipstick was just begging to be tested out. He kissed her lightly, placing his right hand between her legs for a moment.

'Come on darling, let's get moving, you don't know who might see us round here,' she said, looking to the rear out the back window.

He slipped the engine into gear and drove off into the countryside and the anticipation of a fun afternoon. Everything went according to plan.

'Isn't this wonderful, darling. We could spend the rest of our lives like this, we get on so well and like the same things,' said Brian, leaning over her prostrate body. They kissed passionately and within minutes were enjoying the fruits of illicit sex; at which she was very good, and had an insatiable appetite for more, and more.

Brian had been married twenty years. He had no complaints about his own wife except he was bored with her. They had grown apart since their son had grown up. He had joined the army and was out in Afghanistan, and enjoying it. Brian's wife Melanie was a hard worker, and kept a good table. But he wanted a change, and his choice was Mary. He tried again to convince her that she would have a better life with him. Mary was still undecided. The truth of the matter was she enjoyed the company of Brian, but she didn't love him.

'I can stay out till late tonight Brian. Shaun is attending a Lodge dinner and won't be home till late,' said Mary.

'That's marvellous – come back to my place.'

'Shall we? I love your flat overlooking the estuary.'

'We bought that as an investment – well the wife did, I use it as a summer house at the moment. You can sit on the balcony and have some drinks.'

'That would be nice. I just want to lay back and soak up the sun for now,' she said. They arrived at his house and he made her comfortable on the patio overlooking the Severn Estuary.

He got up and lit a cigarette, blowing the exhaled smoke skywards. He didn't smoke many, about five a day, sometimes less. He wanted Mary very badly. It wasn't just the sexual side of it; he was truly in love with her. He couldn't get her out of his mind. He felt at times she was teasing him, stringing him along. She was available when it suited her, but not when she said she had to be with Shaun. She wouldn't make any sacrifices for Brian. She was scared of the consequences if she were ever found out playing away again. It was as if she wanted the best of both worlds and used him like a toy, which she played with and put it back in its box when not needed.

She was also very jealous and got really mad at him if he fancied another woman. Sometimes, there were long periods when they couldn't be together and she would go berserk if she found he had two timed her; but he could just keep himself living like a monk until she was ready to be with him again.

'Why don't you leave him, Mary, and come and live with me. You say you love me?'

'I do love you, but Shaun is a good husband I want for nothing. On what grounds can I leave him?'

'The grounds that you love me.'

'I can't, besides you know what he said he'd do if I left him for another. Brian didn't know what to do. He felt he aught to dump her and find another; he had tried that before but she had spoilt it for him. He was getting desperate and agitated. He had to do something and soon. He moved down to the West Country when he got a new job with Courage Brewery. His wife Melanie knew he was a flirt, and although she suspected him of having affairs he never brought any trouble home, so she turned a blind eye to what he did, and believed his weak excuses.

Mary glanced at the clock on the mantelpiece. 'I think it is time I was going. It's been a lovely evening, darling.'

'Good heavens! Is that the time,' said Brian, prising himself from the settee where they were both cuddled up, and beginning to doze off.

*

'Here you are my darling. Can you walk it from here.I don't want to get any nearer your house in case we are seen,' said Brian, opening her car door.

'No that's alright. It's a nice night and the walk will do me good.' she said.

'When will I see you again?' he said, giving her a goodnight kiss.

'I will call you, darling, don't worry, it won't be long.'

She got out of the car and gave him a final wave as she walked away. He didn't give a thought to the white van parked in the shadows up the road as he drove past it.

There was a call at the police station next morning at 3 am to say that a Mrs Mary Dagleash was missing from home.

Chapter 11

SOLOMON SAT in his chair and his mind went over the two murders he had on his books with no suspect, few clues and no motive. He knew pressure was building from high up in the force as well as the public. He felt so helpless. This killer was clever. Solly knew they would catch him one day.

His thoughts were interrupted when Josh, his superior officer, walked in and placed some papers on his in tray.

'Solly, another nude woman has been found. She has been washed up at Flat Home Island. You better go over and take a look. That's three unexplained murders, the pressure is on, Solly. The Met are talking about coming here and taking over the search for the killer. The Commander wants results and wants us to solve it. You must come up with something. Do you understand me?' said Josh.

'Yes sir, I do.' He could make no promises, but he knew even the Met couldn't find clues where there weren't any. 'I want this murderer caught, Solly, and quick. You have a week, then you're off the case, Understood?'

'Yes, sir,' he said, rising from his chair. He went into the outer office where Mitch was talking to Wendy.

'Come on, Mitch,' said Solomon. 'We have another case, just like the rest. I want you to drive me over to Burnham on Sea, where the sea rescue craft is due to bring the woman's body in on the next tide.'

The local and the national papers were full of the murders. The Police Commissioner had been on TV to explain the difficulty of catching this killer who left no clues.

'We have helicopter patrols out all along the channel coast and the estuary. There are sea patrols out. We must catch him eventually,' said Solly.

'It's a nasty rocky coast around that port, it could play havoc on the skin of the corpse,' said Mitch.

'You're an authority on the rock formations around this area are you, Mitch?' said Solomon with a definite hint of sarcasm.

'No, sir but I went to a convent school when I was a boy in that area.'

'Oh I see, Watch that caravan pulling out,' he said, in an alarmed voice..

'It's alright sir, I saw it.'

They arrived at the scene of the crime. They were just in time to see the rescue boat pull in at the jetty and unload a green body bag. The bag was placed on a collapsible trolley. Solly went over to inspect the corpse. If Mary Dagleash had been pretty before, she wasn't now. Her empty eye sockets staring skywards. Her eyes had been pecked out, and she was horribly mutilated by the effects of the sea.

'This one has only been in the water about two days, very recent. I don't expect the police have seriously considered her a missing person yet. She has taken a horrible beating off these rocks,' said the doctor. 'This is another one for you Solly,'he asked. 'What's that three of them now? Any answers?'

'No. I wish I had. Some one is out to kill young married women; especially in this area. We have no reports of the same thing happening like this elsewhere. Who found the body?'

'The local Coast Guard found her through his binoculars. He phoned us and Sergeant Scrivens was first officer on scene.'

'So we have no witnesses, no evidence at all?'

'There is something, Solomon. This girl has been killed by a hammer blow like the last one. Only she must have had thick hair because it took two blows to kill her. The killer really smashed her skull in. There must be blood on the floor where she was killed. It was a bit clumsy compared with the other two.'

'That's interesting, but it doesn't help find her killer,' said Solly.

Mitch leant over the body and saw that like the others someone had snipped her hair.

'I want to know if she has had sex recently and the DNA.'

'What have you in mind sir?' asked Mitch.

'I am trying to find a pattern in their sexual activities. We know the second woman didn't have sex with Wayne because he told us that he had taken her out and although it was his intention, it didn't happen. He also admitted to having sex with the first girl – what was her name?'

'Fiona Walters, sir.'

'Yes, that's the one. Wayne is dead so he is off our list of suspects.'

'It's not much to go on sir, whether they had sex.'

'We don't know who she was seeing. If we get a sperm DNA at least we have a clue as to who he is. So you see, Sergeant, it is important.'

Having done all they could with no witnesses and no evidence that hadn't been disturbed by the sea, the two detectives returned to their office.

'At least we are pretty certain it was the same person killed the three women,' said Mitch.

'Plus, I think that female reporter hit the proverbial nail on the head when she said the killer was out for vengeance for having an unfaithful wife himself.'

'So that's the motive we're sticking to, is it sir?'

'Yes, until a better one comes along.'

'Christ! There must be hundreds of husbands who have been cheated on and know it,' said Mitch.

'Well, that's the motive the papers have printed. They have a theory that the killings are revenge killings and that the killer is getting his own back for his own wife's unfaithfulness,' offered Solly.

'I agree with the papers, sir. It seems the most likely reason.'

'I also think he is a local man who has a good knowledge of the roads round this town.'

'Yes sir, also he is someone who can keep an eye on the comings and goings of the unfaithful couples so he can plan his murders in advance.'

'I wonder if this victim has ever been to the Wicked Elf pub.'

'I wonder if the killer frequents it,' said Mitch.

'Or works there,' suggested Solly.

'It's open again now sir, isn't it, after the death of Wayne Coldcrow?'

'Yes, his killer comes to court next month. He has already pleaded not guilty to the stabbing; cheeky bastard,' said Solly.

'When are you bringing Justin Long in for questioning?' asked Mitch.

'When he comes back into the country; he's on holiday at the moment. We'll grab him as soon as he arrives.'

*

Brian Wilcox was most frustrated. He had tried to contact Mary with no success. He had telephoned but her mobile was switched off; which was most unlike her. One day he rang her house on the offchance she would answer; and put the phone down when Shaun answered.

'That's twice today someone has rung and put the phone down,' said Shaun to the Family Liaison Officer, sent to his house once the body had been found.

'Is that right, someone wants to speak to Mary, not you sir. It's important we find out who it was. I will do a trace call. We will in the meantime contact the GPO who will have a register of all incoming calls. He wasn't on his mobile, was he?'

'No, Sergeant, he wasn't.'

Brian didn't know what had happened to Mary. He contacted the friends she mixed with. On the third day after her disappearance he was told she had been murdered .It was also in the local paper. Brian was devastated with the sad news. He really loved Mary and would have done anything to get her to move in with him.

He wondered if what he knew about her might help the police capture her killer. As far as he knew she had no enemies, yet he also knew that the present spate of murders of young women had no bearings on one's enemies. The papers said that all the women murdered appeared to be having extramarital relationships with other men. He knew Mary definitely came into this category.

In which case if he wasn't caught soon there could be thousands of women murdered on that theory. He knew it would only be a matter of time before the police contacted him. He wondered whether he ought to contact them.

*

Solomon and Mitch drove to the Dagleash address. A uniformed officer stood outside the house and the area down the road was taped off as a scene of crime. It was a three-bedroomed detached bungalow. A driveway led to a garage at the rear. The windows were curtained so no one could see inside. They stood there five minutes ringing the bell, but no reply.

'He's in the house, sir. I haven't seen him leave today,' said the PC on duty.

'When did you last see Shaun Dagleash, Constable?'

'Last night at nine o'clock, sir.'

'Alright, thanks.'

'Go and have a look round the back, Mitch.'

Mitch did as he was told. The back area was beautifully laid out and spotlessly clean, a little vegetable garden with two fruit trees backed onto a lawn. There was a large shed with its door swinging open. Mitch thought this strange, the owners were so tidy. He went to close the door and nearly vomited when he saw a man hanging from the ceiling of the shed.

'Sir, come here quick,' he called. Solly sensed something was not right and joined Mitch. He looked in the shed.

'Bloody hell!' He exclaimed. 'The poor bastard has killed himself'

'Why, because he killed his wife, and the other two women? Or out of grief at loosing her,' asked Mitch.

'If it's out of grief, how did he manage to find out we had found his wife, or even if it was her?'

'I think I know, sir, I bet it's a local radio station who has picked up on the news that another woman's body has been found, and Shaun Dagleash has assumed it's her and took his life. We don't know what their relationship was like. Did he suspect her of having an affair?'

'Yes, you're right, Mitch. These questions need answering. Phone the station and report this hanging. Call in the investigation team, we need access to the bungalow.

The area was soon cordoned off and Mr Dagleash body removed to the morgue. It was photographed and the scene of the hanging carefully investigated in case there was any doubt that it was suicide and not murder. The bungalow was opened up and men and women in white paper suits entered the house, looking for clues about its normal occupants. The rooms were tidy and the beds unslept in. Empty and part-empty coffee cups littered the area around where one supposed Mr Dagleash sat while trying to find out where his wife had got to.

The comprehensive search of the bungalow and its contents revealed a little blue diary hidden away in the back of the wardrobe in Mary's bedroom. Thankfully she had used it to open her soul, and reveal not only her love affairs but whom she was seeing. She had been a very unfaithful wife it seemed, and she was seeing at that time a Mr Brian Wilcox.

Further reading into the diary revealed she had considered leaving her husband in favour of Brian. There was no notice in the diary of Mr Dagleash suspecting her of any affairs. He must have been a very blind and trusting individual, commented Solly; handing the book to Mitch. He flipped through her diary. Inside the back cover was a small photo of a man. There was no name attached to it.

'Did you see this sir,' he asked, passing Solly the diary.

'No! But I bet he's our man. Get the office to enlarge this picture. It will identify him.'

'Perhaps her husband knew she was being unfaithful and killed her.'

'I don't think so, Mitch. If he did, who killed the others?'

'Yes! Of course.'

Solly's phone rang; he didn't like the mobile ringing when he was busy in an investigation but he realised what a blessing it was to get

vital information to his attention as quickly as possible. He spoke to
Wendy.

'Sir, I have some important information. It concerns Justin Long's
stepbrother Johnny. I have found out that he accidentally killed Mr
Long's mother in a water-ski accident while holidaying in the
Maldives.'

'Is she the woman whose lover Justin killed with a rock?'

'Yes sir, the same woman.'

'Good work, Sergeant. By the way. I believe Justin Long is on
holiday; out of the country.'

'Yes that's right, sir.'

'When did he leave?'

'Wait sir, I will check ... Ah here it is. He left from Bristol Airport
at 6 am the day following the death of Brenda Marlow.'

'Thank you. We will be with you soon. I want another meeting of
every on at 4 pm,' he said, switching off the phone.

'Sergeant, I want you to trace a Brian Wilcox. It seems he was the
lover of Mary Dagleash. Bring him in for questioning. We have found
a picture which we think is of him.'

*

Solomon came into the interview room with Mitch in tow to speak to
Brian Wilcox.

'Hello, Mr Wilcox, I understand you are the man friend of Mary
Dagleash. Do you know she has been found dead – murdered?'

'Yes I just heard. I am very upset, Inspector. I was in love with
Mary and wanted her to leave Shaun and marry me.'

'Was she going too?'

'No, she kept making excuses, including that her husband had
threatened to kill her if she was found out with another man.'

'She has done this before then?'

'Many times I'm afraid. She just can't do without love and sex,
and he's not giving her much of either.'

'And you were?' He didn't reply.

'When did you last see her?'

'Friday night.'

'Did you take her home?'

'Nearly, I dropped her off a few hundred yards from her house.'

'Did you see any vehicles?'

'It was late at night, there was no one around. I passed a white van
as I drove off. It was parked in the shadows, I didn't get the number.'

'Alright we have your name and contact numbers, have we Sergeant Mitchell?'

'Yes, we have all of those details, sir.'

'I want you to go with the forensic team who are at the crime scene and show them where the van was situated, at least as near as possible. There may be tyre marks or blood spots. Sergeant Mitchell will go with you,' said Solly.

'Yes I will do that,' said Brian.

'Have you ever met her husband?' asked Mitch.

'No, but I understand he is unsociable, and very depressive, not good company,' replied Brian, as they came out of the interview room.

*

The police interviews of the residents of the street where Mary lived revealed little information; except at one house where they gave a positive ID of a white van seen in the street late the night she went missing. It was hard to identify as the light was out where it was parked, and it wasn't there long.

One resident in the street said he saw the van but said he couldn't give the number or the type of van, just that it was a small white one. The time it was seen was 10.45 pm when he looked out to see if it was raining. He thought no more about it except it was unusual as everybody in that road used their own garages. When he looked again about twenty minutes later it had gone.

'Might be purely innocent and coincidental,' said Solomon. 'It's not much help as we have no information on it. Put it on the picture board and check to see if anyone owns a van like that in that street.'

'It might be a hired van,' offered Mitch.

'Could be, Mitch. Get a team to check out garages or firms that had a van like that hired out.'

'Yes, sir,' he said, getting a number of DCs together.

'We have some pictures on the CCTV of a white van in the area on the night Mary Dagleash went missing,' said DI Clifford. 'Not in the road itself, but in the main road adjoining it.'

Just at that moment, Josh the Superintendent came out of his office.

'We have Press and a TV conference tomorrow morning, Solomon. I want you and Lieutenant Clifford in attendance.'

Solomon acknowledged the order. 'The Divisional Commander is calling here to speak to you. I want Sergeant Mitchell to be in attendance and DI Collins.'

Solly turned back to his room full of detectives.

'We have the serial number of the van sir,' said DI Simon Collins.

'Well done, that's a break,' said Solly. 'That's good news, Simon. Give it to Sergeant Morrison, she can do a check on it.'

'I'm afraid it isn't, sir,' said Simon. 'We have done a check and find they are false number plates.'

'Damn! What trick hasn't this killer thought of,' said Solly. 'I want all the vehicles at the Wicked Elf checked for forensic evidence and DNA.'

'When sir?' asked Wendy.

'Now!' said Solly.

*

'There was nothing to match the clothes of the missing women found in our sweep along the Severn Estuary,' said Simon.

'I didn't expect you to find their clothes, but the search had to be made. Have you got the results of the handbag?' Josh asked Detective Inspector Solomon.

'Yes, sir, we have a list of telephone numbers and names which we're working on, they look promising,' said Solomon.

*

'I have never seen the boss in a state like that said DPC Bryant to a colleague, he's really agitated.'

'Pressure from the top,' said his pal. 'That's what that is. It gets to all of us eventually.'

'Mitch, make up the Crime picture board. I want to see all those concerned in these murders, including the husbands. There was insufficient evidence to be able to pin it on anyone yet,' said Solly.

Mitch, having had it agreed with Solly, arranged with the transport division to carry out a mock attack on a woman PC to try and copy how the killer carried out his surprise attacks and how long it would take to do the task with one man and then compare the time with two men.

They found that with two men the killing and transporting away from the scene was nearly halved as with an accomplice in the van to grab the body, drag her inside whilst the outside man closes the van doors. This just leaves the killer to get into the van and drive away. However, if the location where the murder took place was on a site which had already been specially chosen because it was dark, or in the shadows, and late at night with no witnesses, then the operation could be carried out by one man as long as he was of a strong, sturdy build. Then there wouldn't be the same urgency. Mitch was pleased within the results and reported his conclusions to Solly.

'There is one factor you have overlooked in your experiment.'

'What's that sir.'

'I think it is vitally important that the victim knew her killer. Just imagine she is walking along the road to her house and she sees the van on her side of the road. She is going to avoid someone she doesn't know, especially after three murders. The killer wants her attention. If she recognises him it will be much easier to get her to come round and look in the back of the van.'

'How would he do that sir? I don't understand.'

'Just supposing his name is Joe Bloggs. She knows him as Joe because she is familiar with him, not sexually, but he could be a tradesman. Do you copy?'

'Yes sir, I copy.' Mitch smiled, wondering where his boss had picked up that expression.

'He knows where he needs to strike the killer blow. He only wants to hit her once. So he gets her to come round the back of the van on some pretext or other, presumably one where he requires her help. Then, Whack! He pushes her in the van. Then he closes the doors and drive off.'

'I have an even better idea, sir. If there are two of them, one stays in the driving seat with the engine running. The actual killer pushed the woman into the van jumps in the back of the van himself the driver pulls two ropes closing the doors of the van and drives off.'

'Yes, Mitch, that looks very plausible and practical,' said Solly

'I think that's the way its done sir. The killer knows that his victim is unlikely to be dropped off right out side of her house'

Having completed his copy of what he thought the killer did when he snatched these women, Mitch went back to the office to write his report. In the meantime the forensic found blood stains on the road where they thought the murder of Mary Dagleash took place, and the good print of a heal mark of a trainer; though it might not be the killers.

This information Mitch had obtained with the rehearsals, could prove a great help in catching the murderer. They had to find the correct white van, and the man who owned it.

Mitch had contacted the forensic department before leaving the station. The area round the cottage was cordoned off and now the tapes were being extended down the road for two hundred yards. The search was being carried out by a squad of police detectives doing a hand and knee search along the curb of the road. Dressed in green waterproof suits, their endeavours proved fruitful because blood samples were found. There was quite a lot actually, and this may well have been because the murderer had to strike his victim twice. Was he slipping up? Was his accuracy impaired? Was he panicking? After all, he was only human; though not a nice specimen of humanity.

Chapter 12

'RIGHT, EVERYONE in the incident room as we are going to review the current situation regarding these three women,' shouted DCI Solomon. The assembled room of detectives left the task they were doing, and sat facing Solly and Josh who had come to hear the latest result. The picture board in the room had been made up to date. Wayne Coldcrow had been removed from the board, not only because he was dead; but events were overtaking him with the death of Mary Dagleash.

There was still no suspect. This was infuriating everyone involved in detecting these murders. The Divisional Commander and his team had been down and held a conference with Josh and Solomon. They were very concerned that three murders had been committed, with no suspect or a motive. Although threats had been made about other people taking over the detection of these crimes, it was realised by the Divisional Commander, Henry Livingston, that Josh and his team were working hard on the murders, and had done all they could to bring them to a halt and find the killer.

The area along the Severn estuary was constantly patrolled, and night vision glasses were used by police doing night patrols along the area. The murderer had the advantage, because he could switch quite easily the point at which he dumped the bodies in the sea. It was too long a coastline to patrol effectively and economically every night of the week.

*

Wendy tapped on the DCI's door and placed a sheet of paper on his desk to inform him that yet another unclothed body of a woman had been found off Brean in Somerset. It had been spotted by a passing cargo ship which had stopped and recovered it. They had signalled the coast guard who had recovered the body. The body was now in Taunton Morgue.

'That's strange, we haven't anyone listed as missing from home have we?'

'No, we haven't a missing person listed sir. The last woman was Mary Dagleash,' said Wendy, returning to her desk.

'Thank you Wendy,' said Solly. He called Mitch into his office.

'Not another body sir?' he asked.

'I'm afraid it might be, Sergeant. I'm getting very disillusioned with the whole thing. Take your coat, Mitch, it has started to rain. They motored down to inspect their latest victim, before she was dissected by the forensic team.'

As they entered the morgue the body had been laid out for them to check over. It lay on a stainless steel mortuary table and was covered head to toe in a white sheet. As they approached, the cloth was removed to reveal a woman in her late forties, early fifties. She had short brown hair and green eyes. She appeared to be roughly five four in height and weigh about 150 lbs.

'As you can see, Inspector, she has been stuck on the head with a hammer,' said the mortician. 'We think this caused her death just as with the other victims.'

The two detectives carried out a careful inspection of the victim without making any comments or observations.

'Thank you,' said Solly. 'Please send your report to me at this address. I would also like a comparison with her dental records, as we have no knowledge as to who she is.' He handed the Senior Mortician his card. When he and Mitch had seen all they wanted, they left the hospital and returned to their police station.

'What do you think, sir? You haven't said anything about the woman,' said Mitch, looking at him.

'I don't think she is one of ours,' said Solly.

'You don't sir, why?' asked Mitch, intrigued, but not surprised.

'I think it's a lookalike, a copy. Someone is trying to pass off a woman's murder to make it look like it's the victim of our killer.'

'Funny, I thought the same sir, honest,' said Mitch.

'Did you? Go on then, tell me your reasons,' said Solly.

'Well, the first was she was still wearing her wedding ring. All the others had theirs removed. Secondly she had a snip of hair removed and it was cut from the wrong side of the head.'

'Quite right, well spotted, Mitch. The reason why the hair was cut from the wrong side was because the killer had forgotten which side our victims had been struck and having chosen the wrong side, he cut the hair from the opposite side.

'It doesn't mean it's not the same killer, Mitch. They don't have to be consistent in what they do. He may have been unable to remover her wedding ring. Secondly does it matter what side of the head the snippet of hair was taken? Everything else matches.'

Mitch didn't reply to his chief's observation. He was busy with his own thoughts in this case.

'The trouble is we don't know who she is, sir. We will have to rely on dental records if we can't find out any other way,' said Mitch. 'She looked fresh too, don't you agree sir? It didn't appear she had been in the sea very long; not like the other three victims.'

'I agree. Have her wedding ring removed. There may be a clue there,' said Solly.

Mitch got on the phone to the hospital and gave instructions for the ring to be removed and sent over immediately to their police station.

Later that afternoon Solly was notified that a gold ring was in an envelope in his desk. He got a magnifying glass from his drawer and inspected the ring. Sure enough he could clearly see some engraving. It read 'Carl and Tracey'. He sniffed. The hay fever count was high today. This didn't tell him much. Once more there were no clues as to who she was, though the name Carl would be of great advantage once they had a surname. Her picture was put on the police web to see if that would help and the local Somerset papers gave a report of her being found and asking for assistance.

*

'Sir, Justin Long is back in this country. Do want him brought in for questioning?' asked DI Collins.

'When did he arrive back?'

'Yesterday, it seems. We asked Mrs Long to ring us when he came home.'

Solly and Mitch looked at each other. 'During Justin Long's absence there had been two more deaths. He couldn't be responsible for those, could he?' asked Mitch.

Solly didn't answer, but spoke to Simon on the intercom.

'Yes please, Simon, right away. Let me know when you have him.'

This case of the serial killer was really beginning to get to him. He remembered years ago when they were searching for the Yorkshire Ripper how long and tedious that had been. He hadn't been involved but he had read and studied the report. So had this killer, it seemed, because he had done his homework and was leaving no clues.

An hour later Simon told Solly that Justin Long was in a cell, waiting to be interviewed.

Once again it was Solly and Mitch who carried out the interview. Having got over the preliminaries involved in interviews Solly started the questioning.

'We are trying to solve the murders of four women, Mr Long. Where have you been these last ten days?'

'Away on holiday.'

'Where?'

'On the continent touring round.'

'On your own?'

'Yes! Why is that a crime?'

'Don't be flippant, Mr Long,' said the Chief Inspector. 'Were you ever in the police force?' Justin Long's face reddened at this question.

'Why, yes I was for a while.'

'Why did you leave?' There was a pause. One could see he did not like this line of questioning.

'I was sent to prison.'

'Why?'

'For murder.'

'Of whom?'

'My mother's lover,' replied Justin Long.

'Tell me about it Mr Long.'

'My mother, Alice Long, was having a love affair with a man in the village. We had a pub in Penalworth in Cornwall. He was a regular customer.'

Justin paused, wondering if he had to give more details.

'Go on, Mr Long, I want the whole story,' said Solly.

'There's not much to tell. I was driving on my way home from where I worked in the Met. As I went down the hill into our village I passed a car with a man driving and saw mother with her head on his shoulders. I was stunned. I wondered what could be going on. They didn't see me. Once they were out of sight I turned my car round and followed them, keeping a safe distance.

'They turned off along a dirt track. I knew they couldn't be going far as it went nowhere. I waited five minutes, parked up and followed them. They were in a sunny glade, surrounded by bushes and already they were both engrossed in the act of fucking. He was on top.' Justin wiped his eyes at the memory of it.

'Take your time, Mr Long,' said Solly.

'I just lost my cool. I picked up a big rock and dashing into the glade, smashed it down on his head, killing him instantly. I remember it as if it was yesterday. He just collapsed on top of my mother. "You dirty bitch," I shouted at her. I was in tears seeing what my mother was doing. She was naked, lying on a blanket. She was in shock. Together we rolled him off of her.'

'"What have you done, Justin?" she shrieked. She was sobbing. It was all very traumatic.'

Solly could understand the man's feelings at coming across a scene like this.

'What did you do next?' he asked.

'I told her to get dressed and I would cover the body up. Which I did, using branches.'

'What about his car. I suppose it was his?' asked Mitch.

'Mum drove mine home and I drove his some distance away and hid it in some woods. I couldn't think clearly. When I got home, Mum was already up in her bedroom sobbing.'

He paused again as if his mind was far away to that tragic day.

'Go on,' said the Inspector.

'Well, as is often the case in extramarital affairs, the husband is the last to know. Many people in the village guessed Mum was having an affair with him. When he didn't come home and nobody saw him, the police were alerted and someone told them about the affair. Mother was questioned by the police when they called at the pub. Dad had heard nothing about the incident till then. He was devastated.

'I heard her sobbing in the lounge where they were interviewing her. Although it was lunchtime, Dad closed the pub. He was at a complete loss. I decided to tell the police everything. I stormed into the lounge where mother and the detectives were and confessed to the whole thing ... That's about all there is to tell. The judge was very understanding and could see my point and I only got fifteen years. Six with good behaviour.'

'And then you went and joined the oil rig,' added Mitch.

'Yes that's right.'

'What do you think of women who play away from home like your mother did?' asked Solly.

'I despise them,' he said. 'I think they're scum, so are men who do the same.'

'I hear your mother was killed by Johnny your brother in a water-ski accident out in the Mediterranean area,' said Mitch.

'Yes it was unfortunate. It was off Majorca. The rudder stuck on his water ski and he slammed into her as she was swimming. She was concussed and never recovered.'

'Very sad to hear that, Mr Long,' said Solly, very sincerely. 'I would like to take you back to the night that Fiona died. You do remember her, don't you, Mr Long?' asked Solly

'Yes of course. Why, how can I help?'

'You passed his car in the town at 11.05, yet you didn't fill up at ASDA according to their CCTV till 0010 hrs. Where were you for that hour?'

'Do I have to tell you?'

'No you don't have to, you are not being charged, just questioned,' advised Solly, adjusting his chair position.

'Then I don't wish to say where I was. I would like to keep it private.'

Mitch decided on a new line of questioning.

'Are you gay, Mr Long?'

Justin blushed. He didn't answer right away. 'Yes I am gay,' he said.

'Do you want to tell us now where you were?'

'No,' he said again.

'Alright, Mr Long, you are free to go. Thank you for your help,' said Solly, gathering up his papers.

*

As he entered the incident room after interviewing Justin Long he was greeted by Wendy with a contented smile on her face.

'We have the name of the woman found off Brean, sir, and the name and address of her husband.'

'Thank you, Wendy, that's good news. Leave them on my desk,' said Solly, disappearing into Superintendent Josh's office for a consultation.

*

Carl woke early. He couldn't exactly remember a lot about the early hours when he fell asleep, completely whisky-soaked. His mouth tasted like a gorillas armpit. He rubbed the stubble on his chin and lit his last cigarette. Eileen would be on the phone organising his day. He would tell her he wasn't well, and to take a few days off. No that would be no good. He had to convince himself and others that his wife was away visiting her sister. She often went off with little or no notice, and it wasn't unusual for him to come home and find the house empty.

There was a ring at the door. He looked to see who it was; he was relieved to see it was Mrs Ellis the cleaner. He let her in.

'Good morning, Mr Barnhoff. What a cold one, isn't it?' she said, taking off her coat. 'Shall I make you a coffee sir?' she asked.

'Yes, do me a coffee and some toast would you.'

She sensed something wasn't right. The atmosphere was different.

'I brought that wool that your wife asked me to get. I hope it's the right colour,' she said, heading for the kitchen.

'She's away I'm afraid. She went to her sisters last night. She was gone when I got home.'

'Oh well I will leave it here till she returns.'

*

It was six days later that a blue Rover 75 saloon drew up in the drive way and two gentlemen in suits came to the door. Carl answered the door.

'Good morning. Are you Carl Barnhoff?' asked Solly.

'Yes, that's right, and you are?'

'Detective Chief Inspector Solomon, and this is Detective Sergeant Mitchell,' said Solly, showing their ID cards.

'Is your wife in, Mr Barnhoff?'

'No, she is at her sisters. What do you want her for? She hasn't been speeding again, has she? She is a devil for speed,' he said, with a big grin.

Solly ignored the speed comment. This matter was too serious.

'When did you last see her, sir?' asked Solly.

'Nearly a week ago tomorrow.'

'Did she say when she was coming home?'

'Not for another week at least. Why all the questions?'

'Mr Barnhoff, your wife was recovered from the sea off Brean. She was dead and had been murdered.'

'What, like those other girls that were murdered? Oh how terrible.'

He pulled his hanky from his pocket and turned away sobbing.

'Oh dear, I can't believe it; my precious love.' He turned to the inspector. 'You are certain, aren't you, Chief Inspector? I mean you are certain it is her. This is just terrible. But how did it happen? She took her car and a few things. She wasn't staying long. I was away on business when she left. She had gone when I came home. I didn't bother to phone her, and she knew I would be out most of the time in her absence. Come in, please, where is she now? The body I mean.'

The two detectives walked into the lounge.

'Has she ever done anything like this before?' asked Solly.

'Oh yes, about every two months she goes to her sisters. Sit down please. Do you want coffee?' They both declined the offer.

'Are you happily married, Mr Barnhoff?' asked Mitch.

'Yes, yes, of course we were. Why? What makes you ask that?'

'It's one of the things we have to know, so that we get a true picture.'

'Is that her picture over there?' asked Solly.

'Yes,' he said, handing it over to the Inspector.

'She was a very attractive woman, Mr Barnhoff,' said Solly, as he returned the picture.

'May we look around?' asked Mitch.

'Of course, anything to help catch my wife's killer. When can I see her?'

'Soon, we will need you to identify the body.'

'Of course, Sergeant, just let me know when and where. Here are my wife's car details, Chief Inspector,' said Carl, handing over a piece of paper.

The two detectives looked around, taking their time. It was when they got to her bedroom that evidence that she had no intention of staying became evident.

'What have we here, Mr Barnhoff? It appears your wife was planning to move out of this house,' said Solly.

'Yes it looks like it, Inspector. I haven't been in her bedroom since she left for her sisters. We sleep in separate rooms because I keep her awake all night snoring.'

'Can you explain why everything is packed?'

The wardrobe was practically empty, only a few oddments remained; possibly because they were too small for the lady, or very out of date. All personal items had been removed. The jewellery box was empty, only a picture of her and her husband remained on the bedside table. In the corner of the bedroom was a very large blue suitcase, bulging with what one must suppose was Mrs Barnhoff's personal belongings. It was evident that Carl was not aware of his wife's impending departure; or perhaps he was.

With out asking they went out side and seeing the garage, tried the door, only to find it was locked. It was a spacious two-door garage, made to hold two or more cars. Carl was standing at the house doorway watching them.

'Did you know your wife was leaving sir? What was she doing, going on holiday?'

'Yes, we were going to take a cruise when she came back from her sisters.'

'Oh yes, where to?'

'Barbados.'

'Have you booked it yet?'

'No, my wife was seeing to that.'

'She has emptied her wardrobe and taken her winter clothes, that's rather odd don't you think, Mr Barnhoff?'

'Yes, I suppose it is.'

'Have you packed your case yet sir?' asked Mitch.

'No, I was going to do it today, or rather my wife was.'

'Has your wife any special friends, particularly of the other sex, who are not your friends?'

'I don't know what you mean?'

'Well sir, my wife has men she knows and has long conversations with in town, or in a U3A circle or photographic club, anything like that. Has Mrs Barnhoff the same?' said Solly.

'No, all our friends are mutual, we know each others, that's all there is.'

'We will need to question you again, Mr Barnhoff. Let us know where you are and don't leave the area until we tell you,' said Solly.

They shook hands, and the duo left the premises.

*

'What's this then, Solly, number four for the serial killer, and none for us?' said Josh, as he entered Solly's office.

'It appears that way sir, though my sergeant has his doubts; we will see.'

'I have had no new suggestions on how we might solve these murders, Solly; but we have to, and quick. The press are having a hay day slagging us off as incompetents,' said Josh.

'We are searching for a white van which might have been the one used in the murders, but without a registration it's hopeless,' said Solly. 'He must make a mistake soon, but I expect more murders till then.'

Josh nodded his head in agreement and shuffled out of the office, deep in thought. There was a knock at his office door and Wendy entered his office.

'Hello Wendy, have you got the forensic results of the vans and cars at the Wicked Elf?'

'Not yet, sir, I will give them a ring. There is a letter arrived, sir. It is addressed to you private and confidential.'

'Oh is it? Thank you, Wendy,' he said, looking at the handwriting. It had been distorted on purpose. It was readable, but written like a five year old might have written it. There was no point worrying about fingerprints because the writer would have ensured that his weren't on the letter, and there had been so many people handling the envelope that it would have been nigh impossible to single out the culprit.

Solly used his paper knife to reveal the letter. When he opened it he was surprised to find it was a poem not a letter and had been made up of newspaper cuttings. It read:

ThReE arE dEAd
PoNdER Why
WiVes ARE sLy
KiLL ThOSE that LIE

At last someone had come out into the open. The killer was as frustrated as they were that they were making no progress, and this letter was sent to tease. He took the letter straight into Josh.

'Sir I have just received this poem,' he said handing it to him.

Josh adjusted his spectacles and read it through carefully three times before handing it back.

'It's a riddle of sorts. It seems to be aimed at giving you a motive. What do you think? Can you deduce any clue in those words?'

'The theme seems to be wives that lie.'

'Which ones don't?' asked Josh smiling. 'It appears genuine, Solly. What do you intend to do?'

'I know a very good psychologist, sir; I would like to call her in. She is very good.'

'Is it Stella Mooney?'

'Yes sir, do you know her?'

'Know her? I used to have a crush on her. I thought she might be retired by now.'

'She isn't, can I contact her?'

'Of course. Stella is semi-retired, but is only to willing to give a hand on an interesting murder case. We have her number on file,' said Josh.

Solly rang the lady's number after leaving Josh's office.

'Hello, Detective Chief Superintendent Solomon. Of course I will help you. I would be delighted to. I have been following these murders with interest. Can you get the file on this serial killer to me? When I have read it I will contact you.'

'Please call me, Solly. All my friends and colleagues do.'

'Of course I will, my dear. I look forward to working with you Solly,' she said.

He felt so much better now. Why hadn't he thought of her before? She was the answer.

'Sir, there is a report that a boy of twelve is missing from home, said Inspector Charlie Findus. He was the replacement for Simon, while on a course.

'Don't bother me with missing persons, Bob. There is a department to handle that,' said Solly, a little annoyed.

'I know sir, but this boy lives less than three miles from Carl Barnhoff's house. I thought you ought to know.'

'Yes, I see. Thanks Bob, we will call. Give Mitch the details please.'

'I have the details here, sir. The boy's bike has been found but not him,' said Mitch.

'Where was the bike found?' asked Solly.

'Near to his house in a ditch.'

'Right! Come on Mitch, we will go over and see his parents, but first we're going to have a look at the latest body found in the sea, and we will call on the missing boy's parents afterwards.'

As they drove over to the mortuary they passed several newspaper sellers advertising the news that a fourth body had been found and no murderer. It came up on the news on the car radio. Solly listened, and without a comment to Mitch, turned it off.

'What do you think of the killer sending us that poem, Mitch?'

'He wants to give us a lead. It's no good him killing women if he's getting no publicity to go with it sir. He knows we are stuck. This is his way of giving us a chance.'

'It doesn't tell us much.'

'Not yet, sir, but I got a hunch there will be more of these poems,'

'You and your hunches,' he scoffed. 'Here we are,' he said, pulling up and parking. The pair of them walked through the doors of the now very familiar mortuary.

Dr Chris Sharky was in the room sorting out instruments.

'Hello, Solly and Mitch,' he said with a smile. 'This is becoming a habit.'

'I know, we can't keep meeting like this,' added Solly, shaking his hand. 'So what's new with this one, Chris?'

'Firstly she still had her wedding ring. Secondly she has been hit with a hammer, but with so much force the hammer has actually entered her head. The killer was desperate that he didn't need a second chance. Also the marks on the skull where the hammer has struck show that it is a ball pein hammer, not a flat-headed sort used on the other murders. And thirdly, the killer did cut a piece of hair; he nearly scalped her. Once again, unlike our regular killer, this one took it from the opposite side of her head.'

'Yes, we noticed most of these facts. Indeed, the wedding ring helped us to trace her. So you think that this is a copycat murder? A lookalike?'

'Well, it could look like a good idea to the murderer, you know, put the blame on someone else.'

'I don't think the murderer I have in mind is quite that clever. Come on, Mitch, we will go and see him.'

'Thanks for your help, Chris. The body hasn't been identified yet, has it?'

'Yes, Mr Barnhoff has seen his wife and identified her.'

*

'Where to now sir?'

'You have the address of that missing boy with you, Mitch?'

'Yes you have something on your mind have you, sir?'

'It's just that it's so close to Barnhoff's house and it happened on the same night. It is unusual. There might be a connection, we'll see,' said Solly.

There is a possibility that this Barnhoff chap is the serial killer and has deliberately killed his wife and the other three women,' suggested Mitch.

'No! I don't think so, you're snatching at straws, Mitch, be realistic. If that were true, he would really be implicating himself, wouldn't he.' Having said that, Solly was pleased his sergeant was thinking ahead.

'Apparently his bicycle was found in the ditch just outside the house,' said Mitch.

'Was it indeed?' Solly got on the phone, contacted the SOCO and gave him details of the house and he wanted a search of the area.

'Here is the house coming up on the left, sir.' Solly didn't reply but, having made sure there was no traffic about, swung his car into the drive and without a word the two of them alighted from the vehicle.

Mr and Mrs. Clements came to the door. She was full of tears. He had a very stern face; both of them were young, in their mid thirties, Mitch guessed. The four-bedroomed detached house and gardens put them in the 40% tax bracket. Solly did the introductions, his manner was very different from when he spoke to Carl Barnhoff.

It was gentle and sympathetic.

'Still no sign of your son then, Mr Clements?'

'No, Inspector. I don't understand it. His bike was in the ditch outside. I naturally brought it in when I found it.'

'Where had Peter been that evening?'

'Up to his friend Simon, about a hundred and fifty yards up the road. I told him not to go by bike because he had no lights on it; but he went just the same,' said Mrs Clements.

'Have you spoken to his friend?'

'Yes, Inspector. He couldn't help. He said Peter had left him at 10 pm.'

'Can I see the spot where you found the bicycle?'

'Certainly come this way,' said Mr Clements. They walked down the path and though the gate at the bottom of the drive. 'It's along here,' he said.

They walked along. Solly and Mitch, being trained in detective work, were looking for signs that an untrained person would not recognise.

'This where I found the bike.'

'The exact spot?' asked Solly.

'Yes, Inspector,' he replied.

Solly leant over the ditch and looked down into it.

'Get the forensic team down here right away. I want a fingertip search of this area. The forensic team are only up the road.'

'Yes sir,' said Mitch obediently. They all went back into the house.

'Can I have a picture of your son please? I will see you get it back,' said Solly.

'May we see his room?' asked Mitch.

'Of course, come on I will take you,' said Mr Clements.

Peter's room was as one might expect. Football posters adorned the wall, and a lot of posters on space flight.

'I see he was interested in space travel,' said Mitch.

'Yes, he wanted to be a space scientist when he got older. He was always reading about it.'

'Did he keep a diary?' asked Solly.

'Not to my knowledge, Inspector,' said Mr Clements.

'Thank you, that will do fine, Mr Clements. Oh by the way, do either of you know a Mrs Tracey Barnhoff?'

'Yes I do inspector, she is the secretary of our WI,' said Mrs Clements. 'Why do you ask?'

'It might help me out on another problem, that's all,' he said, with a warm smile.

Mr and Mrs Clements looked at each other, wondering whether they ought to tell the Inspector the scandal surrounding the Barnhoff's.

'She has had a hell of a life with him. He is a womaniser. It's a wonder she hasn't left him before now,' said Mrs Clements.

'That's interesting,' said Solly.

Chapter 13

THE DETECTIVE DUO got in the car and headed off for the Barnhoff residence. Solly phoned for a police car and team to take Carl back to the station for questioning. As they drove into the drive of his house, they saw Carl in his shirt sleeves, raking up the garden.

Carl's house was an enormous five bed late Georgian style reproduced in about 1880. As one entered the main gate a double driveway led off on the left for entering and the right for exit. Large flower-planted lawns and gardens lay like a large carpet in the front of the house. It was obvious that somebody had spent a great deal of time and money on its upkeep.

'Hello, Chief Inspector. I have been to identify my wife. What a tragic loss it is for me. Life is so unkind, but I suppose I must come to terms with it and make the best of what I have left.'

'You're still a young man, Mr Barnhoff. How old are you?' asked Solly.

'Fifty three this year,' he replied.

'Did you know the killer of your wife left her wedding ring on her when he killed her.'

'No. She wasn't wearing it when I saw her at the morgue.'

'No I had it removed to help identify her. There were several other differences which cause us concern, Mr Barnhoff.'

'Oh, what are those, Inspector?'

'The hammer was a different type to the other three murders.'

'We would like to have a look around the grounds, Mr Barnhoff.'

'Why? You don't think I killed her, do you?'

'We can't rule out any possibility sir. Have you the keys to the garage?' Mr Barnhoff was becoming very flustered.

'Why on earth would I do such a thing to my little treasure? To even suggest it is absurd. I loved my wife,' he said, reluctantly handing over the keys to the garage.

There was a funny smell in the garage, not the sort one associates with oil, grease and petrol. Having had a good look around they walked out into the grounds. Mitch saw a drum blackened by fire which had been used for burning refuse. He walked over to it and poked around the wet black embers. He would love to dig around the house garden and garage and had a strange feeling that this disappearance had more to it than they had been told.

'Are you finished, Mitch?' asked Solly.

'Yes sir, though I would like to do an in-depth search of the premises. He doesn't act like a man worried about his wife. He isn't under any stress; he has asked us no questions. I think this one stinks sir.'

'Alright, Mitch. I know you and your hunches. Let's see if you're right.'

'Would you like to get your coat, Mr Barnhoff we want you to come along to the station for some more questioning?'

'Are you charging me, Inspector?' His tone had changed, he became defensive and aggressive. At that moment the police car drove into the driveway.

'No sir, we are just taking you in to help with our enquiries.'

'Why can't you do it here?'

'No, it has to be at the station.'

'I think I will phone my solicitor to meet me there.'

'By all means, sir,' said Solly.

Carl took out his mobile and gave his solicitor instructions to meet at the police station. It was fortunate that Carl's solicitor was at the station when the police cars pulled up.

'Hello, Chief Inspector, pleased to meet you, my name is Gladstone, Bertie Gladstone.'

Solly shook his hand and introduced Mitch. The four of them and a uniformed PC went into the interview room, where Solly and Mitch were to conduct the interview. Solly opened the proceedings in the correct formal manner giving the location time and who was present.

'Are you charging my client, Chief Inspector?' asked Bertie Gladstone.

'No Mr Gladstone, we are just trying to ascertain the facts leading to Mrs Barnhoff's disappearance.'

Mr Gladstone didn't comment further.

'Did you say you were at home when your wife went out the night she went missing, Mr Barnhoff?'

'No, she was gone when I arrived from work.'

'Have you anyone who can verify that?'

'No, I came home on my own.'

There was a knock on the door and Wendy poked her head in.

'Sorry to interrupt sir, this has just come in. I thought you ought to see it,' she said, handing Solly a sheet of paper.

'Thank you, Sergeant,' he said, sitting down.

'Did you go out at all that evening, Mr Barnhoff?' asked the Inspector.

'Only into the garage and the garden.'

'It was dark, wasn't it. What business had you in the garden?'

'There was some rubbish I wanted to burn up.'

'What! Clothes?'

'Yes.'

'Whose clothes?'

'Nothing special, some bits my wife asked me to dispose of when she was packing for our holiday.'

'Have you still got the clothes you were wearing the night she disappeared?'

'No, they were tatty so I burnt them as well.'

'All of them?'

'Yes.'

'Shoes as well?'

'Yes.'

'I see,' said Solly. 'I might as well tell you, Mr Barnhoff, that I have a search warrant here to search your house,' he said, handing it to Carl's solicitor. 'The forensic team are on their way now to see if there is any clue that would explain how your wife ended naked and dead in the Bristol Channel.'

'I had nothing to do with it.' Barnhoff said, loudly and indignantly.

'Nobody is accusing you, Mr Barnhoff, but we can leave no stone unturned,' said Solly, very coolly.

'Have you any more questions. I want my client released,' said the solicitor.

'Not so fast, his house is a suspect scene of crime, he can't go back there until forensic has declared it clear,' said Solly.

'But you are not charging him.'

'No, but we're holding him for further questioning. He should be clear to go tomorrow. Did you know they have found your wife's car, only about three miles from your house, Mr Barnhoff?'

'Well, I feel better about that. It confirms she did go out and visit a friend.'

'You said she was visiting her sister, that's a contradiction, isn't it?'

'That's where I understood she intended to go. She was obviously side-tracked and called on a friend before going to her sisters. I don't know I find it all so confusing,' said Carl Barnhoff, resting his head in his hands.

'When one tells lies it is easy to lose track of what one has said. It needs a good memory to be a good liar,' said Solly, staring him in the eyes.

Carl Barnhoff looked away and mumbled something about not lying; which didn't sound very convincing.

'Did I tell you we have found a car like your wife's car and some one has set it on fire,' added Mitch.

'What do you mean, somebody set it on fire?'

'It looks that way.'

'How strange. But why. What had they to gain? Perhaps it was vandals, Inspector? It's all very mystifying.' said Carl, trying to look confused.

'Do you know the friend she went to call on?'

'I think it was Mrs Clements down the road,' he mumbled, uncertain of his facts.

'Never mind. We will soon find out. We are retaining you, Mr Barnhoff. You will have to stay in a cell tonight, I'm afraid,' said Solly, closing the interview and leaving the room. Mitch and the PC on duty took control of Carl. He had to give a DNA sample.

Solly felt he had at last made a breakthrough regarding the numerous unsolved murders on his plate.

*

'How are things going, Solly?' asked Josh, as Solly entered his office.

'It looks as if we may have a wife killer, sir.'

'Any particular wife?'

'His own at the moment; but there may be others.'

'Very encouraging. If you do charge him, Solly, I want a press conference straight after.'

'Of course,' said Solly with an understanding smile. He had no sooner got back from getting himself a coffee when Wendy caught up with him.

'Sir, that boy's body has been found, partly clothed, his head smashed in.'

'Where was it found, Sergeant?' Solly asked.

'Not far from where the burnt out car was found, sir. A woman walking her dog found the body – well, the dog unearthed it. The crime officer is there now, together with a doctor and the forensic team.'

'This is hotting up, thank you, Wendy. I want a meeting of everyone this afternoon at 3 pm. We have a guest speaker coming to see us.'

'Yes sir, I will arrange it,' she said, with a smile.

*

Solly was busy writing up his reports when there was a tap at the door. He looked up and saw a senior aged lady in her mid sixties. She smiled at him.

'Good afternoon, are you, Solly? she asked.

He rose quickly from his chair. 'Mrs Stella Mooney?' he asked.

'That's right,' she came forward with her hand extended. He took and kissed her on each cheek – as was the fashion.

'I am so pleased and honoured to make your acquaintance,' he said, pointing to a chair for her to sit.

She smiled. 'Thank you. I hope I can be of help. Here is the file you let me have. It was very graphic and detailed.'

'Can I get you some refreshment? Tea or coffee.'

'No thanks, I had some earlier. Solly, I think you have a grudge killer on your area. I feel he has a vendetta against certain women, and the only link I can come up with is that all three of these women were married, and were having fun with other men playing away from home. Two of them had sex with another man before their deaths. I think this killer is against any woman he can kill who is having an affair.'

'Yes, I must admit we had come to the same conclusions. We decided that must be the motive as we could find no other that fitted the crime,' added Solly.

'I have given it a lot of thought. He selects his victims carefully. He knows where they live, what time they will be home, and the route they will take.'

'So you agree he is local?'

'I wouldn't be surprised,' she said.

'Anything else?'

'Yes I wouldn't be surprise if he had an accomplice to help him.'

'The thought had been suggested, because we thought it would be quicker. But that's very unusual isn't; I mean having two killers?'

'I know, but he has to act quickly because of the short time he has from the time of hitting them to getting them into the van. He has to work fast.'

Solly could not swallow this reasoning. It would be even more unusual to have two killers working together with the same motive; but he didn't argue with her reasoning.

'I have a meeting in five minutes. Would you be kind enough to speak to my team?'

'I would be delighted.'

'Right, if you will come with me we'll go through. Ah here is my Superintendent. I believe you know each other.'

Josh was coming towards them with a big welcoming smile on his face

'Hello, Stella. It's been a long time since we last met. How are you?' He kissed her fondly on her cheek.

'It's lovely to see you, Josh. You must be near retiring age,' she joked.

'Only six months left. Crime today, well there is just too much of it. I think I will be glad for a rest.'

He followed them through to the incident room where every one was seated awaiting their guest speaker. Solly thanked everyone for being there and introduced Stella as a crime psychologist.

'Good afternoon. I have been a crime psychologist for thirty years and have helped to solve many murders in that time; including serial killers.' She referred to the picture board which had just been made up to date.

'We already have four unexplained deaths, possibly five with the murder of the boy – they could be linked. Never rule anything out. I have read and studied the report and I think we have a killer out for revenge. A revenge he inflicts on married women; two of whom we know were having sex outside of marriage, the third might have been the same but for an accident. We don't have a suspect as the one possibility, Wayne Coldcrow, was murdered and his killer is awaiting trial.

'I would suggest that the person we are looking for is tall and well built. He has to be, to handle a dead weight and get her into his van quickly so he isn't spotted. This I imagine is the sequence of events. The van doors are open, she passes, he strikes, kills her, grabs her, into the van, shut the doors and drive off. The time for this operation I would estimate at ten to fifteen seconds maximum. Now if he had an accomplice driving the van he could reduce it even more.'

'We have actually carried out timed trials simulating the murder crime and we concur with your timings,' added Solly.

'Permission to speak, sir?' asked Wendy.

'Yes, sergeant .What have you to say?' said Josh.

'I think that the women knew their killer. So much so, that they were not afraid of him when they met at night.'

'What makes you think that?' said Stella.

'Well, if this were the case, and the victim was not frightened of him. He could invite them to look at something in the back of his van, I would also suggest he had the van doors open. The inquisitive victim comes round the back of the van. He whacks her on the head, grabs her, and slides her into the van, shutting the doors before driving off.'

There is silence in the room. Everyone is going over what Wendy has said.

'Very good,' said Solly. 'I think that suggestion is perfectly plausible.'

'So do I,' agreed Stella.

There was a muttering around the room while she took a sip of water. Many had considered the possibility of there being an assistant; and many doubted it.

'We have what we believe is a white van near to where the third victim was last sighted. This is quite possibly the murder van. However I have given this matter a lot of thought and have put myself into the killer's shoes. And because of this if it were me I would not use the same van twice. I would do my utmost to confuse the police; at least at the start.'

'What would you do?' asked Solly

She turned and looked in his direction.

'I would hire the vans, wash and clean them out afterwards and return them. That way there would be no trace of the van, or the number plates.'

'I just hope for our sakes the killer isn't as clever as you, Stella,' said Josh.

The room burst into laughter.

'Thank you Stella, any questions from anyone?' asked Solly.

'Yes ma'am, what about the poem we received,' asked PC Ruby Howlett.

'You are not the first detective squad to receive a cutout poem from the killer; it has gone on for years. It usually shows frustration by the killer in not being recognised. From his point of view he is getting his revenge for a matter which concerns him, but he wants recognition for it. Also, he needs the publicity to stimulate his ego. It's important to him. The more murders he commits the less bothered he is about getting caught,' she said.

'That's a very interesting theory,' remarked Solly. 'Thank you, Stella, you have been most helpful, and have put some good ideas into our heads which we will work on. Ladies and gentlemen, show your thanks to Stella in the usual way.'

They all stood up and gave her a resounding round of applause.

*

'Sir, there are two reports on your desk from forensic.'

'Thank you, Sergeant,' he replied. He picked up the two reports and read them. The contents were very welcome.

'Mitch, read these reports, and tell me what you think,' said Solly. Mitch read them both through and handed them back.

'Very interesting, are you going to interview Mr Barnhoff again? Only he is due for release tomorrow, sir.'

'I know that, Sergeant,' Solly always called him by his rank when he was annoyed with him. 'Get his solicitor and him into the interview room and we may be able to get this matter settled. I want it done today.'

'Right sir, I'll get on to it,' said Mitch.

*

At five o'clock that day they were all gathered in Room 2 for the interview. Josh was watching the interview via the two-way glass build into the wall. Once again Detective Chief Inspector Solomon, Sergeant Mitchell together with Mr Barnhoff and his solicitor were seated either side of the table. Carl was dressed in a white paper overalls. Solly opened the proceedings as usual.

'Mr Barnhoff, we are investigating the death of Peter Gary James Clements and that of Mrs Tracy Barnhoff,' said the inspector.

'My client has assured me he has no knowledge of either of these killings inspector,' said Mr Gladstone.

Solly ignored him.

There is evidence from the sand and mud found on one of the front tyres of your wife's car that it had stopped outside or near the premises of Mr Clements.

'Who's he? I don't know a Mr Clements,' said Carl.

'Does your wife know people of that name, who live near you?'

'Possibly, I don't know all her friends; besides. I understood her car was set on fire. How could anyone get evidence from burnt out tyres?'

'This tyre was in a puddle and the bottom part didn't catch fire. When it was checked by forensic the tyre marks and residue from the spot the boy was snatched matched up. This proves the vehicle had been there at some time.'

'Why Inspector, that could have been the day before. It doesn't prove anything apart from the fact it had at some time been there,' said Mr Gladstone, very confidently.

Solly looked at Carl's face; he seemed to have brightened up. 'If that's all you have, Inspector I suggest you release my client, you haven't sufficient evidence to retain him.'

'Wait! I haven't finished! Blood spots were found in the ditch where the boy's bike was found. We have a forensic report that confirms they were those of Peter Gary James Clements,' said Solly.

'It still does not prove this was carried out by my client. You will have to release him. You have no evidence that Mr Barnhoff was driving that vehicle that night. It must have been his wife who was visiting Mrs Clements, and when she stopped the car, possibly to speak to Peter, the killer struck, killing them both.'

'Highly unlikely and difficult,' said Solly. 'Imagine trying to kill two people in the dark, outside of the victim's house. Use some common sense please,' said Solly.

The lawyer realised his stupidity and said nothing.

'The in-depth search we did in the area revealed a clue which proves beyond doubt that your client was responsible for these murders.' Solly placed on the table a small plastic bag, in it was a St Michael medallion on a silver chain. 'This medallion was found in the ditch.'

'It could belong to anyone inspector,' said the solicitor.

'Let me finish. Firstly it had Peter's DNA on it. He must have grabbed it as he fell. Secondly it is inscribed on the back "To Carl love Tracy". A strange silence came over the room after this revelation.

'Mr Barnhoff I am charging you with the deaths of your wife Tracey Barnhoff, and of Master Peter Clements, and the possible murder of three other women killed in similar circumstances namely Mrs Debbie Carter. Mrs Jessie Barlow and Mrs Mary Dagleash. Read him his rights, Sergeant Mitchell,' he said rising from his chair.

'Wait! Alright I admit the killing of my wife and the boy. If I make a statement will it help my case?' said Carl Barnhoff, who was now sweating profusely.

'If you plead guilty it will certainly help your case. Are you willing to tell us what happened?' asked Solly.

'Do you want all the details?'

'Yes we do, and a written statement signed by you.'

'I agree.' They all sat and listened while Carl related the gruesome details.

'My wife and I had words that night over dinner and she accused me of having an affair with my secretary.'

'And were you?' interrupted Solly.

'Yes I was, and I loved her more than my wife. So that night I persuaded her – my wife, that is – to come to the garage where I struck her a hard blow with my hammer, killing her outright. I stripped her naked and cut a piece of her hair off like the killer of those other women. I put her in her own car and drove it to the coast about five miles away and pushed her into the sea. I then drove back home and had the brilliant idea of leaving her car near her friends house.

'As I was getting out of the car this lad Peter rode by on a bike with no lights. He said, "Good evening, Mr Barnhoff." I realised he had ruined any chance of my getting away with the murder. I called him over and asked him to help me find my keys which I said I had dropped. He got off his bike and put it in the ditch, as he came towards me I hit him with the same hammer I had used on Tracey.

'He grabbed at me as he fell to the floor; that's when I must have lost my medallion. I put him in the car and drove off. I didn't know what to do. Then I decided I would bury the boy, and set fire to the car; which I did. When I got home I burnt all my wife's clothes she had been wearing, and mine as well. The rest you know, Inspector.'

'When you have signed your confession you may go back to your cell,' said Solly.

He was glad, and relieved to have got a result so easily. This murderer, unlike the serial killer, was desperate and he bungled it, whereas the serial killer was shrewd. He knew exactly what he was doing and when and where he should strike next.

Chapter 14

S OLLY CALLED the press conference for 10 am next day and the room was full of press men wanting answers. Josh sat with him listening.

'What's the latest on the man you brought in?' asked a man from the *Daily Clarion.*

'We have charged him with murder not only of his wife, but Peter Dickenson, the twelve-year-old boy.' A reporter from the *Globe* stood up she was a pretty girl with long flaxen hair.

'I am from the *Globe.* Can you tell me if this man is responsible for the other killings?'

'We are still investigating,' Solly replied.

There were three other questions then Solly closed the meeting. The paparazzi wolves had been fed. He had satisfied their hunger for news, but only for the moment; they would be back.

*

When Solomon and Superintendent Josh entered the Serious Crime Room the hum of voices decreased to a murmur. Wendy had made the board up on the wall so they could all see the pictures and the progress.

'As a result of Mrs Stella Mooney's talk to us the other day I want to find out what you think of her theories, are they practical and do they help you. I'm sure you have all discussed what she said so I would be interested to know where we go from here,' said Solly to the 25 detectives assembled. They were not all involved directly with this case all the time but had been called in to help out.

'What about the killer's motive?' he asked those assembled

'Sergeant Mitchell. Do you think it's realistic that he is out for revenge on women who are playing away from home, in other words having extramarital relationships.'

'I think it is a sound motive and one we should work on sir,' he replied.

'Do you all agree to this?' There was a murmur but no comment.

'Come on, I want an answer. Hands up those who think we should use this as our killer's motive.' Most of the hands went up in a casual manner.

'Right, now regards the vehicle. Do you think that her theory about hiring different vans is a sound one.'

Once again there was a show of hands.

'Good, at least we are agreeing in principle. I want you to watch out for cafes and places where likely victims might be found. I know it's a delicate subject but we are doing it for their own good. I want a team to check out on foot not by telephone those that are hiring out white vans in the last fortnight like the one seen when Mary Dagleash was killed. It's going to be a lot of walking and talking but it has to be done.'

'Sir, we had the report back from the forensic laboratories who have been working on the poem you received. They have some DNA but not enough. They say it appears genuine and they think there may be more,' said DI Bob Findus.

'That's all I need, a bloody poet,' said Solly, which encouraged a room full of laughter.

*

Jeffrey Kantar and Betsy Hedges were on the same committee in the council. In fact she was his private secretary, Jeffrey was nearly fifty, tubby and going a little bald and grey, but still a fine specimen of a man and very active especially on the Bowling Green. Betsy was forty and had worked in county councils since leaving school. Her husband Dick was a junior school teacher, and served on the board of Governors of his school. Betsy was of medium height with an attractive figure for a mother of twin girls aged fourteen.

Jeffrey had been divorced for five years. His wife finally decided she had had enough of his philandering ways and put a stop to it by divorcing him. As so often happens in life when two people work close together and find they like each other a lot, eventually leading to a drink after work or a meal, and progressing from there to a mutually convenient bedroom, Jeffrey and Betsy had been having a very seductive time for three undetected years. But like all good things it could not last with out detection indefinitely; in fact they were thinking of ending it by mutual agreement.

'I think if we are ending our wonderful relationship we ought to celebrate it with one final fling. Do you agree, my love?' asked Jeffrey.

'Sounds wonderful. Like you said, it's better to end it on a happy note than us being discovered and the resulting upset that would follow. We have been lucky and have had a wonderful three years.'

'We'll still be friends though, won't we,' said Jeffrey.

'Of course we will, my lover. That will never change. What do you plan for our last night?'

'Let's go out for a dance. Do you remember the pub we went to a few weeks ago? The Wicked Elf? Let's go there for a start off,' said Betsy.

' Good idea, then back to my house for a farewell kiss.'

'That sounds super; especially the goodnight kiss,' she laughed. "When shall we do it?'

'Can you get out Friday night? We could have another lengthy council meeting with dinner after. We have used that excuse before and you have always been home for eleven at night.'

'I'll try, Dick likes to play bridge on Fridays and he's never home much before eleven. Yes my love. I will say goodbye to my husband, and I will bring a change of dress. I will park in that little car park at the bottom of Bradwell Hill. That's where you will drop me off and I will pick up my car. Is that alright?'

'It sure is, my lovely,' he said, running his hand up her skirt.

'Jeffrey! Not here,' she laughed, slapping his hand.

*

'Where are you meeting tonight, Betsy?' asked Dick, her husband.

'I told you, dear, we're meeting and having dinner at the White Bear Hotel in Chigsbury.'

'Only, I could pick you up.'

'No dear I have already made arrangements. Thank you anyway.'

'What time will you be home?'

'I won't be late. I will be home by 11.30 at the latest. Mum is staying the night and the twins are at dancing classes.'

'As usual you see to everything,' he said with a smile. 'Well, I'm off to my bridge night. Give me a kiss goodbye.' She gave him a quick peck and went back to brushing her hair.

*

Jeffrey picked her up at the little car park. It was a very unobtrusive venue. It only held twenty cars, and there was no charge, which was a rare thing in those days. She took the dress she was wearing that night to work with her because when she next saw her husband Dick, she planned to be wearing it to support her excuse for being out late.

Dick was a good husband. He loved his family and especially his twin girls Bobbie and Marcia. Dick was a small-framed, wiry sort of man, and was quite happy dressed in cords and a jumper. He found contract bridge a very exhilarating game, even better than chess. He hadn't been playing long but had studied the subject and had been to evening classes. Because of this, every Friday night he couldn't wait to get to the club, meet his pals and try and win the evening bridge session.

Once Jeffrey had Betsy securely fastened into her safety belt he gave her a promising kiss.

'Where are we going?' she asked.

'To the Wicked Elf, remember we said we would go for a dance, then back to my house for a farewell cuddle.'

'I'm sorry we're calling it a day my love, but we both know it makes sense. It would be cruel for Dick to find out and our marriage to dissolve because of what we are doing.'

The car park was full – well, nearly – and music could be heard coming from the skittle hall which was converted on a Friday night to a dance hall. They had been there before several times. They only stayed at the pub an hour.

'Let's go back to my place. I have a nice supper laid on with champagne,' said Jeffrey.

Jeffrey's home was a two-bedroom apartment, newly built at Redcott. It was sumptuously furnished with the latest gadgets, subdued lighting and a clean perfumed fresh air dispenser which helped to relax them both after their supper and champagne.

They left at 11.00 pm as it wasn't far to the car park. When they got there he dropped her off, but not before a loving kiss goodbye. She set off across the dimly lit park to where her car was parked, which was the only one remaining, apart from a blue van parked next to it. She passed the van and that was the last she remembered.

*

The Friday selected by Jeffrey and Betsy for their night out at the Wicked Elf also happened to be the night that Big Mac decided he would meet with some pals at the same location. He was leaning on the bar chatting when he saw Jeffrey come in with a lady he did not know, but knowing Jeffrey's reputation for girlfriends he wasn't surprised. He was intrigued as to who she was. He turned to Taffy, a forty-year-old roofing contractor friend of his. He had been divorced three years ago and was constantly looking for the right girl to replace the one he had lost.

'Hey Taff, whose that hen that Jeffrey is with. I'm sure she's been in my café before now. Do you know her?'

'Yes, he's been knocking her off for years. I don't know how he's got away with it, Its Betsy something. I know she's married. I think he's a doctor.'

'She's good looking too, isn't she.'

'Not bad. She looks a bit too classy to be in here though. Some men get all the luck,' said Taff, turning back to his pint.

The pub was cool tonight now that spring was well on its way. It wasn't so packed, though most of the regulars were there. Joyce and Debbie no longer came to the pub after the murder of their friend Fiona. Jerry Long had been in earlier, but when he saw he had sufficient staff he said he was going out on business and would be back later. Elsie, his wife was used to him leaving the bar for her to run. He preferred working in the kitchen.

'I think she's been in my café before now,' said Big Mac, more to himself than anyone else. He had a good memory for faces usually, but this one had him stumped.

The pub was in full swing with dancing, drinking and laughter when Wendy and Mitch walked in. They had been going out regularly since the night Wayne was stabbed, and they liked the Wicked Elf, despite its reputation. There weren't many places that a couple could go and have a fun evening out like this one. Besides, they liked the privacy – no coppers spying on them.

Mitch nodded to Big Mac when he saw him, but didn't speak. He went to the bar and ordered a fruit juice for Wendy and a pint for himself. It had been a month since the serial murders started. He saw Justin flit in and out the bar. The restaurant was busy tonight. They chose a table and surveyed the collection of dancers and customers. Being police men and women they just could not escape the habit of constantly taking in everything that might one day have a bearing on a crime case.

In fact, since Fiona's murder and the stabbing of Wayne Coldcrow, the customer numbers had increased. What a morbid lot people were, thought Mitch.

After finishing his first pint he invited Wendy up for a dance. It was a slow smoochie number of which there were plenty during the evening. Everybody seemed to like Matt Monroe, Sinatra and music from the sixties and seventies. He held her close. The sweat smell of her perfume gave him the desire to lay down with her and physically express how he felt for her.

Wendy was playing everything rather cool. She didn't want to rush into anything. That was why she still kept her flat and Mitch stayed in his; though he had suggested they move in together. She said she wanted to wait. She wanted to be sure. It wasn't as if they weren't lovers, they were; and very good and mutually satisfying ones too. They faced each other, smiled and kissed. Both felt that their friendship would develop one day into a full blown romance. Neither had declared their love for each other.

To practical Wendy, her definition of love was what you did to help someone; not a lot of silly worthless romantic garbage. Whereas Nigel (Mitch) was a true romantic. He loved amorous passionate poetry and speaking soft tender words into a girl's ear. The music ended and the crowd on the floor dispersed.

Wendy, who was more involved with her work than Mitch, who knew when to switch off, suggested a stroll in the car park. Mitch agreed and they walked outside. A full moon beamed down on them, as if showing its approval for two young lovers being out together.

'What are we looking for?' asked Mitch.

'I don't know exactly, but this is too good a chance to miss. I want to see the car park at night.'

Mitch looked at her. Funny woman he thought, but he didn't comment further.

'Look, there's a white van. I'm sure it's different to the one we checked out with forensic. I wonder why they want it, and did it really need changing. Let's have a look at the tax disk. It appears to belong to a garage. I think we ought to have it checked over Mitch. Soon this killer will get careless and leave us clues. The more information we have now the better.'

'Hello! What are you two doing snooping around my car park?' asked Justin Long, appearing out of the darkness.

'Nothing,' said Mitch, quickly recovering from the shock of Justin appearing on the scene.

'We were just admiring your new van, Mr Long,' said Wendy.

'Oh! It's you two. You're doing a bit of snooping in the dark, are you.'

'Not at all, we have come out for some air. It's a nice van though, isn't it?'

'Come off it. People don't come into pub car parks to admire vans.'

'Why did you change it? There was nothing wrong with it, was there?' asked Wendy.

'No but we like to change vans regularly.'

'I see, what you use it for, Mr Long?'

'Look! Bugger off. I'm not standing answering police questions at night. I got a pub to run,' he said, stalking off into the darkness towards his pub.

Mitch and Wendy looked at each other, and burst out laughing, as they too returned to the pub.

*

There was a letter on Solly's desk when he came in the next morning. He picked it up and looked it over. Straight away he knew who it was from and its contents. He opened it and read the contents:

ThREe have Gone aND nOW its Four
How MANy More I tEll U
LoOk for oNE DressEd In bLue

So now it was a game, a quiz a puzzle; and he was going to provide the clues. It would mean they would have to dance to his music. Solly didn't like that. Firstly he could be leading them a merry dance all around the houses. The killer must be local, and educated he guessed. He looked at the poem again. *Three have gone and now it's four.* Was the killer implying the death of another woman, he wondered?

Look for one dressed in blue. What did he mean by that? Was it a clue to his identity? Or was it the next victim? he wondered. But his victims were naked. If it was a clue to the killer's identity it didn't give much away. How many people were there dressed in blue – policeman, fireman, airman, sailor and so the list goes on. Well, it might help, thought Solly; putting the letter back in the envelope ready to show Josh when he came in later.

'Can I have the latest list of missing persons? Only those women who might be targets for our killer, Wendy,' asked Solly. She was busy working on a computer.

'Yes sir, we are working on the white vans available. We have found 356 which are of the same type and are going around asking questions at the garages.'

'What are you hoping to find?'

'Well, sir, I have told my team to look for the slightest mark which could be a missed blood sample that hasn't been washed off. There must have been a spurt of blood when he hit them.'

'Yes I agree. That's cool,' he said, with a smile.

'Oh another thing sir, we, that is Mitch and I were at the Wicked Elf last night and noticed that they have changed their van again. I have a note of the number.'

'Keep on with this van tracing, Sergeant. It's our best hope of finding one or more involved in these murders,' said Solly.

It was just at that moment that a uniformed sergeant came into the incident room to report that a married woman had gone missing and her husband had been harassing the police to find her.

'Have we got a name and details?' asked DI Simon Collins, who had recently returned from a course and was now eager to catch up on the murder investigations.

'Yes sir. It's a Richard Hedges and his wife's name is Betsy Hedges. They live in a village off the A38 named Foxton. 26 Ropse Lane. I took his phone number and mobile sir.'

'Thanks, well done, Sergeant,' said Simon, gazing down at the facts handed to him by the sergeant.

'Are you busy, Sergeant Morrison?' he called to Wendy.

'I am available, sir, I have some work to do, but could do with a change.

'What is it?'

'Another woman has gone missing on Friday night.'

'Is there sir? Where from home?' she asked, gathering up her coat.

'We have no proof that she has gone missing from home. I want us to go and see her husband.'

Chapter 15

WENDY AND NEIL MITCHELL were partners now. They both kept their own houses; for the moment anyway because of the state of the economy house prices were dropping like overripe apples off a tree. They were so compatible in what they liked, and they enjoyed being together, that it was inevitable right from the start that this was the way it was going to be. Wendy and Neil were in love, and although they didn't advertise the fact, friends and workmates could see they were very close.

It was policy in the force, that policemen, working on the same case, should not be married or living together. In fact very often it was not unknown to separate them, sending one of the partners to another station nearby. Because of this the couple did not advertise the fact that they were living in the same house most of the time, though Wendy kept her flat going.

'I'm going to Mother's when I have washed these few things,' said Wendy. 'She's not been well and I haven't seen her for a week. You are going to your Freemasons lodge tonight and I have some work to do at home so I will stay the night there and see you in work in the morning. Your clean shirt is hanging on the wardrobe.'

'Thank you, darling, give your mum my love,' he said, giving her a kiss before he left the room to get ready.

Wendy's mum was sitting with a blanket round her knees and the heating turned off when she arrived.

'Mother, what are you doing? No wonder you have a chill, get that heating on right away.'

'It's the cost, my dear, heating is so expensive.'

'Come on, Mother, you can afford it,' said Wendy, setting the central heating regulator. 'Have you eaten?'

'I had a cup of tea this afternoon. You don't feel like eating when you are cold.'

'Nonsense, that's even more reason to eat. I'll get you something. She went into the kitchen and prepared some scrambled egg for her. Wendy was the youngest of Pearl Morrison's children. She had two sons, both of whom worked for the NHS.

Wendy was twenty eight. She wasn't exceptionally pretty but one might describe her face as businesslike. It always seemed to have something on its mind which was reflected in the furrows on her brow. She had been in the police force ten years, and loved it. She cleaned around the house and tidied up, making sure she had plenty of food in the house, but she felt reassured when her mother told her that usually next door provided her midday meal.

Having seen she was comfortable and warm Wendy set off home it was only about a mile so she walked it. It gave her time to think about her future with Neil. The traffic was light tonight; after all, it was 10.30. She didn't give a thought when she passed a blue van with its doors open and blackness took over her mind from then on.

*

'Where's Wendy?' asked Solomon, the day after she had visited her mother.

'I don't know, she should be here,' said Mitch, looking round.

'Didn't you see her last night?'

'No!' she said. 'She was going to her mother's, because she had been ill, and as her own house is nearby she would stay there, as she had some work to do. It was agreed we would meet at work this morning.'

'Go and find out if she is alright,' said Solomon.

Mitch tried hard to keep within the speed limit as he made his way over to Wendy's house. He had phoned her mother and Wendy's house; to no avail. Mitch pulled up outside Wendy's house and saw that the car was still there. He had a key so he let himself in, hoping to find her asleep in bed, but there was no sign of her. The bed looked as if it hadn't been slept in, though she could have made it. No, he knew she hadn't slept in it. Using his mobile he phoned Solomon. It didn't occur to him at first that Wendy might have walked to her mother's, though she did sometimes if the mood took her.

'Sir, I can't find her, and I can't find any trace of her. It seems quite likely she walked from her mother's to her own house, and if anything has happened to her it could be along this mile walk.'

'Nothing will have happened to her, Mitch. You're getting paranoia about the fate of ladies at night.'

'Nevertheless I want to retrace her footsteps, just to see if there is anything to be found.'

'Alright Mitch, I will send a police car with men in it to help you. Good luck.'

'Thank you sir.'

He didn't wait for the patrol car but set out diligently searching for blood trace or any clue at all to her disappearance. He stopped.

There in front of him blood spots, dried blood spots on the pavement. He looked in the gutter; there were slight traces of tyre marks. He knew it could be anybody's blood and tyre marks, but he had found some distinct tyre marks as a result of the light rain the previous night, but no blood marks. He looked to see if there were CCTV cameras in the area, there weren't any. The spot was between street lights and it was a very minor road. Using his mobile again he phoned Solomon.

'Sir, I have found tyre marks but no blood spots.'

'Say no more,' Solomon interrupted him. 'I will have an investigation team there right away. Where exactly are you?'

'Halfway down Crab Lane, sir.'

'Hold tight, Mitch, I'll be there.'

Ten minutes later the place was swarming with police and forensic men, all looking for clues and gathering evidence as to whether these were Wendy's DNA, and her abductor's tyre marks.

'There is no doubt about it sir, Wendy would have reported in long before now. She had a special sense of responsibility. She is either dead or someone is keeping her captive.'

'Yes, I'm sure you're right,' said Solomon. 'It is of special significance when it's one of your own.'

'Do you mind if I go and interview her, Mother?'

'No that's alright, take a WPC with you.'

An hour later Mitch was seated by Wendy's mum and WPC Sylvia Fletch was seated next to him.

'Whatever could have happened to her, Neil?'

'I don't know yet, chances are she might phone in later. Are you alright? I will get an FLO to come and help you out for a few days.'

'She didn't say where she might be going last night, or in the future perhaps,' asked Neil.

'She said she was going to have her hair done, as it was a mess.'

'And that's all?'

'Yes, as far as I can remember,' she said sobbing.

*

'I'm sorry, Mitch, but it seems she has been abducted,' said Solomon.

Josh was in the room, so was the Area Commander, Bill Bodgers.

The tyre marks were very inconclusive, but there was nothing else to go on.

'Were there no other clues from the site?' asked the Commander.

'No sir, we are looking at all CCTV of that area but of course there was none in Crab Lane itself. We have policemen searching and asking questions all along Crab Lane. They are doing house-to-house questioning and are stopping all cars over a twenty-four hour period to see if any driver remembered seeing anyone or a parked car or van.'

There was a knock at the door Sergeant Toby Melrose came in.

'We have a sighting of a white van, same as was seen when Mary Dagleash went missing. Different number plates though, sir, it's possible he is switching plates as he chooses to confuse us.'

'He's certainly doing that. Thank you sergeant,' said Solomon.

'He most likely has changed the colour of van he uses, now he knows we are checking on white ones,' said Mitch

'It might be blue,' said Solly. 'There is reference to the colour blue in that poem I got yesterday.'

'I agree sir, I think it's quite probable the killer and abductor is driving a blue van,' said Mitch. 'And in the poem reference to blue the killer could be referring to a WPC uniform of blue,' said Mitch.

'Yes, that's quite possible,' said Solly. 'However, if Wendy is still alive and they are holding her as a hostage then I pity them because they have certainly got a tiger by the tail.'

All the talk throughout the station was on Wendy's disappearance, they were waiting for a report of another body being found. They didn't have long to wait.

The first thing was a press conference, where the main subject of questioning was the disappearance of Wendy. Unfortunately, the Police were unable to throw any light on her disappearance, despite heavy questioning and criticism. Her disappearance was also headlines on the news and the daily papers. They knew there was not a lot more they could do till the body turned up, which they expected any day. Mitch was heartbroken with the loss of his partner and spent every day and hour he could spare researching the evidence looking for some clue.

'I feel we have to do some thing positive, sir,' said Mitch.

'Like what?' said Solomon.

'We ought to do a really good search of every house where they lived, their cars and garages, all ex boyfriends and husbands. There must be a link.'

'You could be right but without good reason we can't do it unfortunately.'

*

On the following Monday, after the Friday incident. Detective Sergeant Toby Melrose, who was the temporary replacement for Wendy, came into Solomon's office.

'This character we're looking for, sir, is using any old number plate to hang on his van .We have checked the numbers out with the DVLA and they belong to private registered cars. He must have a pile of them and sticks one on his van as he pleases and as it's usually at night it is not so easy to catch him out.'

Just then Josh walked into Solomon's office.

'We have another female corpse found in the sea off Clevedon; by a fisherman. He managed to secure her and called us up on his radio. A lifeboat is on the way now to recover her; she's fully dressed,' said Josh. Solomon's immediate thought was that it might be Wendy. He went into the main room and called Mitch.

'A woman's body has been found off Clevedon. There is a possibility it could be Wendy's. Don't build your hopes up, Mich,' he said. 'We still have Betsy Hedges unaccounted for. That's been missing ten days. We're going to see the corpse when she is brought in. Come on we'll go now.'

The two of them drove to the Mortuary where the body was to be taken.

'By the way,' he added, 'Superintendent Roberts thinks you should be on sick leave until we find out about Wendy. What do you think, Mitch? Only, he also thinks it may affect your judgement and work.'

'No sir, please let me carry on doing the job. I am alright and whatever the results I can take it.'

'Alright, Mitch, I will tell the Super, and try and convince him. Come on we're going to see the corpse when she is brought in.'

The two of them drove to the mortuary where the body was to be taken.

They walked through the double doors of the mortuary and saw a body lying there under a sheet. The forensic room had numerous doctors working away on different aspects of forensic work. There was a separate room where the bodies were cut up to further the investigations. They were in familiar company so introductions weren't necessary. Mitch was relieved to see it wasn't Wendy. He hoped the longer they waited for a corpse of her the better chance there was that she was still alive and would one day come smiling into the police station as if nothing had happened.

'Who is she, doctor?' asked Solomon.

'A Mrs Betsy Hedges, she's been missing ten days, as you can see there isn't much to look at. The sea and the birds have mutilated her beyond recognition. However there is the dent in the skull caused by a hammer and a snippet of hair as before. I should be certain it's the same killer as the other three. This one still has her clothes on; that's unusual isn't it, Tom?' said Solly.

'Yes, Solly, we may get some of the killers DNA of her clothes. I wonder why he dumped her in the sea fully clothed.'

'We have been keeping a close watch on the Severn estuary for some weeks now. It could be we disturbed him and he panicked,' said Solly.

'It would be marvellous if we could get the killer's DNA,' commented Mitch.

'Is this the woman whose husband hanged himself?' asked Tom.

'No, this is the latest one. She fits the description of Betsy Hedges. Have you found any personal belongings Tom?' asked Solly.

'No nothing! She has been cleaned out. Someone has cut off her wedding ring finger, to get the ring I imagine.'

'That's a first,' said Mitch.

'Yes, that's interesting. It seems the killer is working with us, what with the poems and clues as to who he is. This corpse could have been deliberately mutilated and put in the sea fully clothed on purpose. This is his fourth body. Perhaps he is getting bored. You know, he feels he has justified the reason he chose to kill these women and is getting annoyed that we aren't any closer to catching him.'

'Makes it sound like a disgruntled detective,' said Mitch

'Or a policeman, they sometimes commit murders,' said Tom, listening to the two of them.

'Bloody hell, sir, there's a lot of them to choose one from,' said Mitch.

'I know, Mitch, but if our killer is an ex member of the force he will know how we think and how we work. That's why he has got away with out leaving any clues.'

'I hope he hasn't hurt my Wendy,' said Mitch, looking extremely glum. 'We must catch this nutty bastard,' he said to himself.

'Oh there's one more fact we have found. This corpse was pregnant. Only just by about four weeks but she was definitely pregnant,' said Tom, covering the body with its sheet.

'I wonder if the father knew,' said Mitch.

'Or even its mother,' said Solly.

When the detectives arrived at the office it was to be told that Jeffrey Kanter, who was Betsy Hedges's last-known lover was being held, waiting to be interviewed.

'I blame myself for her death, Chief Inspector,' said Jeffrey Kantar. 'I should have seen her safely in her car, and not driven off leaving her to her own devices. I saw a blue van parked next to hers and didn't give it a thought it might be her killers.'

'We aren't going to be lucky enough for you to tell us the registered number, or type of van I suppose, Mr Kantar.'

'No I'm sorry. I got neither,' he replied.

'What can you tell me,' asked Solly.

'It was our last date; we had decided to split after a three year relationship.'

'I see. Did you know she was one month pregnant?'

'No! It must have been mine as she hadn't had sex with her husband for years,' said Mr Kanter.

'That's what she told you Mr Kantar,' said Mitch, mischievously.

'We will need a DNA sample, Mr Kantar. You can give us one before you leave,' said Solly.

'Can I see her body, please?'

'You mean as a body ID. Yes I don't see why not. I will arrange that also, before you go,' said Solly.

After Mr Kantar had left Solly and Mitch called on Dick Hedges to bring him up to date as to the finding of his wife's body. They were as gentle as possible regarding her description and didn't mention the fact that she was pregnant. Mr Hedges asked to see his wife's body and asked when he might be able to bury her. He was told that all the bodies had to be held in the mortuary until the CSP decided they could be released. He thanked them. He was surprised when he was informed that she had been put in the sea fully dressed. He asked if this was a relative and was assured that Betsy Hedges's body offered the best chance of finding the killer's DNA. He gave a watery smile, and thanked the detectives as he showed them to the door.

*

Solly called a meeting of his detectives when he got back in the office.

'Pay attention everybody. I want to tell you the bad news. There are three lots of bad news. Firstly, Sergeant Wendy Morrison has still not been found and we haven't a clue where she is. Secondly, we have been given seven days to solve these murders, and we have three days left, then we hand the whole lot over to a specialist murder squad, and we won't be able to take any further interest.'

These comments caused a stir amongst the assembled detectives; both points being very important.

'Thirdly, we have recovered Mrs Betsy Hedges from the channel, and she's not a pretty sight. However, the one difference is that this time we must have been close to the killer because he put her body in the water fully clothed. Forensic are hoping to get some of the killers DNA. The Crown Prosecution Service has decided to convict Carl Barnhoff with the murder of his wife and the boy. I feel we have a strong enough and waterproof case for a positive conviction. Now we have four murders and we are no nearer a conviction. I need some ideas from you.'

DI Collins made an observation. 'Well, sir, all the men whose wives and partners were murdered have a motive to kill them for having extramarital sex. Some people can be very unforgiving and these things usually end in divorce. Our killer seems to want to kill any woman who comes into that category.'

'Why, I wonder?' said Solly.

'Perhaps he has had it done on him, and it has made him flip so that he wants vengeance.'

'A reasonable explanation; have any of these been married before and have they got a divorce on these grounds?'

'Let's go over the corpses again. First was Fiona Walters, second Brenda Marlow, third Mary Dagleash. Then Betsy Hedges, and now our own DS. Wendy Morrison.. Four of them have been found in the sea. Three were nude and one fully dressed. Three out of the four had sex with another man other than their husband.'

'Do you think the killer of Brenda Marlow didn't know she hadn't had extramarital sex, and wouldn't have killed her if he'd known?' asked Mitch.

'Possibly, not that it matters, a murder is a murder,' said Simon.

'Let's have a look on the board,' suggested Solly. 'I want to update and refresh everyone's brains as to what has happened to four ladies in our patch, not including our own Detective Sergeant Wendy Morrison. Here are the four ladies, and below are their husbands, and below that are the men they have been having affairs with. Each of them has been murdered after a night out with a male friend and each has been killed on the way home.

'We have no common denominator except that each of them has been stripped naked and dumped in the sea. Except, that is, for Mrs Hedges, who we think may have been left fully clothed on purpose.

Forensic have proved that although they had sex previous to dying, none of the ladies had been sexually assaulted after death.'

'It appears we have a serial killer who is leaving no clues up to now.'

'Are we still using the motive that this is revenge killings for something the killer has a hate for?' asked DC Ginger Lewis.

'It appears we can rule out sex as a motive, Ginger,' volunteered a young detective constable, eager to show he was taking an interest.

Solly had heard enough about theories for the motive and decided to put a stop to any more.

'The motive we are using is vengeance against married women having sexual affairs outside of their marriage. That's final. Any other theories will complicate what is already a difficult case,' said Solly. 'I want to know who killed them – and quick.'

'It could be somebody we have already interviewed, and who we think would never do such a thing. I have just thought of another important factor sir,' said Mitch. 'The killer knows these women and chances are the women know him. So if they meet suddenly; like on the way home and the killer greets them, they are not going to be alarmed.'

'Yes, we have already ascertained that sergeant. What point are you making?' asked Solly, getting a little annoyed going over old ground. 'My point is, sir: where does he know where to pick them up to kill them?'

'Most of them are killed near their homes,' advised Inspector Collins.

'Alright, I agree, but how does he know where they live? I suggest, sir, he must be someone dealing with them at home; like a milkman, that sort of thing. That way he would know the victims and where they lived,' said Mitch, sitting down.

'Yes, Sergeant, perfectly reasonable and a good point. You could also add that the killer must be a self employed man because he is out all day setting the scene. Unfortunately all the men concerned up to now fall into that category,' said Solomon.

Mitch had another thought. 'What about if the killer was also a delivery pizza man. He would most likely use a van. He would be out in the evenings, and may even see his victims leave home,' said Mitch.

'Thank you, Sergeant Mitchell, for your ideas,' smiled Solly.

'I want you to split up into pairs and each pair to be assigned to the menfolk involved with a victim. I want you to go over their alibis, check them out. Be sure you can completely rule them out. At the same time I want you try and find a real suspect, check out their vans. Off you go and do some real detection work

'Mitch! Come with me.'

Mitch followed Solomon into his office and straightaway Solomon poured forth his thoughts.

'I am personally devastated with the loss of Wendy,' said Solly. 'Wendy does not fall into this category that the killer is using to select his victims. He has no reason, nothing to gain by attacking a police woman. I just don't get it. Why was she taken by this killer? What has he done with her body? Where are her clothes? If she has been thrown into the sea where is her corpse? I want answers, Mitch, as I am sure you do,' said Solomon.

'I certainly do, sir, I loved that girl and I haven't given up hope that she may still be alive.'

'Perhaps,' said Mitch, unconvinced.

'Hello, here's another poem. I can recognise the writing now,' said Solly picking up the envelope address to him personally.

tHE nEXt Is MY LAsT
that's aLL I will do
Still hoo I aM u AinT
Got A cLue
Why I KIlLeD EM
MORal jUstIce Was duE
FiFtY ThouSaND PoUNdS
FoR ThE Girl IN Blue

'For fuck sake Mitch, look at this. I think it is a ransom demand. That's why there was no blood at the scene. They abducted Wendy without violence because they are holding her ransom. Also, Mitch, I don't think it is our killer, I think this is a completely different gang of thugs,' said Solly.

'Do you really think so, sir?'

'Yes Mitch, someone is capitalising on the tragic murders we have to solve.'

'I had a feeling she wasn't dead,' said Mitch, with a smile. He was feeling very relieved.

'Mitch, don't get complacent. If we don't find her soon she could well be our next victim.'

Chapter 16

WENDY WOKE to find herself in a very dark room. She was dressed in only her pants and bra. She lay on a bed, which had a pillow and one blanket. Around her neck was a metal collar, which she couldn't remove, because it was padlocked, and fastened to a chain.

She tried to see how far the chain would permit her to go. By fumbling around in the dark she found a flush toilet .She could see light under the door but the length of her captive chain would not allow her to gain access to the door. The chain appeared to be securely fixed to the ceiling because she gave it several tugs but it stayed secure. She lay back on the bed and tried to see what she remembered, and how she got into her present position, and more importantly why?

*

Jill Stanton kissed her mum goodbye.

'There you are, Mum; keep yourself warm. I have filled the larder up so you should be OK over the weekend. Alan is away till Monday. I'm glad he is. I'm really fed up with him ... Now don't cry, Mum. It was him that started it. But I'm going to bloody finish it; two can play his games. I have had several chaps at work ask me out. I might take one of them up on the offer,' she said with a laugh. 'Right I will be off now. You're OK. You have the phone if you need me.'

She kissed her again, and walked to the door. 'Bye Mum,' she called as she closed it behind her. She took out her mobile and sought a familiar number.

'Hello sweetheart, are we still on for tonight? Good! Where are you taking me? ... No besides there,' she laughed. 'No he's away ... I don't know where and I don't care. I just want to be with you. You give me so much happiness and know how to treat a girl. Bye lover.' She sealed her message with a big kiss.

She went to her blue Nissan Micra and got in, fastening the safety belt. These young ones don't know what lovemaking is all about, she thought as she drove off. Her lover was very good. She could hardly wait for 6.30 tonight. Her nymphlike figure was wrapped in a fur-edged coat made by Gyrones, the top London maker. She'd picked it up in an Oxfam shop for a pound – like her shoes, they were a bargain at £2.50, never worn, made by Ashley Barnett. You couldn't go wrong these days buying cheap and fashionable clothes.

Her light brown hair had silver highlights in it. Any man would be proud to be seen out with her. She was beautiful and she knew it. She had been married to Byron for eight years. The first three had been reasonably happy until he started drinking and gambling. He wouldn't listen to reason. Their only child Simon who was now seven lived with his grandmother in Richmond, Surrey, because Jill thought it was doing the child no good being brought up with parents who were rowing and fighting. Lately Byron had resorted to physical violence and had broken her nose last year. She was seriously considering ending it all and going for a divorce like her mother had said she should.

He was away on TA manoeuvres this week, so Jill was making the most of it and meeting her secret love named Arnold Fricker. It was not the most romantic name in the world but she loved him as he loved her. Arnold was two years older than Jill, and at thirty-eight he had a magnificent physique as he was a leading figure in European weightlifting. His hair was a light sandy colour and he was only an inch taller then she was at 180 centimetres.

Arnold was an electrician, and his proficient workmanship was always in demand. He had never married as he had to look after his father who had Alzheimer's disease, and spent any spare time training and working. After she had a bite of lunch she took her car to the main garage for a service and clutch change which meant she was without wheels tonight. She didn't want Arnold to pick her up as her neighbours were always on the lookout for a new bit of gossip, and if she was going for a divorce she couldn't afford any scandal. She walked down the lane and caught the bus into town. It only took ten minutes, and as she got off she saw Arnold standing by his blue Mercedes waiting for her.

'Hello honey,' he said squeezing her slim sweet smelling figure and kissing her warm enjoyably moist lips.'

'Where are we going tonight?' asked Jill.

'I thought you might like to stay at my house I will cook you a nice meal and we can watch a movie.'

'That sounds great to me darling, let's go,' she said, sliding into the grey leather bucket seat, while he stood ready to close her door. Twenty minutes later they were at his four bedroomed Edwardian detached cottage in the country.

'I do love your house darling,' she purred.

'It's been in the family for generations and has been passed down to the eldest child.'

'You haven't got any children. What will happen then.'

'I better hurry up and get some, they both laughed at the implications. The house was warm and quiet.'

'Father's up in his room. I have settled him down for the night,' he said, taking her coat and leading her into the comfortably furnished spacious lounge. The floor was fitted with an Afghan handwoven red and blue embroidered carpet. A simulated log fire kept the chill off the room. Victorian and early Edwardian furniture intermingled with the odd piece of late Georgian furniture added to the welcoming warmth and cosiness; the whole aura of the room was welcoming. Long red embroidered drape curtains kept the room warm, while built in air conditioning maintained a comfortable ambience for its occupants.

'My, this is lovely, Arnold. Why didn't you bring me here before? It's so comfortable. One gets the feeling that you could do anything in this room, don't you think so darling?' she said as she accepted a cold dry martini from him. Nobody had ever treated her like this before.

'Sit there my love, dinner won't be long.' He leaned over and kissed her. Half an hour later after he had made several return trips to replenish her glass and his kisses; he led her through to a tastefully decorated dining room. Jill was most impressed.

'Darling you're spoiling me, I'm not used to being treated like a lady,' said Jill.

The dining room wasn't huge. It would seat six comfortably; eight at a push. There was an oak refrigerated wine cabinet; she learned later that it was designed to keep wines at various temperatures all the time. The subdued illuminated walls were decorated in a royal design paper of excellent quality. In the centre of the room was a pull leaf dark oak dining table with two carvers and four matching reproduction bow backed diners. A single, dual branch silver candelabrum sat in the centre of the table, its two candles flickering from a draught coming through the opened door.

'Would you like to sit opposite me? There are only the two of us,' he said, pulling out her chair for her to sit.

'If I had known we were going to be posh, Arnold, I would have worn my best dress,' she said, with a lavish smile.

He topped her glass up with a chilled Grand Cru Chablis and served her first course – a starter of prawns and other assorted fish in a salad of his own making as was the sauce. Jill tucked in and was a good conversationalist when speaking about an assortment of topics. Arnold kept the courses coming, changing the disc of selected background music occasionally as required. The meal eventually came to an end and the two of them went and had their coffees in the lounge.

'I don't know whether you would be interest, darling, but I have the latest film out on disc which is all the rage. It looks very entertaining. Shall we watch it?' he said, handing it too her to read.

'It looks fine, I would like to see it.' she said, handing it back to him.

'Wait, while I top your glass up,' he said, bringing the bottle over and filling her glass.

'Steady lover, I'm getting tipsy,' she said with a laugh.

'We don't want that, do we sweetheart.' He put the DVD in and sat down. Next, he pressed a button, and a full size screen lowered from the ceiling.

'My, you have all the gadgets, haven't we my love,' said Jill.

'I have nothing else to spend my money on,' he said, in an apologetic manner. 'Shall we make ourselves really comfortable? Sit up.'

He leaned towards the end of the settee and pressed a button. The two centre seats slid forwards and the lower section slid out to support their legs.

'There that's better,' said Arnold, putting his arm round Jill and cuddling close. Jill felt she was in the mood to be seduced, which is what Arnold intended.

'Good God, look at the time,' gasped Jill. 'I must get going. He'll be home soon and will go mad if I'm not there. I'm going to divorce him, but don't want to give him an excuse to make me the guilty party.'

'Alright,' said Arnold, pulling on his trousers. I'll get you home by 11.30. Will that be alright?'

They sped through the countryside to where Jill lived. Arnold suddenly found he could drive her no further. There was a sign reading ROAD CLOSED GAS LEAK.

'It's as far as I can drive you, my love.'

'That's alright. It's not far from home I should be alright.'

She kissed him and left the car while Arnold reversed and drove off.

A short while later a white van came down the road. It stopped, the driver got out, picked up the ROAD CLOSED sign and drove off.

Chapter 17

JOSH CAME into Solomon's office just after eleven the next day.

'I have some bad news, Solly. Wendy Meadows's police jacket, has been found in the Bristol Channel; that's all, just the jacket.'

'Where is it now, sir?'

'It's at the lifeboat station at Cladden on Sea.'

'It could mean she is alive, sir.'

'It is a very slim hope, Solomon. She was taken just like the other victims. Send somebody down to pick her jacket up.'

He said no more as he left his office. This was all getting very mixed up and irritating .Somebody was doing these murders and out of all the men they had considered there wasn't one who had a motive or the opportunity to do them. He sat and went through their names, checking their statements in front of him. He needed a bit of luck. Something must happen to give the police the positive clue it deserved. Even the press had gone cold on the story.

A letter arrived for him the next day and Solly was getting used to receiving poems from the killer. This envelope though was different: its shape and colour was different as was the handwriting. He opened it up and read the contents:

WE have Wendy NicE GiRl To
I shall KiLl ThE GirL In Blue
£50 000 for her return
Or OF HeR FaTE U WilL LerN

Solly got up and went straight into Josh's office. He didn't even bother to knock.

'I have just received this, sir. I think it is a copy cat attempt with the intention of ransom.' Josh read it through.

'So do I, Solly. Get this over to forensic. See what they make of it. Have they got Sergeant Morrison's jacket?'

'Yes sir, they are still working on it. Do you think she is still alive?'

'It seems like it by this poem. The trouble is, Solly, they may kill her; especially if she is a handful; which she will be. And had having killed her they could have us believe she is still alive and we get her back when the ransom is paid.'

Josh paused and Solly followed on in his train of thought. 'And all the time she is dead.'

'Exactly,' confirmed Josh.

'It appears she was taken in the same manner as the other girls.'

'No Solly!' said Josh. 'I have been thinking about that. The WPS was drugged and abducted. I don't think she was hit on the head like the others. Far too risky, they might have killed her. I think she was drugged – chloroform, something like that. I suggest you work on that theory Solly,' said Josh.

He dismissed Solly with a wave of his hand, implying the detective work was up to Solly, and it was up to him to get the answers. 'Keep me up to date, Solly.'

'Yes sir,' he said, returning to his office. He called Mitch into his office

'Read this, Mitch. It has just come in.' Mitch took the letter and his brow frowned as he read it.

'This implies she is still alive sir,' he said, his face lighting up with hope.

'Yes, I would think the same way. I'm sure she is being held somewhere. Also I don't think it's the same party that did the murders.'

'Don't you, sir? No! I think you're right. Someone is trying to cash in on the murders.'

*

It was the morning of the following day that Mitch came bursting into Solomon's office without knocking. Solomon looked up alarmed, and annoyed; for just a moment.

'Sir, traffic has picked up a blue van and in the back was the remains of a policewoman's uniform, less the jacket. Do you think it might be Wendy's?'

'Calm down, Mitch, come in and sit down. As you know we already have her jacket and it's with forensic. In fact the report came in this morning.' He reached for a letter, unopened in his in tray.

'That's good news. Can I collect it sir?'

'They will send it over when they have finished. It will be the same with the clothes they have found. However, you can have the van driver brought in for questioning.'

Mitch was on a high when he went to find out who the van driver was who had found the clothes; even more so when he was told his name was Jack Drakes and that he would be in their police station within the hour. It was an hour later that Solomon and Mitch, together with Jack Drakes, were in the interview room.

Jack Drakes was a scruffy individual, with two days' growth on his chin, untidy blondish colour hair. He wore dirty white shirt, jeans and trainers. He was a small framed man about thirty. Solomon after the usual interview proceedings opened the interview.

'Jack Drakes, it seems apparent that the clothing found in your van belonged to Detective Sergeant Wendy Morrison who went missing two weeks ago. How did you come by it?'

'I found it.'

'When?'

'About a week ago on the sand at Sand Bay. It was in a pile, like someone had gone swimming.'

'Was it wet?'

'No it was dry.'

'What were you going to do with the clothes?'

'I was bringing it to you when the police pulled me in for questioning; apparently a van like mine is linked to some murders.'

'You took your time that's over ten days ago, and you have just decided to bring the clothes in.'

'I didn't place any importance on it at the time.'

'What made you pick the woman's clothes up in the first place? Why not just leave them she might be coming back for them.'

'I dunno. She couldn't have been swimming the tide was a mile out.'

'What about her jacket. Was there any sign of her jacket?' asked Mitch.

'No I didn't see that.'

'Was there any one about, what time of day was it?'

'Late afternoon, about four.'

'What were doing on the beach at that time of day sunbathing?' asked Mitch.

'No I was looking for anything useful I could flog, you know like a beachcomber,' he said.

'Where do you live?'

'Glastonbury.'

'Where in Glastonbury?'

'I share a caravan with this bird,' he said

'What's the address.'

'We aint got one, we live in a field.'

'I don't suppose the van is taxed insured and MOT'ed either, is it?'

Jack shook his head.

'Do you realise you could have helped us a lot if you had reported the clothes you found straight away?'

'I found this in the pocket of the girl's trousers,' said Jack, pulling a sheet of paper from his pocket. Solomon took it and read it.

'Bloody hell, why didn't you tell us this before. Are you daft or something,' snapped Mitch.

'I forgot in all the excitement,' said Jack.

Solomon handed the paper to Mitch to read. Mitch read it. It was an A4 sheet on which had been stuck a message made out of cuttings of letters from a newspaper it read. It was the same that had arrived earlier in the week

I HaVE Wendy. IF yU WAnT hEr BACK a LIVE IT wILL cost YOU tWeNtY gRANd

'What do you make of it sir?'

'Well! He has decreased the sum of money he wants for her. It was fifty grand, remember,' said Solly.

'It means that Wendy is alive, sir,' he said, excitedly. 'I bet she's leading them a merry dance. It must be like holding a tiger by the tail. That's why they reduced the ransom,' said Mitch gleefully.

'Maybe, don't build your hopes up, Mitch.'

'Can I go now,' Jack asked.

'No, you certainly can't.'

'Are you charging me with something? I came here voluntarily. I know my rights.'

'You came here because we brought you in for questioning. You're lucky you haven't been charge with anything yet,' said Mitch.

'Do you know anything about this,' said Solomon, showing the message they had received.

'I can't read it. I can't read anything,' said Jack.

Solly thought he was lying due to the work he had done.

'I see,' said Solomon. 'Well, for the moment we will charge you with driving a vehicle with no tax, insurance or MOT.'

'Does that mean I can go?'

'Once we are satisfied we have all the information about you we require,' said Solly. 'We will close the interview now. Mitch read him his rights and book him in to attend court.'

'How can I get home?' asked Jack. 'I can't drive now.'

'Don't worry we will take you home. I would like to see where you live,' said Mitch.

The three of them got in the police car and under Jerry's directions found the site where the caravan was placed .It was up in the Mendips along a narrow mud track between two fields.

'Is this it?' asked the driver.

'Yes this is home. I don't know how we are going to manage without a van now.'

'Go to social services tomorrow, tell them we told you to come to them and ask them for help, I'm sure they will.'

By now they had reached the door of the caravan. Jack opened it. The smell was horrible; it stank of fish and shit; no one, unless desperate, would want to sleep there.

The two policemen drove back to the station.

'Isn't it terrible the state some people will live in?' said PC Small.

'Indeed it is,' said Mitch. 'Do you know, I have a funny feeling about this case. Why should Wendy's clothes suddenly come on view? Where have they been for the last two weeks or more? How come her jacket was found in the sea separate from her other clothes? I think she is alive and is definitely being held to ransom.'

We must find some way of raising the money, or convincing the abductors that we have the money, and are ready to exchange. Especially, after that demand note we have received confirming they had her, but only asking for half the original figure. I hope forensic can come up with some clues.'

Chapter 18

O N ARRIVING BACK at the station Mitch found that Solly had left, so there was nothing more he could do that night; besides it was his lodge night, and it was tonight they were having a vote whether Solly was acceptable to the lodge. Solly was keen to join Freemasonry, and his detective police sergeant, Mitchell was already a Freemason.

Solly had been proposed by a colleague who had known him for fifteen years and was already a member. Mitch, although a Freemason, was unable to do this as he had only known Solomon some six months, but he could second the proposal, which he had done. It was Mitch who had educated Solly into the merits of joining Freemasonry, though his inspector needed no pressure; not that a Freemason would apply any, it had to be purely voluntary.

Solly had attended an interview board that had assessed his suitability to become a Freemason, and they educated him in a few facts which would be helpful before he finally committed himself. He had made up his mind that he definitely wanted to join.

Needless to say, the ballot proved in favour, and it was only a matter now of finding a suitable date when the Lodge could formally accept him, and the candidate was available. Mitch had great pleasure in telling Solly next day that everything had gone well for him. Solly was equally pleased and wanted to know when the Lodge would initiate him. Mitch was just as enthusiastic to tell Solly about last night, and his theories regarding the loss of Wendy .

'I am even more sure she is alive, sir. Furthermore I think her clothes were deliberately placed so we would find them.'

Solly interrupted Mitch by passing over another A4 sheet of paper on which was a message just like before. It read:

WE hAvE Her And shE wIll End Up IN The sEa lIke the Others If WE don't GeT TwenTy Grand

Underneath it read: 'Park a police car on the sand at Sand Bay where the clothes were found on Thursday afternoon. If you do that we know you mean business and will tell you where to leave the money.' It was written in the same cutout language.

'What are we going to do, sir?'

'We will park a car there are requested and we will be covering the area in plain clothes, making notes. Don't worry, Mitch, if someone has got her, we will find her.'

*

On the Thursday, the police car was parked on the sands where Wendy's clothes had been found. There were numerous police in plane clothes acting as tourists to take pictures of all in sight. At the end of the day, the car returned to base as did the policemen. It was nearly a week later that another letter arrived telling them where the money was to be left; and where to find Wendy.

'What do you think sir?' asked Mitch.

'Well, they have definitely got, or had Wendy, because the uniform we have is hers. Whether it's a catch and they have killed her, or won't return her if we pay remains to be seen.' The press and the news had got the story some how; there must have been a leak.

'Oh I do hope she's alright sir,' said a very distraught Mitch.

'Of course you do, we all do.'

'Still no clues on the ladies in the sea, are there sir?'

'Mitch, you know as well as I do we have interviewed and assessed the likelihood of all the males in this case and there are none of them we can call in and question without being charged by the Police Complaints Commission for unnecessary and undue harassing. None of them are suspect and the killer has left no clues. You will be pleased to know we are no longer under threat. We only have four days left before we hand over all these cases to another specialist force. We don't want that Mitch, so we have to get our conviction pretty damned quick,' said Solly.

The culprits who had taken Wendy for ransom seemed to be getting desperate for their ransom money because when they arrived back in the station the instructions on where to leave the money had been sent. The writer was getting bolder now and the message had come out of a computer printer.

It read as follows:

'On the Mendips there is a long straight road running between Cheddar and Green Ore. There is a pub on the road called the Millionaire's Arms, a mile before you come to it you will see a white post sticking above the wall. Leave a biscuit tin of £25,000 on that spot. Drive off and disappear into the distance. No police helicopters or police to be around when you have gone we will recover the money and tell you where you will find Wendy. No tricks or she dies.'

'Bloody hell, they are making sure we don't catch them, aren't they sir,' said Mitch.

'They are not as clever as we are, Mitch. They just like to think they are.'

'There has been another body found at Minehead, sir, just like the other four,' said a detective constable, handing a sheet of paper to Solly.

'That's sounds strange. I thought we had finished with the dead women,' said Mitch.

'No, the letter from the killer said the next would be the last,' corrected Solly.

'Where is she?' asked Solly.

'She's in the morgue at Taunton.'

'Have there been any reports of a missing woman?'

'Not since Betsy Hedges, sir,' said DI Collins.

Solly turned his back on the assembled detectives, while he thought about the current workload and their priorities. He desperately wanted Wendy back; even if it meant losing the task of convicting their serial killer. What should he do?'

'Simon, I want you to handle this latest murder. Take what staff you need. Sergeant Mitchell and I will continue with the task of freeing Wendy.'

'Alright sir,' said Simon Collins.

*

Wendy shuffled around to try and get comfortable. The thick leather dog collar attached to her neck rubbed it sore and she had to bear the weight of the chain attached to it. She had tried many times to get out of the harness which her captures had placed her in, but to no avail.

It gave her some freedom but very much restricted how far she could move in the little farm cottage where she was being held. Plus the fact she was almost continually blindfolded. She tried to remember how long it was from the day she was kidnapped, but with the room in near darkness it was impossible to calculate night and days.

She remembered just a little of her abduction; her passing the blue van and having a smelly chloroform rag covering her mouth and nose; within seconds she was unconscious. She didn't know anything else until she woke up with a terrible headache to find her police uniform had been removed and she was left in her underclothes. She was pleased and relieved to know she hadn't been sexually molested while unconscious. Her abductors brought her a meal on a tray, but they were clever to make sure she couldn't identify them.

They were permanently masked.

'I'm cold. I need some clothes.'

The man bringing her food tray didn't reply, but five minutes later came back and threw her a tartan skirt too big for her and a woollen cardigan, which she could wear without having to remove the collar. The chain was lightweight but strong. It was long enough to give her some freedom of movement. She had access to a shower and toilet and she could walk twelve paces in each direction; it had all been carefully planned before she was captured.

She tried to talk to her kidnappers, but they said nothing. She had some books and magazines to read by lamplight when they removed her blindfold but they in turn always wore brown knitted balaclavas to hide their features. She had a small black and white television. She thought, they had made arrangements to keep her locked up there indefinitely.

The only two people she saw was a young man whom she heard being called Jerry, and an elder man who seemed to be the brains behind the kidnap. He must have been late fifties; though she had never seen either of their faces.

The house stank; she had never heard a vacuum cleaner. There was the unmistakable ping of a microwave oven during the day, so without a woman in the house most meals were bought in. She was fed up with fish and chips and burgers. They did keep her fed though and supplied plenty of tea; in fact too much some days. They had a big dog, and although she had only glimpsed it once she heard it sniffing round her door at night, and barking outside the house. She felt that even if she was able to make a run for it the dog would get her.

She lay on her makeshift bed of a smelly mattress and stained pillow. Her covering was a duvet which had not had its cover changed since she had been there. This gave her plenty of time to think about Nigel. He was a nice lad and she was sure that if he didn't soon propose to her then she herself would pop the question. Besides, she wanted some kids; life wasn't all police work, she reminded herself. She cried a lot, thinking about her mum and wondering how she was getting on. She knew she could rely on Nigel to see to her needs, but she wanted to come home.

She had seen all about her kidnapping on the telly and how the police thought at first that she was another victim of the serial killer. Apart from a few news snatches, the media seemed to have lost interest in her case, and gave the impression to have written her off as dead.

Then last week there was the finding of her clothes; this sparked new interest in her case and the news suggested she might still be alive and it gave her morale a great boost to think they were still trying to find her.

The door opened and the nasty old man poked his head into her room

'Hello, Wendy. You might be free in a few days if the police do as we have told them.'

'Good! That's good news,' she said sitting up. 'What will happen if they don't bow to your wishes?'

'Then we will toss you naked in the sea like the rest of those women.'

'No! No you can't. I have done nothing to deserve such a fate,' she screamed. He just walked away chuckling.

*

'When is the day for the money to be paid, Dad?' asked Jerry.

'Next Monday at three in the afternoon, we will have to work some way out whereby we don't get caught picking up the money.'

'We aren't letting the girl go till we actually got it then, Dad.'

'And counted it, son,' he said, smiling

*

Detective Chief Inspector Solomon was busy doing some paperwork. He didn't feel well. The trial on his nerves regarding the killing was affecting his health. His diabetes was playing up. He couldn't sleep at night. His blood sugar rate had risen to the mid twenties. He had lost his appetite and was really tense and worried. He knew that if they didn't solve the murders and find Wendy he would have to hand in his resignation; a task he did not relish. Mitch knocked on his door and walked into his office, clutching the latest demand from the kidnappers.

'They want us to leave the money in a tin on next Monday at three pm, sir,' he said, putting the form on the desk.

Solomon read it through. 'I will have to speak to the Commander to have this money released. It isn't as easy as it sounds, Mitch.' He took the sheet of paper into Josh and was told to sit.

'What do you make of it, Solly. Is it for real?'

'I think so, sir.'

'And if we don't play ball and deliver the money?'

'Then I don't think we will see Wendy alive.'

'Do you think this man killed the other women?'

'I don't know. I'm not really bothered about that sir. I want Detective Sergeant Morrison back here, fit and well as soon as possible.'

'Have you worked out a plan of operation?'

'Not in detail yet sir.'

'You get your plan worked out and I will contact Division to make the money available.'

'Yes sir,' said Solly, getting up and leaving his office.

Solomon sat down in his office and called Nigel to sit at his desk with him. This was most unusual for Solomon, but he wanted Mitch to help him hatch up a plan.

'Get me an Ordnance Survey map of the area Mitch.' He went away to the Administration and Stationary Dept to get the map he needed, and ten minutes later he was back at Solly's desk with maps paper and pencils.

'Right Mitch, this is the road in question, and here is the pub he mentioned. You can see he thought it out clearly because the road is straight for at least a mile in each direction. He wants the road clear of cars after the drop.'

'That means we will have to close the road off at each end sir.'

'Yes that's right. It's pretty open countryside round there.'

'Yes, but they have been clever because where they want the drop done is fir wood. He will disappear into that wood with the money.'

'We will have our men circle the wood on foot watching for him to come out. We can't use the helicopters; we daren't endanger the life of Wendy.'

'What about using dogs, sir.'

'Yes, we will use dogs but again it must be done with discretion. If the captures suspect that we have done anything to trap them ... Well, I can't take that chance.'

'Surely we have to make some demands our self. We want to see Wendy at the time of hand over, we can't be expected to leave a large sum of money without seeing what we are buying, and the condition she is in.'

'Don't worry Mitch that is all in the equation, and has been covered for.'

The money arrived next morning and was in a tin as demanded the whole thing locked in a cell for security. Police were already in position and had been since dawn. Everybody connected with this rescue operation were on tenterhooks.

'Sir! A message has come in from the target area that a white van has been seen patrolling slowly in the area.'

'Keep an eye on it. Follow it but don't alert the occupants,' said Solomon.

*

'If you're lucky you might be going home today,' said the old man.

Wendy was excited at this news.

'We are taking you out with us this afternoon; any nonsense on the behalf of you or the police then the deal is off, just hope your mates are sensible.'

Wendy heard the van draw up outside. The two men still kept their faces covered.

'I have checked the area, Dad, like you said the police are going to close the road off at each end so no cars can come along that road.'

'Good, that means they are serious.'

'Why did we only ask for twenty five grand, Dad? We should have asked for a hundred,' said Jack.

'Don't be greedy son. They can take twenty from their tea fund and not miss it. If we ask for too much it makes things awkward. Right unchain the girl and take her out to the van. Make sure you blindfold her, and keep her on the chain.'

Jack did as he was told. She was still blindfolded. Her hands were tied behind her back. They had forced a rag into her mouth and gagged her. Wendy felt completely helpless. She stumbled as she was shoved forwards.

'Get in here, copper,' she heard the lad say, as he helped her into the back of the van. She sat down in the rear of the bare metal surface. Jack leaned over and checked her bonds and her gag, then checked the blindfold she wore.

The trio then drove off to the place of the pickup.

Jack's dad was called Raymond Chivers. Jack was not his legal son, but he had brought him up after his mother had emigrated to France with a man from the circus, leaving Jerry with a friend to bring up. Eventually, when he was a boy of five he finished up in Raymond's care, and nobody new, or cared less in the Council authorities. Jack called him dad, though he did vaguely remember his own father, but not his mother.

Raymond was rough, but it suited Jerry. He was fifty years old and knew the countryside better than a rabbit; which he fed the family on mostly. That and game and pheasant's eggs. For an old vagrant he could knock up a good meal. They made their living like vagrants, buying and selling scrap and whatever they could scrounge. They had the cottage which was very run down, but it was a house. It used to be a farm worker's cottage and Raymond rented it for services to the farmer and fifty pounds a month.

It had been Raymond's idea to catch Wendy, and hold her to ransom. Jack thought Raymond would kill the woman if the money was not paid. He had a cruel mean streak in him. Everything had worked out fine up to now. This was going to be the most nervous part; handing over the girl and collecting the money.

The police had searched the area, and called at the house, but there was no reason to suspect that it was the one that held Wendy. Raymond was out when they called. He didn't invite them in. They looked around the outside area and asked him some questions; Jack acted a bit dumb, and said his mum and dad were out shopping.

There were plenty of isolated cottages, many of them in a poor state of repair. These were once used by farmers for there workers, some were empty.

*

Once they were on top of the Mendips, Raymond took the van to a spot a mile away from the pick up point. He was keeping a careful eye open for trickery on the part of the police; he didn't trust them.

Solly was in charge of the operation. He had carefully planned the whole thing .One thing he didn't want was to jeopardise the safety of Wendy. Once all the men were in position, and well out of sight of the drop zone he had a man with a telescope keeping an eye on the place the money was to be put. The surrounding area was covered so that there was no chance of anyone escaping once the money had been picked up. The force would then close in. A helicopter was in position to be called on when needed, also an armoured back up squad an ambulance and medical staff. Solomon thought he had covered every contingency.

Chapter 19

A T 14.55 PM THAT AFTERNOON, a police car sped towards the drop area and stopped, before depositing a box containing £20,000; right by the post. The man with the telescope radioed through that the drop had been made. Nobody came along the road. The area was quiet. Every one was waiting expectantly for the box to be removed, but not until the police car had disappeared over the rise at the end of the road.

Suddenly an empty paintpot with an oily rag inside it which had been set alight was thrown over the wall on to the road. The black pall of smoke it gave off completely obscured the area in which the money box had been placed. It was Jack who had lit it and thrown it onto the road as Raymond had told him. Grabbing the money box he scooted back to where Raymond and Wendy were waiting.

Solomon saw what had happened and cursed the ingenuity of the criminal mind. Neither he nor anyone else saw the tin of money being taken, or who took it .It took them ten minutes before they could get the oil pot removed and men on the spot.

'Tell the men surrounding the wood to close in,' commanded Solomon. 'Keep the roads closed. Call up the helicopter search.' His radio operator was sending out these signals to all concerned.

'Damn the man. He has our money and Wendy .We must catch them,' he said.

Jack and his dad were both dressed in army surplus camouflage suits and had blackened their faces like commandos would have done. This was all part of Ray's experience he had gained whilst serving two years in the TA as a young man of twenty two. The two men knew the area and cut along the wall keeping low and out of site .They knew the police would be surrounding them and had made their escape plans carefully. Having came out of the wood they paddled up a narrow shallow stream running into a gully. They couldn't be seen from the woods where the police were, as they had made their move long before them.

Emerging at the end of the gully they quickly undressed out of their camouflage suits and were dressed underneath in normal clothes like any other tourist. Hidden in the bushes were two cycles. Raymond put the money in the saddle bag and the two of them set off to join all the thousands of tourists who had come to Cheddar Caves for the day.

Overhead the police helicopter was searching for them, but by now they were one of a crowd.

'We made it, Dad,' shouted Jack.

'I think we have, son.'

'What about the girl? She is still tied up in the van.'

'We will get rid of her later,' said Raymond.

'What kill her?'

'Yes! What else?'

'Don't be daft. We might get away with stealing twenty grand but killing a copper, well that's sheer madness. I don't want any part of that,' said Jack.

'I suppose you're right, alright I will see to her,' said Raymond. Suddenly they came across a police car with two men in the car.

'Keep going; keep peddling,' said Raymond. 'Act normal.'

The policemen looked up but saw so many cyclists up and down the Cheddar valley road that they didn't bother to stop and question them.

'How is the operation going, Solly?' asked Josh, from his patrol car.

'Not very well, I'm afraid. The thieves first used smoke on us, and then when we brought the dogs in to follow them we found they had scattered numerous pots of pepper all along their escape route. Then we found they had paddled through a creek again, the dogs couldn't trace them. We did find the camouflage clothes they were wearing, sir. I assume they are mixing with the tourist in Cheddar now, where there were hundred to choose from.'

'What about Detective Sergeant Morrison?'

'No sign of her sir.'

'You haven't come out of this very well, have you, Detective Chief Inspector Solomon. Keep trying to find the kidnappers and the girl.'

'Yes sir,' said Solly.

He could tell his boss was mad with him. This was all he needed He cursed his misfortune in mucking up the recovery of the money and the capture of the criminals. Also there was the problem of finding Wendy. What had they done with her? He dreaded to think. Morons like that were capable of anything. If they injured Wendy Morrison he would never for give himself; as he felt it was himself who was responsible.

Chapter 20

WENDY LAY BLINDFOLDED in the back of the van. She couldn't get comfortable there was something she was laying on that was sticking in her thigh. She pulled it clear and realised it was a hammer. Her thoughts immediately returned to the police force and her involvement in trying to catch the serial killer. She wondered what the progress was, and whether Solly and Mitch had caught him.

She had slept a little, and apart from the birds singing she could hear no noise; no human voices or traffic. She felt very alone and stressed out. Determined to find a way to pass the time she tried to wriggle out of her bondage. It wasn't too tight, but she found after half an hour of trying that she was exhausted. She felt a ridge in the van where the seams had been joined together so she started rubbing the bindings on her hands up and down this abrasive ridge.

She started making progress and within no time her hands were free. She snatched off her hood and undid her feet, stuffing the rope in the pocket of her jeans. Suddenly she could hear voices of the men returning. It was getting dark by now. She put her back against the back of the van and when the door was open she kicked out hard-hitting Jack in the face and knocking him to the ground.

Raymond turned and ran away. Wendy pounced on the winded young man and dealt him another crippling blow, from a selection she had learned in her self-defence classes. Then she got him in a half nelson hold and tied his hands together with the rope she had freed from her feet. She was in control of the situation now, and she would make damn sure they played by her rules. She ordered him to lie on his face or she would make him. He obeyed her command.

'Where is your mobile? – and don't tell me you haven't got one.'

'In my trouser pocket,' snivelled Jack.

She found it, and contacted her station. It was a very surprised Detective Inspector who received the call. She gave her rank and number for confirmation at their end. When this had been verified, there were questions; as one might expect.

'Wendy, where are you? Chief Inspector Solomon is out with Mitchell and the rest of the available force, trying to rescue you.'

'Well, they haven't been very successful,' she replied.

'Where are we, toe-rag?' she asked Jack.

'Three miles from Priddy on the Charterhouse road,' he replied. She relayed this information.

'Right, Wendy, I will contact the team and they will come to your rescue. Wait there.'

'No, Inspector. The mobile might pack in. I am motoring in the van with my prisoner to Priddy. I will wait on the green.'

She grabbed Jack and forced him into the back of the van. She was about to start the car when her car door opened. A man she knew very well stood there with a pistol in his hand.

'Get out, bitch,' he said.

*

Solly and Mitch were both over the moon when then they received the message from Headquarters that Wendy had phoned in and was in control. Solly tried to phone her using the number she had given when she phoned in, but there was no reply. It didn't occur to Solomon that the owner of the mobile had his phone back.

Wendy was now in the back of the van again as a captive, she couldn't take a chance that the pistol was a replica or a toy; so she obeyed his commands. Chief Inspector Solomon arrived at Priddy, expecting to see the white van there but it wasn't.

'Something has gone wrong, Mitch.'

'Do you think so sir?'

'Well, why isn't she here? She has had plenty of time. Get the helicopter up. We're looking for a white van in a five mile radius from here. Also call up all units to call on all houses in this area and search everywhere. I think she has been recaptured. Mitch, order an Armoured Support Unit in to the area.'

'I already have, sir, on your authority.'

Solly would have like to make some remark about getting too big for one's boots, but decided not too. He knew Mitch was doing his best, and he was proud of his new detective sergeant.

The police helicopter was already in the area looking for someone else, as it happens, when Mitch asked for its assistance.

'Hello Romeo One, white van spotted sir. Over,' came over the radio system, which Solly and Mitch were tuned in to. 'We are following it along a track. The van has stopped. Two men have got out and are dragging a third person from the back. Over,' said the operator. 'One man has seen us and has fired a pistol at us. It missed. We are backing off. Over.'

'I think we have them this time,' said Solly, sending out a message for the Armoured Back up Unit to proceed to the location where the van had been spotted and that they were to take control in rescuing Wendy.

Mean while on the ground Wendy realised that she was in the hands of a desperate man, who being armed, might easily turn the gun on her if he felt he had nothing to loose. She did what he told her and having scrambled out of the van ran into the cottage and allowed herself the humiliation of being fitted with the retaining collar and chain she had worn before.

'What are we going to do, Dad?' asked Jack.

'We will leave her here. She will only be a burden. Now I want you to make a run for it, and you know that cave about a mile away? Go and hide there. Take some grub with you, a blanket off the bed and a bottle of water. Hurry, we haven't got much time. Here, take this mobile. I have another. I will ring you. Now off you go.'

Jack rummaged around to find what he needed and ten minutes later he was gone. The helicopter radio operator saw him leave and reported it to the Group Commander.

'We have just seen one of the criminals running from the cottage carrying camping equipment. He is heading for a wood nearby,' said the pilot.

'Any sign of Wendy Morrison?' asked Solly.

'No sir. I suspect she is a captive in the house. I am going to land nearby.'

'Be careful, he may be armed,' said Solly.

'So are we sir,' came the reply. 'There are two left in the cottage that we know of,' he said.

'Armoured back up unit move in and secure the site,' commanded Solly.

'The occupant has a loaded weapon. There is a female police officer being held captive. Great care must be taken to secure her safety. Please acknowledge.'

'Message received and understood,' came the reply.

'You in the house, come out with your hands up,' commanded Solly, the Senior Crime Officer.

The cottage was isolated. There was no other within a mile. The house was in darkness; only illuminated by a milky moon. It was all very eerie and foreboding. The armoured unit had taken up positions all around the house which consisted of a small lawn front and a small unkempt vegetable back garden. The house appeared to have two bedrooms whose curtains were drawn, adding to the gloom of the place.

Suddenly floodlights illuminated the whole area. It was impossible for anyone to escape undetected. Five quiet minutes passed. The police were waiting. During this period Solly and Mitch with two other police officers turned up on the scene. In the distance one could hear the ambulance alarm ringing as it made its way to the site.

'This is your last warning. Come out with your hands up now or we will come in firing.'

'I have the girl here, coppers. If you try anything she gets it,' came the reply from the house.

'Just like the old American gangster films,' said Solly.

Suddenly Mitch opened the door of the land rover and keeping low down ran for the back door of the house. Wendy was his girl .He couldn't just sit there and see her get killed. He gave no thought to his own safety but only for that of Wendy. He reached the back door undetected.

'Concentrate your efforts on the front of the house,' radioed Solomon to the armoured unit. 'We have a police officer who has taken it upon himself to try and rescue the officer inside – who is his fiancé.'

Mitch tried the back door and, as he expected, it was locked. He looked at the windows to see if an entry was possible through one of them; they too appeared secure. The back door, although locked, was of an old design and in dire need of repair and a good coat of paint. He knew what he needed was a diversion and having said that to himself he heard shots being fired at the front of the house. Two armed policemen came over to assist him.

'Break that back door down,' he told them.

One went over to the door and with his big leather studded boot gave it a mighty kick, nearly taking it off its hinges.

'Wendy,' he called.

There was no reply from her.

One of his men had a torch. 'Get back behind us, Sergeant,' they told him. 'We know our job. Don't interfere.'

Mitch did as he was told. The two men progressed through the rooms, searching for its occupants. Mitch stayed well back as he had been told. Suddenly the lights in the lounge were switched on and the police could see Raymond standing behind Wendy, who stood there with her hands tied behind her back.

'Let her go,' demanded one of the coppers.

'Sod off. I want safe passage from here and I am taking her with me. Come a step closer and she gets a bullet in the head.'

Mitch was out of sight but standing in the gloom of the passageway he could see what was going on. He backed off and saw a side door off the passageway. He took it and it led to the kitchen. He could hear voices, the police were reasoning with the man. He switched the light on, which showed him another door which he reckoned would lead into the lounge where the conflict was taking place. It sounded like a stalemate in there.

Mitch eased the door open. Raymond was standing with his back to Mitch, facing the police. A gun was pointed at Wendy's head. Wendy kicked at Raymond's shin. It was sufficient to change the status quo. Raymond's attention was distracted as the pain shot through his leg. Mitch had to make a quick decision. The two marksmen were ready to fire.

He withdrew into the kitchen. One marksman fired, hitting Raymond in the shoulder. He dropped to the floor, releasing Wendy and the pistol, which as it happens was unloaded and empty.

Mitch rushed to Wendy and hugged her, although her hands were still tied.

'Let me get my hands free first, lover boy,' she said in a very brave voice, considering what she had just been through. In a moment she was free. Mitch took her outside.

'Wait, Mitch, I'm busting for a wee. I'll be back in a minute,' she said, disappearing into the lavatory. She was back soon and taken outside to the waiting ambulance.

'I'm alright,' she said, 'I will drive in the police car with you and the inspector.'

Solly was in agreement. The tin of money was just lying in a kitchen cupboard; it was all there. The operation was a complete success. Chief Inspector Solomon and Josh were delighted. The press was waiting for her when she got back to the police station.

'They have picked up the son, Jack,' said Josh. 'He's in a cell. His father is still in hospital with a police escort.'

'We will interview his son this afternoon, sir,' said Solomon.

'Well done, Solomon. You have turned what appeared to be a disaster into a fine victory. Your capture of the two criminals, together with the recovery of the money and most important the safe return of Sergeant Wendy Morrison, is all highly commendable. You and your officers have our thanks,' said Josh.

The Area Commander also gave his thanks to Solly and Mitch.

'Thank you sir, I will tell them,' said Solomon.

'Can I come and sit in on the interview with the other villain, Jerry?' asked Wendy.

'No, Wendy, you are on a fortnight's leave.'

'I don't need leave, sir. I am perfectly alright and would like to sit in; besides I have knowledge which could be useful,' she said.

Solomon knew it was hopeless arguing with a sound-minded woman; so he gave permission for her to sit in.

'Do you think these are the people that have killed all these women lately, sir?' asked Mitch.

'It seems highly likely. Let's wait and see what comes out this afternoon at the interview.'

*

Two o'clock sharp the interview door was shut. The occupants were Solomon and Mitch

Wendy sat on a chair at the side; she was not involved in the interview. Sat opposite Solomon were Ron Chivers and his council Mr Brian Dark. A constable stood by the door to answer it and maintain order if required. Solomon opened the proceedings in the usual way and there were no comments from the opposition.

'Jack, was it you who kidnapped Detective Sergeant Wendy Morrison?'

'No. It was my dad.'

'How did you do it?'

'He said he drugged her with something that made her sleep.'

'Had he done this before to other women?'

'I dunno. If he did he never told me.'

'Where did you keep her locked up?'

'In the cottage.'

'Did you undress her?'

'Yes,' he said, going bright red.

'Who made out the letters demanding money?'

'My dad.'

'How did her jacket get in the sea?'

'I flung it in.'

'Did you? Why?'

'To make you think she died at sea,' he replied.

'Did you put her clothes on the sand for us to find?'

'Yes.'

'Did your dad go out much at night in the van?'

'Sometimes, Why?' Solly ignored the question.

'Did you ever go with him?'

'Sometimes, not very often. Why? Why don't you tell me the answers to the questions?' he whined.

'We're nearly finished, Jack.'

'Was your dad married?'

'Yes once.'

'Where's your mum?'

'She's dead.'

Solomon and Mitch looked at each other, were they on the right track?

'How did she die?'

'She got cancer or something?'

'Thank you, Jack. We will resume this interview tomorrow. Close the proceedings, Sergeant, and lock him up,' Solomon said to Mitch, as he got up and left the room.

Wendy was sent away with firm instructions she wasn't to return for two weeks. She said that Jack had replied truthfully to the questions as far as she knew, and wished Solomon good luck before she left.

'Thank you, Wendy. Off you go and have a rest,' said Solly.

*

Solly was very relieved that the business of Wendy Morrison was settled. It had been a very traumatic event; very touch and go. DI Collins came along the corridor and stopped to speak to Solomon.

'We have been searching the cottage that Wendy was held captive and we found this assortment of women's clothing and personnel effects.'

'That's it then,' said Solomon. 'It looks as if he was our killer after all. Have the clothes gone to forensic, Simon?'

'Oh yes, sir, they have.'

'Well done, have you finished out there?'

'Not yet, nearly.' Solly was deep in thought as he made his way back to his office. It was possible that this pair could be the killers. He called Mitch into the office and told him his theory.

'A perfectly acceptable explanation, sir, but for one thing,' said Mitch

'What's that?'

'His white van is not linked to any of the sightings of white vans and the number plates haven't been removed or changed.'

'Oh come off it, Mitch. It's the easiest thing in the world to fix a set of number plates temporarily on a van.'

'Yes I suppose so, sir, so you're convinced it's him; the man we shot and wounded?'

'All the clues seem to point that way, Mitch.'

'It would be nice if it were that simple, sir,' he replied.

'Come on, Mitch, let's go and have a coffee – your turn to pay,' said Solomon.

Once they were settled in their favourite café, with coffee and hot scones, Solomon brought up the subject of his application to become a Freemason.

'What's the progress, Mitch? Have they got a date for me?'

'Yes, sir. Our New Year begins next month. I meant to tell you, but what with the excitement of Wendy being rescued I completely forgot. The next Worshipful Master is installed next month, and you will be initiated two months later.'

'That soon; you told me you had to wait three years to get in Mitch.'

'It all depends on the number of applicants waiting to get in.'

'Oh, so you have a waiting list then?'

'Oh yes, some longer than others. Men are very keen to become Masons, and once in very few drop out. We do our best to make them welcome and encourage them to stay.'

'Are there many police in the brotherhood?'

'Yes loads of them, sir, they're good men, why shouldn't they join.'

'I'm looking forward to it,' said Solly.

There was a pause while they drank their coffees and consumed themselves with private thoughts.

'I wonder who did kill Jill Stanton?' asked Mitch.

'You mean the latest body recovered from the channel. She was a pretty woman,' said Solly.

'She was, when she was alive sir.'

So much had gone on lately they had forgotten the five dead women. The last one, Jill Stanton was still in the morgue and the police were waiting for forensic reports on her. Plus they had to interview Byron, her husband.

'We will find out soon enough, Mitch. Did it register with you that Byron's snooker partner is the same Raymond Chivers we have in custody?'

'Yes it did, sir, and the sooner we can interview him the better.'

*

Solomon was well pleased that the abduction of Wendy had been solved and he had two villains behind bars.

'When do you think Raymond Chivers will be well enough to interview, sir,' asked Mitch the next morning.

'I would think he will be fit enough tomorrow. It was a good job we didn't kill him, otherwise we would have lost a useful witness.'

'How do you plan to find the killer of Jill Stanton, sir?

'It is by a system of elimination, Mitch. Firstly, all three could have a motive; Mr Stanton could kill her off because he has found she is cheating on him. Next our friend Raymond Chivers could have killed her, but I can't find a motive at present. And if he isn't the serial killer we are looking for, the serial killer could have killed her to add to his list of wanton women who play away from home. That's the trouble with crime; it's never straightforward,' said Solomon, getting to his feet.

'Byron Stanton had plenty of opportunity and motive to kill her. Shall we concentrate on him, sir?'

'DI Collins has been handling the murder of Jill Stanton. He has interviewed her husband and we have that on file. It appears their marriage was very shaky, and he showed little or no regret when he was told his wife had been murdered. He identified the body, but she was in a hell of a state,' said Solly.

'He never reported her as a missing person, sir. Surely that's strange? Perhaps he hoped she had gone away and left him,' said Mitch.

'No, she was murdered like the rest, said Solly. 'Simon carried out interviews in her road, where a white van had been seen, and someone said when they came home that night they had to do a diversion because the road was blocked by a sign saying there was a gas leak. Simon checked with the gas company, who said it wasn't their sign, and there had been no gas leak.'

'That's it then sir, it's the serial killer again.'

'Yes, Mitch, it's a good job the police force lifted that week. They imposed to solve these crimes because today is the day we would have been kicked off the job. Mitch gave a little chuckle.

'Come on, let's interview Raymond Chivers. Where do you suggest we start?' asked Solly. He was testing his sergeant to see if his reasoning was logical. He had proved very good in the past; but each crime was different and had to be handled in a different way. It usually involved different people each time, with strange personalities.

Mitch knew this and was quite content to answer Solomon's questions.

'I suggest we check out his alibi as to what time he left his pal Ray Chivers. Then we dig out her boy friend and find out what time and when he left her.'

'And where?' added Solomon.

'Yes of course, and where,' said Mitch.

'Next?'

'What I do next, sir, would largely depend on the results of what I have outlined.'

'Very good Mitch, we'll make a detective out of you yet,' he said, with a big smile.

He liked Mitch, and could rely on his judgement. 'Come on then, let's go and find Byron's friend.'

'We have to decide what to do with Jack Chivers and charge him sir. The deadline is tonight at 9 pm.'

'You're right, Mitch, that had slipped my memory. We will do it straight after this, come on.'

'If Raymond Chivers did kill her what motive had he got?'

'Well, we know he's capable of killing someone, he's proved that. But why would he want to kill married women having affairs. I don't think it's him, plus this line of questioning is going to jam up the works, if he has nothing to do with it. If he is responsible for killing the other women then this one is no different. She was playing away from home. Her boyfriend knew nothing about the murder when we told him. He was very upset and said he dropped her off where the road closed sign was,' said Solly.

'I've got a theory, sir.'

'Go on, Mitch. I'm listening.'

'We know Byron and Ray were pals. Supposing Byron told Ray of his unfaithful wife, and Ray offered to get rid of her for a small fee.'

'It's possible, but not easy to prove. So we will go back and do our interview of Jack Chivers,' said Solomon.

Both were busy with their thoughts as they arrived back at the police station.

'We have been doing a search of the cottage that Chivers lived in. We found items of women's clothing whose DNA we don't know yet, and hidden under the linoleum on the floor was Chivers bank book,' said DI Simon Collins, handing the bank book to Solomon.

'What a funny place to hide one's bank book,' said Solomon, flicking through the pages. Having done this he handed the book to

Mitch to have a look at. There was an entry of £5000 having been paid in a month ago.

'All we got to do now is check to see if Mr Stanton has withdrawn that amount from his account,' said Mitch.

'You astound me at times, Mitch. You seem to think life is so simple; so cut and dried. There are many reasons why that money might be in Chivers book and even if Stanton did pay it to him there could also be lots of reasons.'

'Hmm, I suppose so,' said a very thoughtful Mitch, as he browsed through the bank book.

'Two o'clock, Mitch, in the interview room with Jack Chivers,' called Solomon.

'Yes, sir, I'll be there.'

*

Mitch was lonely at work without Wendy. She had gone up North for a week to stay with an aunt; they kept in touch by phone; but it wasn't the same. The period she was in captivity made Mitch realise how special she was, and what a wonderful lifelong partner she would make. He decided he would speak to her on that matter when she came home. In the meantime he had some murders to solve.

He sat in the interview room opposite Jack and his solicitor. Once more Solomon was in command and opened the proceedings.

'Does your dad play snooker, Jack,' he asked.

Jack thought this was a strange question and wondered where he was heading.

'Yes quite regularly, usually on a Friday night,' he replied.

'Does he always have the same partner?'

'Really, Inspector, I don't see these questions have any relevance on the case with my client,' interrupted his brief who was again Brian Dark.

'Oh, but it has, as will be revealed as we go on.'

'Well, Jack, answer my question.'

'I don't know. He has several partners. I heard him speaking to a chap called Byron once about a game. I remember, because I thought what a funny name Byron was.'

'Do you know whether he ever met Byron's wife, or did he mention her?'

'I don't think so.'

'When did he last play snooker to your knowledge?'

'Let me see, must have been about a month ago. He said he was fed up staying in looking after women and was going out for a game. He left me in charge of the girl.'

'I assume you mean Detective Sergeant Meadows.'

'Yes.'

'Did he take the white van?'

'No, we had traded it in for a blue one.'

'Why?'

'He said it was too conspic … something like that.'

'Conspicuous?' volunteered Solly.

'Yes.'

'Have we had the forensic report back on the van, Sergeant?' Solomon asked Mitch.

'I don't know, sir, shall I go and check?' Solomon agreed.

Mitch was gone less than ten minutes. 'Here you are, sir and we have the DNA report on the clothes found at the cottage.'

'Thanks, Sergeant,' he said, taking the papers and flicking through the contents.

'Let's go back to our last meeting. You said your mother died of cancer. There must have been an autopsy on her death. What did it say?'

'I don't know. I never saw it.'

'How long ago did she die?'

'About fifteen years, I think.'

'It's alright, we can get a copy of the autopsy report.'

'You agree you played an active part in the kidnap of Wendy Meadows, Jack.'

'Yes I suppose I did, but I only did what Dad told me.'

Solomon whispered something to Mitch, for his ears alone.

'Jack Chivers, you are charged with the abduction and kidnapping of Detective Sergeant Wendy Meadows, along with your father Raymond Chivers. Read him his rights and put him back in his cell, Sergeant,' said Solomon, getting up and gathering together his papers.

Mitch gave Jerry his rights, and closed the meeting.

*

Mitch, having seen Jerry secure in his cell, came into Solomon office. He was busy reading the papers Mitch had given him.

'Have you read this, Mitch?'

'No, sir, I brought them straight to you.'

'Well, forensic, has proved conclusively that some of the clothes were Wendy's, while others match the DNA of Jill Stanton.'

'Is there any marks inside the van linking it to Jill Stanton, sir?'

'No, only those showing Wendy had been in it, which we already know.'

'Ask forensic to carry out further tests to see if there are anyone else's fingerprints, or DNA, on her underwear or top clothes. I feel we are halfway there, Mitch.'

'Do you think Raymond Chivers is responsible for the entire murders, sir?'

'What do you think, Mitch?'

'I think the finding that the clothes that Wendy was wearing while she was being held captive belonged to Jill Stanton is pretty near conclusive. Raymond and his son – or even just Raymond – were or was responsible for the murders, sir; especially as we found all those other clothes at the cottage. How else could he have got them?'

'Perhaps you're right,' said Solomon, leaning back in his chair and closing his eyes.

Solomon, meanwhile had arrived at his office and was at his desk working when Josh came in.

'We have a press meeting at eleven, Solomon, so I should get your story ready.'

'Yes, sir, of course.' Solomon downloaded the files on the killings and gathered all the information, making sure he was familiar with the possible questions he might be asked.

He and Josh walked into the conference room and it was packed with Press agents, many of whom he knew.

'Have you got the killer of those poor women who were drowned, Inspector?'

'Not yet, but we are close to making an arrest.'

'Is he, or she, a local person?'

'I am not prepared to say.'

'How many in total are there now, Inspector?'

'Four.'

'Are you expecting any more?'

'I hope not.'

'How long has this been going on, Inspector?'

'About six weeks.'

'You got the man who kidnapped your police sergeant. Do you think he is responsible for the other murders?'

'At this stage I am not proposing to add anything.'

'Thank you, ladies and gentlemen,' said Josh. 'That is all we have to say at present.' They left the room.

'We have to get these murders solved quickly because they will be after your blood next time we hold a news report.'

'Yes, I agree,' said Solomon.

Mitch came into Solomon's office after the press interview.

'How did it go, sir?'

'Not too bad but it will be rough next time if we don't get them solved by them. Let's try and finalise Jill Stanton.'

Mitch and Solomon went to interview Ray Chivers, who was out of hospital and in a secure cell in their police station.

It was the usual setup with Solomon and Mitch on one side and a very weary looking Ray Chivers with his brief Mike Findle. Solomon opened the proceedings as usual.

'Do you know a Byron Stanton, Mr Chivers?'

'Yes he's my snooker partner.'

'Have you ever met his wife?'

'No.'

'Has he spoken to you about her?'

'Sometimes, why?'

'I'll ask the questions,' said Solly.

'Do you get the impression he is happily married?' Chivers was getting uncomfortable, he was wondering where this was leading to and what the coppers knew. He looked at his brief for help. Mr Findle nodded that Chivers should reply.

'No, he wasn't happy, they were going to split.'

'What time did he leave you at the snooker club the night his wife went missing?'

'About ten.'

'No later?'

'No.'

'We have found women's underclothes at your house which has the DNA of Jill Stanton. Because of this, we are charging you with the kidnapping of Police Detective Sergeant Wendy Morrison and the murder of Jill Stanton,' said Solomon.

'He's not getting away with it like that. Raymond Chivers paid me five grand to take care of his wife.'

'And did you kill Jill Stanton?'

'Yes, I bumped her off the same as the others.'

'Are you confessing to all the murders?'

'Yes, I might as well. I only have one life to spend in prison.'

'Raymond Chivers, I am charging you with the murder of Jill Stanton, Debbie Marlow, Debbie Carter, Fiona Walters and Mary Dagleash. Read him his rights, Sergeant,' said Solomon getting up and leaving the room.

'Well, that will please everyone, sir, well done,' said Mitch when he met with him later.

'It's not over yet. I know we have a confession but our friend Byron Stanton isn't getting away with it. Bring him in for questioning, Mitch.'

He immediately went and found a police constable to assist him and drove to Byron's house. Mr Stanton wasn't very cooperative and Mitch had to arrest him as he refused to come quietly. He brought him into the station and booked him in as a witness, helping out on a murder inquiry. He was put in a cell to wait his turn to be interviewed. Mitch went and reported to Solomon that Byron was in the cell waiting and a brief was already here to assist.

'Right, Mitch, set it up. I shall be ten minutes.' He went in to see Josh to brief him as to the interview of Raymond Chivers and told him of his confession to all the murders. Instead of Josh giving him a slap on the back, he warned him not to take this confession too seriously, the man might be bragging. He would have to make more serious enquiries to confirm he was telling the truth.

Solomon was a little deflated, he had hoped that it was a genuine confession and he could wrap the murders up all together. He told Mitch to put Byron Stanton in the interview room. Later that morning Stanton's interview began.

'Did you have anything to do with your wife's disappearance, Mr Stanton?'

'Don't be silly. Why should I do that?'

'You told your friend Raymond Chivers you were unhappy with her and wanted to get rid of her.'

'Yes! But not by killing her.'

'Mr Chivers says you paid him £5000 to kill her.'

'Well, he's a bloody liar.'

'Your bank statement at that time you withdrew £5000. Did you pay him £5000?'

'No!'

'It might help your case if you admit it, Mr Stanton. What have you to say?'

Stanton was quiet, thinking. Solomon didn't say a word. The next move was Stanton's.

'I didn't mean he should kill her, just get rid of her. I knew she was two-timing me. She thought she was being clever.'

'If Chivers wasn't to kill her, how did you imagine he might get rid of her, Mr Stanton? I put it to you that Mr Chivers told the truth when he said you paid him to kill her, and blame it on the serial killer; that's what you planned, isn't it? Very ingenious and good timing, but Chivers got greedy, and kidnapped our detective sergeant.'

'He was daft, I told him to do one thing at a time. He drew attention to himself.'

'Then he left the underclothes of your wife at home instead of burning them. The whole operation was a bodge up.'

There was silence in the room for a few moments while the faults in the planning of the killing sunk in .Eventually Solomon addressed Mr Stanton.

'I am charging you with being an accessory before the act of killing your wife. Read him his rights Sergeant Mitchell,' he said, gathering up his papers and heading for the door. He knocked at the door of Josh's office and entered.

'We have a definite confession for the compliance in the murder of Jill Stanton, sir. And we have charged Ray Chivers with the murder.'

'Good work, Solly. Let's hope we have seen the end of the serial killings, and you have found the real murderer.'

Solomon agreed.

*

Wendy was back off holiday with her aunt, and she and Mitch were together again. It was the weekend, and neither of them was on duty. The couple were living at Mitch's house for a week. They did week and week about. It was a fantastically sunny day; too good for staying in really, but too early in the year for barbecues.

'I'm not letting you out of my site. You can't be trusted,' he told her as he hugged her affectionately. 'Oh how I have missed you my love.'

'And I missed you too darling, when I was in captivity. I would lie there in the dark, making plans for us.'

'Were you scared?'

'No not really. Not once I got used to the idea. I guessed what their game was, and knew they didn't have a chance and that it would only be a matter of time before I was released.'

'We have charged Ray Chivers with the murder of Jill Stanton and it was Jill's husband who paid him to do it.'

'Very nice, well done. It's great to be back to work. I will take more care in future, when walking down quiet roads in uniform.'

'You better,' he said, slapping her bottom as she passed.

'Excuse me talking shop when we're home, but what's the progress on those four girls who were murdered?'

'Well, we're working on it all the time, but we can't find a link to tie it down to one person. Solomon thought he had the man when he interviewed Ray Chivers and even charged him with the murders after he confessed, but I don't think his confession will hold water in court; and if that gets thrown out, then maybe the killing of Jill Stanton would too.'

'You definitely believe he did it then?' said Wendy

'Yes! don't you?'

'I think we might have missed something, Mitch.'

'Go on, tell me more.'

'No, I don't want to make my views public. It wouldn't be fair on Solomon.'

'Alright, I will ask Solly whether you and I can interview him again, because we have a theory.'

'Yes, I'll go along with that. No more shop. Dinner is ready.'

Mitch got the keys from the office for the cottage at near Priddy where the Chivers family lived. If Chivers had done the murder as he confessed to then hopefully, the hammer would still be in the house. For some unknown reason, the finding of a hammer was overlooked when the house search was done, and this was a vital clue in the conviction of Ray Chivers.

Wendy had told Mitch she was sitting on a hammer when captive in the van. He must find it and pass it to forensic. It was imperative that one of these murders be solved, and as Wendy pointed out, there were too many loopholes to be sure of a conviction.

He opened the door of the cottage and told PC Tommy Lewis his driver to search downstairs while he concentrated on the garage and out buildings. Mitch opened the garage door and there lying on the workbench was a hammer. He put it carefully in the plastic evidence bag, and continued his search. He discarded another hammer he found as it was too light and had a broken shaft.

Having done a good search, he was about to close the garage door when his eye caught the shaft of what appeared to be a hammer, sticking out from a pile of rubbish that had been pushed in a corner.

There were rags and tins and a coke bottle but there was no mistaking the handle of some tool which just had to be a hammer.

Mitch was excited as he went to pick it up because he felt this hammer had been hidden. It was going to be thrown away with the other debris; but at first sight there didn't appear to be anything wrong with it. It was a perfectly good ball pein hammer with a one pound head on it. That too went in a bag as evidence.

The house search had already been done very effectively. It was just specifics, like the hammer, that they were looking for. The other girls that had been murdered had been hit with a flat-headed hammer, and Mitch couldn't find one anywhere to match it. Neither could Simon Collins in his search of the house.

'I didn't find a hammer, Sergeant, but I found a pair of scissors which I thought might be useful.'

'Well done, Simon, yes they would have used that to cut her hair. It's been a good day's result. Let's get back to base. Mitch was well pleased with what they had, and having shown the items to Solomon, had them sent round to forensic for DNA testing.

The DNA results from forensic were never that quick in coming through, even when they were being produced as a priority; simply because the work involved took a long time and the laboratories had to be certain, beyond any doubt, that their findings were waterproof and were infallible when challenged by the defence barrister in court. It was Wendy who received them first, and having read them, she hurried to Mitch forensic findings.

Mitch in turn couldn't believe his eyes when he read the DNA results and hurried through to Solomon's office where he knew the details would be received with likewise incredibility.

'Here are the forensic DNA reports on the hammers we found at Chivers house, sir.'

Solomon took them and started reading.

'Well I'm dammed, so it wasn't Raymond Chivers, but his son who was responsible for the murder of Jill Stanton. The hammer showed Jill's blood and hair, but Jerry's fingerprints and DNA.'

The results certainly shook the investigating team. Everything pointed at Raymond Chivers, and he was covering up for his son all the time. Nobody was disputing that Ray was very involved and that he accepted the contract; but it was his son Jerry who actually killed her, and cut the hair off.

Jerry, who acted so innocently and gave the impression that it was his dad who made him do things he shouldn't do. Nobody makes you into a sadistic killer.

'Have Jack Chivers brought back here from Pentonville Prison where he is being held. We want him for questioning on the charge of murder,' instructed Solomon.

Jack's father, who was still in the cells at the police station, was told of the results and that the police now knew for certain who had committed the murder of Jill Stanton. Raymond didn't dispute it. He had tried to save his son from being accused and was willing to take the blame on himself; which though foolish, was very commendable. When Josh was told of this latest result, he just went back into his office, shaking his head with disbelief.

'What about the other murders of the four women, sir. Are you still going to accept Ray Chivers's confession to them?' asked Mitch.

'In view of recent events I know it would be folly to do so. For a start off he had to be in the right place at the right time to facilitate the murders. No, I am firmly convinced the real murderer is still out there and still looking for victims.'

'Perhaps he is controlled by a full moon, sir. I have heard of killers murdering on the night of a full moon,' said Mitch.

'I think you will find, Mitch, that they do it because they want to on the night of a full moon; not because some trigger in their brain tells them to.'

'Oh I see,' said Mitch, returning to his desk.

The next day Jack Chivers was available for interview and he was placed in the interview room with his brief Mr Brian Dark.

'What is it this time, Inspector? My client has already been charged with assisting in the kidnapping of your lady police sergeant. I have no knowledge of any other offences.'

'We want to question him regarding the murder of Jill Stanton.'

Jack didn't say anything; he just sat there looking at the ceiling. He knew why he had been called back to this inquiry.

'Where were you on the night of 5th June this year at around 10 pm ?'

'I don't know, that's ages ago,' said Jack, in a much stronger and aggressive voice than the wimpy one he had used previously.

'Were you out in the white van, or if not white, any other colour van?'

'I might have been, as I say it was a long time ago.'

'Do you recognise this hammer? For the benefit of the tape I am showing Mr Chivers a hammer in an evidence bag Exhibit 1,' said Solly.

'I've seen a lot like this one,' he said, handing it back to Solomon.

'This hammer was found in your garage and furthermore, it has not only the hair and blood of Jill Stanton but your fingerprints and DNA.'

'Do you recognise these scissors?' he said, showing him the ones found in his house. Jack shook his head.

'They too were found in your house, with Jill's hair on them, and your fingerprints. Also in the house, articles of ladies' underwear clothing were found with your DNA on, together with those of Jill Stanton.'

'It's not me, it's my dad. He got me to put my dabs on them after he killed her. He's trying to blame me for the murder. It's a setup,' shouted Jack, standing up.

'Sit down and shut up,' said Solomon. 'Jack Chivers, I'm charging you with the murder of Jill Stanton. Read him his rights, Sergeant.'

'I didn't do it, I tell you, I been framed. It's a set up. I should have got all that five grand my dad got. I been robbed and framed.' He was still protesting his innocence when placed in the cell waiting for his return to prison.

'Nobody mentioned to him the five grand in his father's bank account, so he's further incriminating himself,' offered Mitch, when they were back in Solomon's office.

'Well, apart from the trial let's hope that's the end of that murder,' said Solomon, putting the file away. 'Who's coming for a drink to night?' asked Solomon. There was a loud chorus of 'I am's.

Josh came into the office. 'Would you mind leaving us alone, Sergeant,' he said to Mitch.

'Right now, Solly,' he said as soon as Mitch had departed. 'I am under pressure from the top to get these serial murders solved otherwise the boys from the Met will take over and we don't want that do we?'

'But sir, I have charged Jack Chivers with the murder of Jill Stanton,' said Solly, feeling that he was being put under undue pressure. 'Besides, tomorrow is the last day for a charge against the serial killer.'

'Ah! I have good news for you there, Chief Inspector. The Area Commander is pleased with the results up to now and the finding of Detective Sergeant Morrison, so he is extending the time he gave you to two weeks,' said Josh with a satisfied smile. 'So I want you to put extra personnel on the case, include overtime if you have too. I think we have about two weeks at the most. I am trying to prevent a press conference on us, because that can also do us harm.'

'I agree, sir, but any leads we had have gone cold. The killer has been inactive and the Jill Stanton murder was a spanner in the works because although it wasn't linked, it was made to look like it was.'

'Yes, well that's all over, bar the court case, which I think you have pretty well buttoned up and water tight. Think over what I have said. Keep me informed, Solomon; preferably with good news.'

'Yes sir,' said Solly, as Josh was leaving. Solomon didn't know what to do for new ideas, then luck suddenly played into his hands.

Wendy knocked at his door.

'Come.'

'Sir, another body has been found naked as before. It appears to be the work of our serial killer.'

'I cannot say good, Wendy, because that would be morally wrong and unprofessional; but I must admit I am badly in need for some new evidence to catch this killer. Put any details you have up on the board in he incident room and we will have a discussion with the crew this afternoon.'

'Yes sir,' she said, leaving the door for Mitch to come in.

'Come on, Mitch, a lady has been found by a fisherman off the island of Steep Holm. How she managed to end up there, heavens knows. Apparently she was caught up in his nets. If this is the serial killer it makes five murders. That's five widowers, some with children. Not a nice legacy and we are in the hot seat to get this killer caught and bloody quick. I was given a warning this morning by the Chief Superintendent, that if we don't solve it then London CID will take it over.'

'Have we got a name for this woman, sir?'

'Elsie Maxwell is the name Wendy gave me. She disappeared two nights ago.'

'That was Friday. It appears they all went missing on a Friday. There must be a link there, sir.'

'Good point, Mitch, and worth following up. Let me know how you got on.'

'Where is the body now sir?'

'In the mortuary at Weston super Mare. That's where we're heading.'

The body of Elsie Maxwell lay on the mortuary table, naked, staring at the ceiling through eyes that could no longer see.

'Good heavens, she's young isn't she, Chas?' said Solomon, to Chas Priest, the duty mortician.

'Yes, she's only twenty-six. It's a terrible waste of life. This killer must be caught Solomon. The women of the West are terrified to go out alone.'

Solomon didn't reply – what was the use? He, like everyone else, knew it was up to him and his team to solve these murders – nobody else.

'Are the marks the same Chas? You know a hammer mark and a piece of hair cut off the head?'

'Yes identical. She must have put up a bit of a struggle as we have found a fine sliver of skin under one fingernail, whether it's of any consequence we do not know. She too has had sex before her death, her body is badly bruised, which could be caused by an assault on her or by the sea, we will investigate.'

'I know you will, Chas. We are desperate for some definite clue to work on. Let me have the DNA report as soon if not quicker. My team have been given only so long to live.'

Chas smiled understandingly. He knew the pressure Solomon was under from the hierarchy.

'I'll do my best, Solomon.' Solomon and Mitch took their last look at the sad figure of Elsie and swore they would leave no stone unturned to solve them.

Chapter 21

'LET'S GET BACK, Mitch. I want an Operational group meeting of all concerned for 3 pm.'

Wendy was waiting for Solomon when he got back. 'I have some more information on the girl you have been to see in the morgue, sir. She is not married. She lives with a bloke but isn't married to him.'

'The killer has made a slip; he must have thought she was married. It's the first case like this. It's only a matter of time, but we haven't very much of it left,' said Solly, popping a couple of Paracetamol tablets in his mouth to help relieve a bad cold.

'She is so young, sir,' said Mitch. 'Usually they are much older women.'

'Who was her partner and where did she live?' asked Solomon.

'105 Gravel Pit Road, South Clevedon,' replied Wendy, referring to her notes on her laptop. 'We'll pay a visit. No better still, you and Wendy go and interview her partner. Do a good job of it, Mitch. I need clues so I can get a conviction.'

*

That afternoon he and Wendy drove over to the house which was a street of early-twentieth-century terraced houses; ideal for first-time buyers, though many of them were being advertised to let. Mitch knocked on the door and a man aged about thirty answered it. He had brown hair and wore T-shirt, jeans and trainers. He was quite handsome, in spite of the stud he wore in his top lip.

Mitch introduced himself and Wendy, then embarrassingly had to ask the man his name, because they had no record of it.

'Derek Shaw,' the man replied. 'Come in both of you.'

Once Mitch and Wendy were seated, Derek opened the conversation.

'I suppose you have come about the disappearance of my partner. Have you found her?'

'Yes we have, Mr Shaw. I am sorry to have to tell you she is dead. She was found in the sea off of Steep Holm Island in the Bristol Channel. She was naked.'

He bent his head in sorrow, holding it in his hands. He didn't cry but seemed genuinely filled with grief. Wendy looked around the room. It was tidy and comfortable, with a simulated gas fire in the grate, a settee and two armchairs; the floor was fully carpeted. On the mantelpiece were birthday cards.

'Whose birthday was it?' she asked, indicating the cards.

'Hers, she had been out celebrating with my brother, they went dancing.'

'Oh. Did she often go out with your brother?'

'No, but I couldn't go. I had a committee meeting at the Rotary Club so she went with my brother.'

'Where had they been, anywhere special?' asked Mitch.

'They went to the Wicked Elf, a little pub out in the country. They have dancing there.'

'Yes, we know it,' said Wendy, casting a glance at Mitch for confirmation.

'Had you been to this pub with her yourself?'

'Yes many times.'

'Had your brother taken her there before?'

'No never. It was her idea they go there.'

'So people at the pub would associate you and her as a couple, and your brother as a new man on her arm?'

'Yes I suppose so,' he said, wiping tears from his eyes. 'Do you think the killer was there?'

'It's a possibility. The other ladies who had been killed had visited the same pub.'

'Have you any idea who done it?'

'No, but we are working on it.'

'What, like the other four that got murdered? You aren't getting far. How long is it now – six weeks, maybe longer?' He was obviously uptight at the slow rate of finding the killer.

'Can you remember what she was wearing that night?' asked Wendy.

'Grey skirt, white blouse and jumper with a coral necklace.'

'Have you a picture of her we can borrow?'

'Yes, here is a recent one,' he said, taking it from his wallet and handing it to Wendy.

'She was very pretty, wasn't she,' said Wendy.

'Did she come home with your brother?'

'No, she met her best mate and said she would be coming home with her. So my brother Keith came home on his own. I waited up till one, and phoned him. He was as surprised and worried as I was that she hadn't come home. It seems she didn't come home with her friend because when the dancing finished, her friend couldn't find her, so after waiting for half an hour she came home on her own .Keith had already left for home earlier.'

'So we don't know who brought her home. We would like a talk with her best friend. Do you know who she is and where we can contact her?' asked Wendy.

'Yes, it's Chloe Burns. She lives just at the end of these houses, at 26,' said Derek. 'We were thinking of getting married next year and having some kids. Please try and find who killed her,' he said, with tears rolling down his cheeks.

'Can I have your brother's name and address? We need to talk to him,' said Mitch.

Derek gave him the details which Mitch wrote in his memo pad.

'Thanks, I think that will be all. Oh yes, we need someone to identify the body. As you are her partner, will you do that?'

'Yes of course. Will you contact me and tell me where and when.'

'Of course,' replied Mitch, opening the door for Wendy to leave. 'We'll do our very best to find out who did this, I assure you. I feel it won't be long, thanks to your help. Here is my card, give me a call if you have anything you feel may help in this inquiry.'

'Her friend won't be home till six, she is working. She is a lucky sod. I lost my job yesterday, after fifteen years with the firm. No job, no pension and no prospects.'

'Join the police, you're young enough,' said Mitch, shaking hands with him.

'That's an idea. I might do that,' he said with a smile, as he saw them to the door.

*

'I feel sorry for him,' said Wendy. 'He's lost his girlfriend and his job. Some people are very unlucky.'

'Don't tell me, my little bluebird. I know only too well when I nearly lost you. I didn't know what heartache was till then.'

'What shall we do? Shall we go back and come out another day, or wait for her?'

'Let's go for a coffee and come back,' said Mitch. They sat there drinking their coffees and talking about the force and the case in hand.

'I think we ought to go dancing this Friday, Nigel; what do you say?'

'I agree, we need to have a good look at the Wicked Elf. It appears that all the dead girls have used it in the past. Perhaps there is something we are missing; something of importance right under our noses. Shall we try our witness and see if she is home?'

They found the house and a car was parked outside which suggested someone was home. Mitch knocked the door and it was answered by a middle-aged man about fifty, Mitch thought.

'Good evening, sir. I am Detective Sergeant Mitchell and this is Police Woman Sergeant Meadows,' they both showed their ID cards.

'How can I help?' he asked, chewing on a partly eaten digestive biscuit.

'Is Miss Chloe Burns in? We would like to ask her some questions?'

'Chloe, someone to see you,' he called. 'Come on in, the pair of you. Excuse me finishing my tea, only I have a bowling match tonight. I'm Chloe's father. What's she been up to now? Not another driving offence?'

Chloe appeared, her hair was wrapped in a towel, and she had obviously just washed it.

'Hello, what do you want?' she asked her dad.

'It's the police, dear. I told you they would catch up with you one day,' he said, chuckling to himself as he disappeared into the kitchen.

Chloe was unable to throw any further light on the proceedings of the night at the Wicked Elf, except to say she saw the owner of the Silver Spoon café there.

The detectives thanked her and left.

*

'What's the program for tomorrow sir?' asked Mitch

'Well, you know it's the trial of Jack Chivers for the murder of Jill Stanton. Go over your evidence, make it watertight. I don't want to lose this one, through some mistake on our part.'

Mitch picked up the notes and took them to his desk to familiarise himself with.

Wendy came over. 'Hello, lover boy, what are you doing?'

Mitch smiled up at her. He loved her more, every day. She just seemed to know what he wanted, and what he shouldn't be doing.

'I'm revising my evidence for tomorrow.'

'Good, I hope he gets sent down.'

Mitch and Solomon sat together in his office till late, going over all the points they could think of ready for the next day in court. They arrived in court in good time and met the prosecuting barrister.

'I'm afraid I have a bit of what might be bad news, Solomon.'

'Oh what's that?'

'It seems the defence have a witness we knew nothing about.'

'Who's that?'

'The lad's partner.'

'I didn't know he had one,' said Solomon, looking at Mitch.

'I knew he was living with someone months ago before the abduction. They lived in a dirty old caravan up in the Mendip Hills with no services or sanitation. I advised him to get out and contact Social Services. When I went back a week later all signs of habitation had gone. There was just a dirty muddy patch there, that's all.'

'I wish you had said something before now. What difference will it make too our case, Councillor?'

'I don't know. It depends what she says.'

'Will you be calling her up?'

'If I think she will help our case, then yes I will.'

Solomon cursed, and turned away deep in thought. This appeared to be a spanner in the works.

Meanwhile, back at the court the case against Jack Chivers for the murder of Jill Stanton was about to start. There weren't many in the public gallery. These murders were becoming so common that they had lost the imagination of the public who were tired of them, and wanted them solving, so they could walk the streets in safety again. Mitch sat there on his own for ten minutes before Detective Inspector Collins came in to join him. Solomon had phoned Josh who was very understanding and said he would prefer to have an officer there with Mitch.

The court opened with the usual ritual and straight away the prosecution came in heavy with the evidence against the accused. The clothing was of great importance. The fact that it was Jill's clothing and DNA traces of the accused had been found on them. The defence council tried to wriggle out of it saying the DNA was so slight it was of little significance and that it could have been caused by the accused sneezing near it, not even knowing the clothing belonged to the victim. The trial then went on to the murder weapons and how there was unmistakable evidence that Jerry had handled them, as his prints were clearly visible.

The prosecution made a great show of these facts to the jury, who seemed very impressed. Mitch and Simon Collins, the Detective

Inspector, were pleased the way it was going. The council for the prosecution sat down, as he had no further evidence. It was the turn of the Defence.

'My Lord. I would like to call Miss Stephanie Rolls.'

She was summoned and was made to enter the witness box and take the oath. Having ascertained who she was, the defence went on to question her regarding her relationship with the accused.

'Were you living with Jack Chivers?'

'Yes sir.'

'Did you go with him to his father's house at any time?'

'Yes often. We hadn't got any electric in our caravan so we went over there at night to watch telly.'

'Have you ever seen this hammer,' he said, holding up exhibit A. The Clerk took it and handed it to Stephanie to see it.

'Yes sir.'

'Where did you last see it?'

'In Mr Chivers's house.'

'Where? And when, exactly?'

'He handed it to Jack to put in the garage, one evening when we were over there.'

'How did he hand it to him?'

'His dad, Mr Chivers, held the head of the hammer and Jack grasped the wooden handle.'

'Was Jerry wearing gloves at the time?'

'No don't be silly. It was indoors.'

'So Jack's prints would be left on the hammer.'

'I suppose so.'

'Where was Jack told to put the hammer in the garage?'

'He was told to hide it under some rubbish for the dustmen.'

Thinking her evidence was finished she started to leave the witness box.

'Thank you, Miss Rolls. I haven't finished yet.' There was a mumbling of voices in the court after the evidence just produced. The jury were very impressed. Mitch looked at the DT who was not happy. The Defence Council continued with his evidence.

'Do you recognise these scissors, Miss Rolls?' he said, handing to the clerk a plastic bag which contained them. 'This is "Exhibit B" M'lord,' said the defence council.

'Yes, they look like the ones. His dad gave them to him to cut some pictures out of a magazine.'

'When Jerry had finished cutting, what did his dad do?'

'He put the scissors in a bag which I thought was funny at the time. Then he took them out of the room.'

'Members of the Jury, these scissors not only have Jack's fingerprints on, but forensic have found traces of the victim's hair. No further questions, M'lord,' said the council, taking his seat.

The judge had to sound the gavel for silence as this fresh evidence was produced.

'Are you implying, Mr Tetley, that the father was deliberately implicating his son Jack in this crime, and setting him up as the murderer?'

'It certainly looks that way your honour,' replied the defence council.

'Have you any questions for the witness, Mr Smith?' asked the judge.

'Yes, Your Honour,' he replied.

'Miss Rolls, when did the incident with the hammer happen?'

'About three weeks ago.'

'Can you be more precise?'

'Yes, it was on Wednesday, the 23rd of June.'

'You're sure of that date, Miss Rolls?'

'Yes. I am sure.'

'No further questions, M'lord,' said the defence council.

The judge dismissed the witness. Suddenly the prosecution council addressed the judge.

'Your Honour, the evidence from this witness has placed the prosecution in a dilemma. Can we adjourn for 24 hours? The judge agreed to adjourn to the same time next day. The prosecuting council came over and spoke to the detective inspector, and Mitch.

'If we don't destroy her evidence, we have lost this case. I leave it to you both to find out if she was at the house on the night she says she saw this happen. It all looks too well prepared.'

The two police officers said they would, and departed.

Mitch and DI Simon Collins were stuck to know where to start looking for additional information which would win the case for them. It seemed they had exhausted every avenue of their enquiries. The evidence that Miss Rolls had given appeared unshakable. They decided to each take a separate line of enquiry and to meet up that evening to consolidate what they had found out.

Unlike the previous hearing, the court was packed the next day. DI Collins met up with the prosecuting council and briefed him as to the new evidence they had uncovered. The court opened in the usual manner with them all standing as the judge entered.

'Will you call your first witness, Mr Smith?' asked the judge.

'Yes My Lord. I call Miss Rolls.'

Miss Rolls was taken to the witness stand and reminded that she was still under oath. Mr Smith opened his questions.

'I have been to see your mother, Miss Rolls. Will you confirm your mother is Janet Rolls of 34 Queensway Avenue, Weymouth, Dorset.'

'Yes, that's right.'

'Your mother told us that you were not allowed in the house of Raymond Chivers, because he disliked you and you never got on together. Is this true?'

'Yes,' she said in a low voice, her head lowered. She knew she had been caught out in a lie.

'Speak up please, so the jury can hear.'

'Yes,' she repeated loudly

'That being the case, all the evidence you gave us yesterday must be a pack of lies, and you are guilty of perjury?'

'Yes,' she said, starting to cry.

'So you didn't see the hammer and the scissors?'

'No.'

'Why did you lie, Miss Rolls?'

'To help Jack out of a mess. He said we would marry and go away together after the trial if I helped him incriminate his dad and get him off the hook. He told me they were both in on it but his dad had got the money, and was keeping it, even though it was Jack what did it. Also I heard the two of them arguing over the money.'

'Thank you, Miss Rolls. No further questions, M'lord.'

The defence had no questions and the jury were out for only half an hour before finding Jack guilty.

The date was set for the trial of Raymond Chivers and Byron Stanton, both who were implicated in Jill's murder. The results were very much appreciated by Solomon who thanked his two colleagues for digging up the information from Rolls's mother; without this, he would surely have got away as not guilty.

The good result of the conviction of Jack Chivers for the murder of Jill Stanton took some pressure off Solomon in the finding of the serial killer. In fact the papers had found other juicy items of interest now. There were still five unsolved murders on Solomon's plate, which he was responsible in solving.

*

Detective Chief Inspector Solomon was not feeling well. The pressure of work and from the press and his bosses made him feel he wanted to throw his hand in; and yet he knew that come what may, he had to see this serial murder through to a successful conclusion; then he could have his rest and a holiday. His office was empty. He had just had a meeting with Josh and his sergeant Mitch, discussing the current events and the likelihood of catching this man – or men – responsible for the serial killings of the five women.

Just then a young detective brought in his mail and on top of the pile was an envelope he recognised. It was poems from the murderer, or someone who wanted Solly to believe he was the murderer.

He opened the envelope, taking care not to disturb any regular fingerprints which might produce evidence. The A4 sheet was laid out in the same familiar manner.

I HaVE dONE
Tis 2 Hot 4 ME
JUsTiCe IS mine
I Hope 2 be
Let OF scOtt free

Solly, pushed the letter into the out tray on his desk. The killer, if it was him, wasn't helping much. He could be leading a completely false trail for the detectives. One thing was certain and that was the line ''Tis too hot for me.'

Solly had tried to make it too hot for him. There were evening patrols of police cars prowling the streets at night; a field patrol with night sights, scouring the banks of the Severn; helicopters and sea patrols ran up and down the estuary. He had made it very hot for the killer. Wendy tapped his office door before entering; she gave him a familiar smile to which he responded. He liked her a lot, and now she was wearing an engagement ring. There was no publicity as to who it was from, as she and Mitch did not want to advertise the fact they were now a complete couple.

'I thought you might be interested, sir, only I saw the owner of the Silver Spoon café this morning, driving a white van.'

'Did you indeed? Put it on the board. Did you get the number of it?'

'Of course I did sir, and the make.'

'Well done, it might come in handy,' said Solly. 'Ask Mitch to come in please, Wendy,' he asked, as she left his office.

Mitch tapped the door and entered.

'You wanted me sir?'

'Yes Mitch. Do you fancy going for a coffee this morning,' he asked. Mitch was a little surprised but knowing his boss he knew there was more to it than coffee.

'Yes sir. Where are we going?'

'To the Silver Spoon, we have been there before.'

'What time sir?'

'Now I think. It should be quite busy. Do you know he drives a white van?'

'No. I wonder why, it sounds strange for a café owner ... I'm ready when you are, sir,' said Mitch.

The two of them drove to the well-established café in the High Street in Solly's blue Rover 75. Solly was right in saying he thought the café would be busy, as indeed it was. There were lots of women, some with young children all sitting round drinking refreshments and chatting. It was very noisy. Outside stood three young women smoking and chatting. He supposed it was like this most mornings. Besides, the prices were very reasonable.

They went up to the counter and stood waiting as Big Mac served his thirsty girls. He guessed that the topic of the murdered wives was very predominant on all their lips. He would love to have sat amongst them, listening to their theories as to who was responsible for the killings. They went up to the counter.

'Good morning, gents. What is it, coffees?'

'And two tea cakes please,' added Mitch.

'Take a seat and I'll bring them over,' said Mac.

The police officers both noticed his arm was bandaged up.

'What happened to your arm, Mac. Had an accident?' asked Solly

'Yes, helping Johnny change the tyre on the white van. Got my arm trapped. It bled very badly, blood everywhere. I thought it might mean A&E, but young Johnny fixed me up. It's getting better, I'm pleased to say.'

'Good!' said Solly, as he wandered over to where the chatty ladies were seated. Solly wondered what the subject of conversation was amongst them.

He headed for a table which had recently been vacated, He chose it because it was right next to where the ladies were sitting.

The chatter dropped as they took their seats. The ladies looked at the pair suspiciously.

Solly smiled at them.

'Good morning, ladies, enjoying this sunshine?'

There were one or two replies.

'I'm feeling in a generous mood. Would anybody like more teas or coffees?'

'Thanks, I'll have a top up,' said a buxom brunette whose thumb was constantly hovering over the text keys on her mobile.

'Anyone else?' asked Solly.

'We are not keen to talk to strangers,' said a young mum with twins in a pushchair.

'Why not, because of the murders,' asked Mitch.

Mac came over and put their coffees down.

'Get another coffee for this lady, and anything that the others want,' said Solly

'Are you alright, Detective Chief Inspector?' said Mac, with a grin, knowing he had disclosed their identity to all in the café.

'Oh you're the police, that's different,' said the woman with the mobile.

Many of them laughed at this, and some more took up the courage and changed their minds, taking advantage of the detective's offer.

'Have any of you any ideas as to who our killer might be?' asked Solly.

There were some murmurings, but nobody wanted to speak out what was on all their minds.

'What's your name madam?' he asked the big brunette.

'Jennifer Gordan,' she said. 'And I'm a single mum. I'm not having an affair, and I don't and can't afford to go out,' she added with a grin. All the women laughed at her confession.

'Have you any theories?' asked Solly.

'No not really. We all thought it was that chap, Wayne, until he got murdered.'

'Have you ever been to that pub?' he asked.

'No never, but it's got a reputation for ... you know what.' She said trying to make a point without committing herself.

'Have any of you any ideas as to who might be behind these murders?'

'No not really, but we're scared,' said a pretty blonde girl, with a little boy, whose nose she was constantly trying to stop running.

'Alright, thank you for your help,' said Solly.

He was just about to rise out of his chair to leave when Mitch gave out a moan and collapsed face down on the table, gripping his stomach.

'Mitch! What's the matter?'

'Stomach cramp sir, hurts like hell,' he gasped.

The inspector felt his pulse. Big Mac was looking on.

'Mac, get an ambulance quickly,' said Solly.

'OK! Leave it to me.' The ladies looked on, suggesting a variety of possible causes from indigestion to food poisoning. The ambulance was there in ten minutes and two medics rushed in.

'Looks like appendix trouble,' said the senior one. 'Hold on sir, we'll soon have you in hospital.'

Minutes later he was on a stretcher and on his way to Taunton Hospital.

Chapter 22

D I COLLINS called Detective Sergeant Morgan over to his desk.
'I am still waiting for your report on the clothes found on
the banks of the Avon estuary, Sergeant.'

'Sorry about the delay sir, but it was due to a shortage of staff at
Forensic, they used the excuse of Government reduction of staff.'

'We have all suffered from that. Did you get copies of the tyre
tracks you found?'

'Yes sir, the trouble is finding a vehicle that matches them.'

'This is very frustrating. How this killer can get away with them
for so long beats me. He's so cocky with it, sending poems and
leaving clues. This must be one of the longest criminal searches in
history,' said the Inspector.

He sat there for a moment, not saying a word, thinking over any
avenue they had not perused.

'I want you and I to go over to where you found the clothes and
have another look around. Perhaps we have missed something,' said
the Inspector.

'When, sir?'

'Right away. There's no time like the present, bring a coat, rain is
forecast in that area.'

'Yes sir.'

They drove along towards the Severn Estuary, chatting away
about the crimes they were investigating. They were about three miles
from the location they wanted to search, when the sergeant, suddenly,
and without warning, stopped the van.

'What's the matter, Sergeant? Why have we stopped?'

There is a little stone cottage down in the valley, with a white van
parked outside, and the van has something written on the side of it.'

'So what!' We can't stop for every tradesman van,' said the
inspector.

'I have a gut feeling about this one, can we make a slight detour?'
The inspector looked at his watch.

'Oh! Alright then.' The police car made its way to the cottage.

The police officer got out of their car and went to inspect the
white van. Written on the side of it was .

PIZZA DELIVERY: A SPECIALITY OF

THE WICKED ELF PUBLIC HOUSE

'Wow! What a surprise,' said the Inspector, as he looked inside the van and round it.

'There are some good tyre prints too,' said the sergeant. 'I can photograph them.'

'Yes go ahead. It's got a flat front tyre; I see. I wonder if there is anyone at home.'

'The tax ran out last week sir.'

'So they're not making much money delivering pizzas with this van, sergeant.'

'No sir.'

Despite several attempts at bell ringing and knocking, nobody came to the door. The blinds were drawn. They circled the cottage, making notes and taking photographs.

'Come on, there's nothing more we can do here today. Let's be on our way,' said DI Collins. They continued their journey to the estuary.

'Here is the spot, sir. See the vehicle has driven nearly up to the water.'

'Yes it would need too, if one person wanted to drag, or carry a body to the water's edge.'

There were no visible footprints, but the grasses along the river bank had been compressed.

'What have we here?' said the Inspector, lifting a plastic bag from under the grasses. 'I trod on it.'

'What is it sir?'

'It's a hammer, a gift from heaven. It must have fallen out of the van when he was dragging the body out.'

'Fantastic, sir, well done.'

'Yes, I just happened to tread on it, and in a plastic bag as well.'

'Which should mean the entire DNA is intact. Come on, sir, let's get back and give this to forensic. This is a break we have been waiting for,' said the sergeant.

*

Superintendant Josh was very happy at the news of the finding of the hammer. This should really find the killer of the girls. The hammer was sent straight to the science forensic laboratories who were expert at getting the facts. Solly couldn't believe his good fortune and heartily congratulated DI Collins on his find.

It was two days later that Wendy tapped on Solly's door with the good news.

'Sir, I have the details of the hammer, from forensic. It is unopened, and has been send over by courier.

'Thanks, Wendy,' Solly felt elated as he took the letter to his superior Josh.

'This is what we have been waiting for sir,' said Solly, handing the report over. They both sat down, Solly waiting till Josh had read the report.

'Hm! There is still work to do, Solly,' he said, handing the report over for him to read.

'Yes, the hammer has fingerprints, blood DNA, and even strands of a woman's hair. Armed with these facts, you must pinpoint who it was. There are no magic answers.'

'No, sir of course not, but this evidence is a great help.'

He got up and returned to his office; feeling a little deflated.

As he passed Wendy, he signalled for her to come into his office.

'Sit down, Wendy. As you know we have the forensic reports on the hammer. It seems as if all the clues are there all we have to do is match them and find the killer. You have on file the DNA records of all our suspects. I leave it to you to give me a name.'

'Yes sir,' she replied, getting up.

'Another thing is, don't tell a soul about the hammer. I don't want the press round here asking questions, not yet anyway.'

'I understand, sir,' she said, as she left the office.

*

DI Collins called Sergeant Morgan to his office.

'I want you to go back to that cottage we stopped at yesterday and see if anyone is at home. I want that van checked over as it may have been used to transport a body. Next, I want you to go to the Wicked Elf and find out what you can about who was driving it and left it there. You got all that?'

'Yes sir.'

'Right, off you go. Take a detective constable with you.'

The two police officers set off for where the broken down van was located. There was no sign of the van when they arrived at the cottage.

'Come on, Tony,' said Detective Sergeant Morgan, 'We'll see if anyone is at home.'

This time the bell was answered straight away. A middle-aged lady came to the door. DS Morgan introduced the pair of them to the woman.

'What do you want?' she asked.

'We are investigating that white van we saw here three days ago.'

'Oh that. I was glad to see the back of it, littering up my garden.'

'I see it belonged to the Wicked Elf pub.'

'That's right, a man rang the bell and asked if he could leave it as it had broken down. But it was here a week before he collected it yesterday.'

'What's your name, Madam?'

'I'm Mrs Short Janice Short. Come on in and talk. It's cold out here.'

They entered the lounge. It was comfortable with a well-used three-piece suite and other furniture. The room was full of the appetising smell of a beef casserole.

'Do you live alone here, Mrs Short?'

'Yes I do. I was widowed five years ago. My husband was a baker.' There were pictures in silver frames of children.

'You live here all alone then. It must be scary and lonely,' said the sergeant.

'No, I got used to it. My two children live away from home, but I see them sometimes.

'What did the man look like that left the van?'

'It was hard to make him out. He wore a hat down over his eyes and a scarf round his face. Oh and he couldn't shake hands because he had had an accident and damaged his hand.'

'What could he be doing down here? I wonder,' said the sergeant.

'He said he was delivering pizzas, when he got the puncture.'

'Are there any more houses round here?'

'There's one over the back, about two miles away.'

'Who lives there?'

'I dunno, it's just been sold. Oh and borrowed my bike to get home.'

'Did he indeed?'

'Yes, and brought it back. Don't bother checking it for prints. He was wearing gloves. Besides it was a shorter chap came and recovered the van.'

'Right! Thank you for your time. You have been most helpful,' said the sergeant.

They both shook hands with Janice, and drove away.

'Drive down this road a couple of miles. I would like to see the new owners of the house.'

'Right, Sergeant,' said the constable.

Ten minutes later they arrived at a small, two-bedroomed cottage. A man in jeans and a T-shirt was up a ladder, adjusting the guttering. He came down when the police car drew up.

'Hello gentlemen, what can I do for you?'

The sergeant greeted him and introduced the pair of them. They shook hands.

'My name is Ben Nevis. I know it's a mountain; my parents had a sense off humour.'

'Not your fault, Ben,' said the sergeant smiling.

'No! I only got to live with it. How can I help you?'

'Did you have a pizza delivery last week, or at any time recently?'

'No, we don't like them. Why?'

'We're trying to trace the driver of a white van seen in this area.'

'No, he might have called on the house a couple of miles away over there.'

'No, he didn't – we checked.'

'Is that all?'

'Yes, Ben. I will never forget you.' They all laughed, and the policemen said their goodbyes, and drove back to the station.

'So he wasn't delivering pizzas.'

'No, Sarge.'

Then he was up to something else. I think it was the van which dropped the last woman off in the sea, and left the hammer.'

'Certainly looks that way, Sergeant.'

DS Morgan reported to DI Collins, who seemed to be awaiting their return.

'Well! How did you get on?'

'The van has gone sir. The occupant of the house is a middle-aged lady named Mrs Janice Short. She said a man called one night and asked if he could leave his van there as it had broken down.'

'How did he get home?'

'Apparently he borrowed Mrs Short's bicycle, which a man has returned. And she said he was wearing gloves.'

*

Solly drove back to his office knowing it would be some time before his sergeant would be back to work. He reported to Josh on his arrival, and was told to take Wendy Morrison on as a replacement.

'By the way, Solly, we have found tyre tracks down by the estuary which match those of one of the vans we checked on. Unfortunately it's a hire van.'

'Damn!' said Solly. 'Just when we needed a break. Can they name the person who hired it?'

'No the licence was false. But they did give a description of him. He was six foot tall wearing a motorcycle crash helmet, and he was thick set. They also said he spoke with a foreign accent, but he couldn't keep it up, so he was putting it on.'

'Do you think this is our killer sir?'

'Could be, Solly, but not much to go on I'm afraid.'

Solly walked back to his office and called Wendy in.

'I'm sorry to tell you, Wendy, but Mitch has been taken to hospital by ambulance.'

'Oh no! What's wrong?' She uttered, shocked at the news.

'They suspect appendix trouble.'

'Can I see him?'

'We will phone the hospital later and you can visit him this evening, I expect. Don't worry. He's in safe hands. Sit down, I want to talk to you.'

She sat down, but she was not her usual alert self. The news of her fiancé had greatly upset her.

'You have been given to me to replace Mitch until he is well enough to return.' She looked up surprised. This was a lucky break. It was a pity about Mitch.

'Thank you sir,' she said, with a weak smile.

'Have you heard they have found tyre tracks that match a van we checked on and a vague description of the driver?'

'No, I didn't know sir. Can we improve on that?'

'Let's think about it. I feel we are not far off catching our man,' said Solly.

'What about the van that I saw Big Mac driving. Why would he need a van?'

'I know, we were going to question him when Mitch was taken ill. I'm busy this afternoon. Ask DI Collins to go with you and speak to him. Besides it might be better you going, as he is getting familiar with Mitch and I.'

'Right sir. Is there anything else?' She was switched on, this girl; he was pleased to be working with her.

'No, that's all sergeant, off you go,' he said, with a smile.

*

DI Collins wasn't available. Wendy was told by his secretary that he had gone to investigate the tyre tracks that had been discovered. At 2 pm that same afternoon a police car with Wendy and Solly in it stopped outside the Silver Spoon café. The driver stayed with the car. Solly and Wendy entered the café. It was empty of customers, which was not uncommon at that time of day. A woman stood behind the counter.

'Hello,' she smiled. 'Can I help you?'

Simon and Wendy produced their warrant cards and introduced themselves.

'We would like to talk to Mr MacDonald. Is he in?'

'He's taking a shower. I'll call him,' she replied.

'I think it may be wise to close the café while we speak with him. It won't take long,' advised Wendy.

The lady went and put the closed notice on the café door. She called her husband.

'He won't be long,' she smiled.

Just then Big Mac appeared.

'Hello! It's the boys in blue again. What's up now?'

'You were seen driving a white van this morning, Mr MacDonald, was it yours? Only, we're checking every white van in the area as we have had several sightings of these vans where women have been murdered,' said Simon.

'And your van does not appear to have been checked by us,' added Wendy

'Yes, it's mine. I didn't know you were checking them, nobody told me. It's out the back if you want to see it,' he said.

'Why do you need a van when you own a café? I wouldn't have thought there was much call for one,' said Wendy.

'Ah! Well, that's where you're wrong, young lady. If you had done your homework you would know I use the van for delivering hot meals in the evenings,' he grinned at her.

'And how would I know that?' she replied.

'Because, I advertise it in the local paper. Look!' he said, taking a paper from under the counter and showing her where it was advertised. Wendy was ready with another question.

'That means that as you are so efficient, Mr MacDonald, you must keep a register of every person and their addresses so assist your deliveries.'

'That's right,' he replied.

'We would like to see it, will you get it for us,' said Simon.

Big Mac went white. 'I can't. I haven't got it.'
'Where is it?'
'My assistant has it.'
'Who might he be?'
'Johnny Long, at the Wicked Elf.' Big Mac replied.

Chapter 23

SOLLY AND WENDY drove over to the hospital that evening and were surprised to find Mitch sitting up in bed.

'I thought you were ill,' said Solly.

Wendy dashed over to her sweetheart, and gave him a big kiss.

'I have been so worried about you darling,' she said.

'I'm alright,' said Mitch. 'I did have a strangled hernia, but I had keyhole surgery and am much better, I should be home in a couple of days.'

'That's good news. Wendy has been standing in for you. I should be careful Mitch she is very efficient, she might replace you,' he smiled.

Mitch was keen to be brought up to date on the murders and showed interest when he heard of Big Mac's involvement.

'Yes! and another thing sir. He has a gift of words. Have you seen the framed poems around the walls of his café?' said Mitch.

'Yes, I have noticed them,' said Solly, pulling up two chairs. 'I have here a copy of the latest poem I received,' said Solly, handing it to Mitch. He read it through and handed it to Wendy to read.

I HaVE dONE
Tis 2 Hot 4 ME
JUsTiCe IS mine
I Hope 2 be
Let OF scOtt free

'I have been thinking sir, having read that poem,' said Mitch.

'Steady, Sergeant, that's not good for a man in hospital,' interrupted Solly.

The three of them laughed at Solly's remark.

'No seriously. This poem the killer sent you, sir,' said Mitch.

'Yes.'

'Well, the bottom line said something about getting off scot free.'

'Yes, go on.'

'Well, I think this was an intentional lead to the Scotsman Big Mac.'

'What! Like a confession that he is the culprit.'

'Or, it could be someone trying to pin the murders on him, particularly as he is a poet,' said Wendy.

'Yes interesting trains of thought – both of them,' said Solly, feeling very pleased with his two assistants.

*

Seven days later Mitch was back at work. He shouldn't have been but he refused to miss out on what he felt was the climax of the murders.

Wendy came into Solomon's office looking quite perturbed.

'Hello, Wendy, what's wrong?'

'Sir there are five men downstairs demanding to talk to you.'

'Who are they? What do they want?'

'It is a delegation of all the menfolk of the five women who have been murdered by the serial killer. They are not a happy crowd, sir. They insist they speak to you and demand an explanation as to what you are doing to find the murderer.'

'Put them in the interview room, Wendy. Mitch and I will be down in a minute.'

'Right, sir,' Solomon put his head outside his office and called Mitch over.

'It looks as if we have a revolt on our hands. I have never known anything like this before. Come with me we will go and talk to them.'

'Good morning, gentlemen,' said Solomon, when he and Mitch entered the room. All the men had been provided with seats, and didn't look very happy.

'Gentlemen. I understand your concerns at the slow rate we are getting results in respect of these five murders, but this killer is leaving no clues we can work on. He kills his victims at night on their way home, strips them naked and throws their bodies in the sea.'

'Why does he put them naked in the sea?'

'That way he ensures any DNA he might have put on them has been washed off.'

'Does he sexually assault them?' asked Roger Carter.

'There is no evidence of that.'

'What about these white vans he is suspected of using?'

'Yes, we have seen white vans on several CCTV cameras, but they are different types with different vehicle numbers. We have no evidence to link any of them.'

There was silence in the room for a moment whilst the men digested this information to try and find a loophole or some new unexplored avenue.

'When can the bodies be released? We want to bury our women folk,' asked Roger Walters.

'I will look into that for you and try and get them released.'

'What's the motive behind the killings? Why is he doing it?' asked Derek Shaw, the partner of the last victim.

'I was hoping you didn't ask this question. All the ladies were showing signs to the killer that they were having extramarital affairs.' This caused uproar in the room.

'How dare you suggest that my Mary was having an affair? She loved me. We had a normal sex life – she didn't need anyone else,' said Shaun Dagleash.

Other men were disputing Solomon's suggestion for the motive as absurd.

'Well, I am sorry, gentlemen, that's the way the evidence points. Some of the ladies were found with other men's sperm in them. I don't want to reveal who unless I have to.

'What about my partner, Inspector? You said mine was an exception,' said Derek Shaw.

'Yes, Mr Shaw. Your partner might have been raped after she was killed, or while she was unconscious. There is evidence of skin under her nails, which we hope is that of her attacker.'

'But why pick on her?'.

'I think primarily because he always associated you being with her and the night she was killed she was with your brother, so the killer thought she was playing away from home.'

'Yes it sounds reasonable, Inspector. So what more can we do to catch this killer?'

'Quite honestly we are stumped. We have a DNA sample now from the skin taken from under Elsie Maxwell's fingernails, but no suspect to match it too. We have your entire DNA on file and we know there is no match there.'

'Will you keep us informed, Inspector?' asked Arthur Marlow, as the men got up to leave.

'Gentlemen, I promise you no stone will remain unturned and I will let you know any positive results.' They thanked them both and left the station.

Wendy was waiting outside the interview room, looking very anxious.

'Sir, we have a match on the hammer confirming the DNA and fingerprints.'

'Are you sure, Wendy? That is good news. Both of you come into my office, sit down. Well, come on, who is it?'

'Its Big Mac sir,' she said.

Solly and Mitch looked at each other. Both felt disappointed it was him.

'You're sure, Wendy.'

'Definitely sir.'

'Thank you. Leave the letter on my desk and you can both go.'

The two sergeants left the office. Solly went and knocked on Josh's office door.

'Come in, Solly. What's new?' he asked, indicating that Solly be seated.

'Sir, we have a name which links to the DNA on the hammer.'

'Have you indeed, and who is it?'

'It's a Mr MacDonald at the Silver Spoon café in town.'

'Right! Call a meeting of the whole team we need to discus this matter before we go galloping off after this man.'

'What time sir?'

'Give me an hour, Solly.'

*

Everyone connected with the murder team were seated in the office at 11 am. Solly opened the meeting and brought it up to date regarding the hammer. But no suspect's name was released, Solly didn't want the press hounding him until he was ready to arrest the culprit.

DI Collins stood up.

'Sir, I have additional information.' He went on to relate the findings of himself and DS Morgan. Then DS Morgan stood up, and updated the officers on the broken down pizza delivery van.

'Well done, everyone. You have been working hard. We have a suspect and will be bringing him in. Until he is charged I don't want his name known.'

A murmur went around those gathered who didn't know the name of the suspect, and thought they should. The meeting closed.

'Can we bring the suspect in sir?' asked Solly.

'In view of the additional information revealed this morning, then yes go ahead. I want to be in on the interview,' said the Superintendent.

Solly thought it wise that he and Mitch were not in the team bringing in Big Mac. He sent DI Collins and DS Morgan to bring the suspect in.

The arrest was made and Big Mac, despite protesting loudly, was placed in a cell. The arrest of Big Mac was soon on the local radio and television. The world press were demanding information and a meeting with Solly and Josh.

*

Big Mac was brought into the interview room, loudly protesting his innocence. Solly and Mitch were to carry out the interview. Big Mac's solicitor was present.

Solly started the interview proceedings as per the book.

'I haven't killed anyone, Inspector,' cried Mac.

'We have brought you in for questioning because there are several pointers that suggest you may be the man we are looking for regarding the killing of five ladies. We have found this hammer,' said Solly. 'I am showing the suspect exhibit A.'

'Is this yours?' Mac looked it over.

'Aye! It's mine how did you get it. It's been in me garage. I can tell because there is a piece of the handle missing at the end.'

'It was found in a plastic bag in the reeds on the bank of the Severn Estuary.'

'I have never been there,' said Mac.

'On the handle are your prints and blood samples of one of your victims.'

'That's a load of rubbish. Someone else has used it. Not me.'

'Where were you on the night of Friday, 19th November?'

'At home, I know because I couldn't drive because of my damaged arm.'

'Have you a witness to that fact?'

'Yes, my wife. She and I stayed in and played Scrabble.'

Solly and Mitch looked at each other. Mac had a reasonable alibi. He could have been set up. They couldn't charge him The defence would pull the case to threads.

'All right Mac, you are free to go,' said Solly.

A look of great relief came over Mac's face.

'I think someone has tried to set me up, Inspector, and I am going to find out who.'

'Don't do anything. Leave the case with us,' said Sergeant Mitchell.

'You didn't charge him then, Inspector,' said Josh to Solly.

'No sir, we couldn't. He had a good alibi. He's not our man, I am certain of that,' said Solly.

'Never mind, keep at it,' said Josh, disappearing into his office.

*

Solomon and Mitch were sat in his air-cooled office going over every item associated with the murdered five women. As far as they could tell, they had covered every loophole and individual. They had blood tested and DNA'ed all the men; there were no clues as to a possible suspect. They had gone over their stories of where they were on the night their partners were murdered and these alibis were pretty watertight.

'Have you considered, sir, that most of these women; in fact all of them have at some time used the Wicked Elf pub. There must be a link between the murders and the pub, something we have overlooked.'

'What have you in mind. Mitch?'

'Well, who would be better than the person working behind the bar at seeing the comings and goings of the clientele?'

'So what. He or she wouldn't know the women were married or whom they were married to.'

'Perhaps not, but they would see who they were going out with. I think we agree, sir, that our killer is a man with a revenge vendetta. Who is out to get his own back on those types of girls he married. He has an unforgiving nature. So he will be keeping a careful eye on his prey. Do you know there has recently been a change of landlord at the Wicked Elf, sir.'

'No, and I never met the earlier one, did you, Mitch?'

'I saw him but never spoke to him. He was interviewed by Wendy.'

'Perhaps we slipped up there; he might have held some vital information.'

'Shall I go and look up who the previous landlord was, sir.'

Solomon nodded.

Mitch was only away a few minutes. 'It was a Mr Jerry White. However, he was trading as a publican using the name of Jerry Long. That was the name over the door.'

'Never, are you sure?'

'Yes of course I am sir, why?'

'Hmm. I wonder why he changed his name, and then changed it back when he left the pub,' pondered Solly. 'Well, if it is the same one he owned a pub in Cornwall. Colein and I used to stay there. His wife went off the rails and started playing away with a chap from the village. Jerry said he would never own another pub; fancy that, I don't believe it.'

'So perhaps he is our murderer?'

'If only it was that simple. Find out his forwarding address, Mitch.'

'Well we must treat his father Jerry as suspect number one.'

'Now we know who he is I agree we must. When you find out where he is living bring him and his wife in for questioning. Make that a priority task, Mitch.'

It didn't take long to find where Jerry had moved to. Mitch phoned the Wicked Elf and spoke to the new landlord who had his forwarding address.

'It's not far from here, sir, we could drive over and interview him.'

'Alright we'll go over this afternoon.'

The sun shone on Solomon's car, as the pair of them drove to north Bristol up the A38. The address was easy to find as the house stood alone and showed that the owners had invested wisely in their choice of a five-bedroomed detached Edwardian house, fenced off from the nosey passing traffic by a smart, well-trimmed green hedge. A cobbled driveway led from the front gate around a small lawn on which was a water garden and fountain.There was a double garage to the left of the property. Jerry must have put all his hard-earned savings into this retirement retreat.

Mitch closed the wrought-iron gate, while Solly drove and parked by the garages. He got out of the car and waited for Mitch to join him. They walked to the white panelled door decorated wit black simulated iron studs and rang the bell. The door was opened by Jerry, who took a moment for his brain to register where he had last seen Solly's face.

'Detective Inspector Solomon, what a surprise. I never expected to see you again. I suppose its business, is it? Police business?'

'Hello Jerry, yes you're right, it is police business. I have been promoted. It's Chief Inspector now. Can we come in? This is Detective Sergeant Mitchell.'

'Fine, nice to meet you come on in.'

'Where's the wife, Jerry?'

'Which wife? I have had two.'

'Both of them.'

'Well the first one, who you met, died in a boating accident in Tenerife. Very tragic, but that was three years ago.'

'I'm sorry to hear that, Jerry.'

'Yes she never really recovered from that horrible affair in Cornwall. The one my son took the blame for.'

'Well, he did carry out the killing of her lover – didn't he? What was the sentence your son got?'

'Fifteen years. It would have been more but the judge took kindly to his admitting the murder and the fact that it was a natural reaction after having seen his mother engaged in sex with a man other than her husband. Anyway, how can I help you?'

A young lady came into the room, dressed as a maid.

'This is Flicky, my house helper. She looks after my needs. Get us tea for the three of us Flicky please,' he said.

'You recently were the landlord at the Wicked Elf, weren't you?'

'Yes I only moved out about a fortnight ago.'

'You told me you were not going back into the pub trade after that murder in Cornwall.'

'Well, I never intended to, but this little bargain came on the market. I could see the potential so I snapped it up. I turned that place around, Solomon. I converted an old skittle alley into a Friday night dance club. It brought them in by droves, ran the disco myself, extended the car park and made a lot of money. I already had this place on mortgage but when I sold up I paid it off and now it's all mine.'

'Very nice too,' said Solly, looking round at the recently decorated room and furniture.

'You changed your name as well I see. It was Mr Long, and there was a Mrs Long.'

'Oh don't talk to me about her. She ran off with a customer and really left me in the lurch.'

' So you're on your own now?'

'Yes, and enjoying it.'

'What can you tell me about the five murders, which although not directly attached to your pub, were, in nearly each case, the last place the victims were before dying.'

'What do you mean, Inspector?' said Jerry, moving himself forward in his chair giving the impression he was very engrossed in what Solly was saying.' You're not accusing me of anything are you Inspector.'

'No Jerry. I want your assistance, because apart from the killer, you might have been the last person to see them alive.'

'I was rarely in the bar. I had staff to run the place. Once I got the disco started I handed it over to a young chap, he was much better than me.' The tea arrived and the conversation lapsed for a moment.

'Have you got a white van, Jerry?'

'I did have I sold it when I sold the pub. It was pretty clapped out anyway.'

Mitch came up with a question. 'How many children in your family, Jerry?'

'Two boys, Justin and Johnny. Justin helps in the kitchen mainly and Johnny works in the pub running a taxi service and helping with a hot food service ran by Big Mac at the Silver Spoon café.'

'How did your youngest son treat your new wife after the killing?' asked Solly.

'He was very upset, and was very annoyed at his mother, in fact he never forgave her playing away, and rarely spoke to her after that. Surely you don't suspect my sons of being the murderers, Inspector?'

'We can't rule anyone out. We must find out who the killer is. How old is Johnny?'

'Thirty, he is the younger of the two. Here is a picture of the two boys, taken with their mother five years ago. How I wish we could turn the clock back.'

'Do you keep a diary, Jerry?'

'No I don't, why? Look, my sons had nothing to do with these murders. You might be running short of suspects but don't start accusing my boys.'

'We are dealing with facts, Jerry. There have been five murders nearly all of married women who have played away from home. Your sons are not suspects, but we can't rule anyone out.'

'Even me?'

'Yes Jerry, even you.' Solomon got up to leave. 'Thanks for your hospitality and help, Jerry. It's been nice meeting you again. Let me know if you think of anything which may help.' He shook hands, and Jerry saw them out.

'What do you think, sir, about his son Johnny?'

'It's quite possible. We know he is mad at his mother. It seems strange how she drowned so suddenly after the murder, and did she commit suicide? Look into it, Mitch; see what facts you can find on her death.'

Solly called a meeting of all his officers involved in the serial murders the next day. The incident board was brought up to date and had the addition of the Long family.

'Has anyone here any pointers to add which will help us solve these murders. Sergeant Mitchell what have you discovered about Justin Long?'

'I have found one date on which he visited his father at the Wicked Elf and that matches the death of Jill Stanton. I have shown his picture to many people who might have known him, in particular the bar staff at the pub; some of which are still employed there. Apparently Justin Long was involved with another chap in a fight in the bar. It wasn't over a woman, it was over a young man.'

'Is he gay?'

'No sir, his brother is. He admitted it when we interviewed him,' said Mitch. 'Anything else of interest we can follow up. I know the leads are cold now, but it is never too late to solve a crime. I know it's boring and you all want juicy new crimes to work on, but we can't leave this one. I want you all to team up in pairs and requestion those concerned. See if their stories are still the same. It's nearly three months now, they need good memories.'

Josh was at the back of the hall listening. He didn't interfere; Solomon was quite capable of handling this. CID had decided not to interfere and leave it to the local police, they realised the chance of a conviction had gone very cold. There was an air of despondent gloom in the incident room. No one wanted to work on this old case.

Josh decided to intervene in the group conference. 'Now listen, all of you. It's your responsibility, every one of you, to do your utmost to solve this crime. The killer is out there somewhere. He may feel he has got away with it and let his guard down. It's up to you to trip him up. Detective Chief Inspector Solomon is still working hard. It's up to you to support him. I want this solved by the end of the week. Look at the board, study the clues, divide yourselves into pairs and find that murderer. There will be another meeting like this in a week's time. I want results and we will keep on working on it till we get them.'

It wasn't often Josh addressed the assembled police team but he could see Solomon was at his wits' end and needed help; that's why he put pressure on them.

Chapter 24

SOLLY COULD SEE through his office window that Wendy seemed agitated about something so he beckoned her in.

'What's up, Wendy? You seem all on edge.'

'Well, sir, Wendy and I have got engaged and would like you to come to a little dinner party with us to celebrate.'

'That's very nice of you and Mitch. Of course my wife and I would love to come. Congratulations. Is she happy?'

'Yes, sir, very happy.'

'When is the party, Wendy?'

'Next weekend, sir. It is Saturday night at the Golden Globe, 8 for 8.30.'

Solomon wrote the date in his diary. 'I will tell her when I get home.'

'Mitch and Wendy are getting engaged next weekend and we have been invited to their engagement party.'

'That's nice for them, they have had a pretty rough time of it what with her getting abducted, that must have been terribly upsetting for both of them,' said Colein.

'They seem to have got over it,' said Solly.

*

The day of Mitch and Wendy's engagement party arrived. The occasion certainly made a change from trying to solve murders. Wendy had taken the day off to prepare for the engagement. She had been wearing the ring for a month, but didn't advertise the fact they were engaged. If anyone spotted it, she explained it was one her mother gave her, and didn't elaborate on it.

There were ten guests there at the party. Wendy had arranged a sit down reception dinner at the pub.

Solly and Colein gave the engaged couple a silver decanter which was her mother's. They never used it, but it was still a valuable gift. The evening was a great success, and all enjoyed themselves.

'Have you fixed a date for the wedding?' asked Solly, loud enough for all to hear.

Wendy blushed. 'No, we need to do some saving first,' said Wendy.

Her mother stood up. She still looked very pale.

'Wendy and Nigel, here is your engagement present. I want to give it to you while I am still able to,' she said, sitting down.

'Can I open it, mother?'

'Of course you can.'

Inside the package was a note to them both and ten thousand pounds in cash.

'Mother you shouldn't have.'

'Go ahead, take it, and bring the marriage date forward. I want to be there before I die.'

Wendy ran round the table and kissed her. 'Yes, we will bring the date forward. How about Easter this year?' She looked across at Mitch, who smiled, and nodded his agreement.

'That's it then, my dear friends, we shall be getting married next Easter,' said Wendy, excitedly.

The party broke up soon after that, and they all made their way home.

*

'Mitch, I think we aught to speak to Johnny Long. Find out his address and we will question him. If he's not the murderer, then let's cross him off the list,' said Solomon. 'Besides we have this new information from Big Mac that Johnny is involved in delivering hot food at night to houses in the area. He knows the customers and where they live. He has already killed his own mother whether by accident or not is immaterial.'

Mitch had Johnny Long brought into the police station for questioning. He had his own solicitor present. Solomon was out working on other police matters so Mitch enlisted the help of Wendy in the questioning.

The four of them sat in the interview room, two on either side of the table. Mitch opened the interview in the traditional manner, mentioning all those present.

Johnny sat there, leaning back in a relaxed attitude in his chair. His fair hair was receding from his forehead, leaving him a high forehead below which was a pair of pale blue eyes. He was thin-faced with a day's stubble, and wore a clean, open-necked white shirt and jeans. He appeared a confident man with a casual air about him. One could imagine him as a businessman, certainly not a manual worker. He used his brains more than his physical energy to earn a living and overcome problems.

Johnny Long was the last person one would imagine a serial killer to look like. He gave the impression he had far more important things to do in life than bump off middle-aged tarts, who were two-timing their husbands.

'Thank you for coming in and helping us with our enquiries, Mr Long regarding the murder of five women in this district.'

'That's alright, call me Johnny, they all do.'

He still carried that same silly grin as when he was first interviewed. Mitch didn't feel comfortable about this interview. He knew he had to keep a tight reign on the questions or Mr Long would take over.

'Where do you live at the moment, Mr Long?' asked Wendy.

'With my father.'

'Just the two of you?'

'Yes.'

'And before that?'

'In the Wicked Elf.'

'With your stepmother, Mrs Elsie Long?'

'That's right, you know all that. Remember you and that DI interviewed me,' Johnny replied, looking very disinterested in the proceedings.

'I know, Mr Long, but we have received fresh evidence which means we have to question you again,' said Mitch.

'Did you ever attend the dances at the pub on a Friday night?'

'I might look in sometimes; I wasn't really interesting in getting involved with anyone there. Besides I ran a taxi service and delivering hot meals for the Silver Spoon café.'

'How long have you been doing that?'

'Over a year,' he replied.

'You have a register of all your customers and where they live, haven't you?'

'Yes.'

'Where is it now?'

'My dad has it.'

'There are a lot of people who share the knowledge encased in that book,' said Mitch.

'I suppose so. So what?'

'Why would your dad have the register of your customers?'

'Well, he sometimes helps out delivering.'

'Does Big Mac take deliveries as well?'

'Yes sometimes,' said Johnny, reaching for his mobile. Mitch leaned over and took the mobile from the very startled man.

'You're not phoning anyone from here. You can have this back when you leave.' said Mitch.

Just then the door opened and Solly entered the room. 'Carry on, Sergeant,' he said to Mitch.

'Were you with your mother when she died?'

'Yes I was.'

'Tell me about it.'

'What's that got to do with the murders?' said Johnny, looking at his solicitor for help.

'Yes, Sergeant. I agree with my client. What has that to do with the murders?'

'Johnny's mother was involved in a love affair with another man, outside of her marriage, just like all of these women were. There was a murder committed by her son Justin on the man she was cohabiting with. I am given to understand that Johnny had no time for his mother.'

The solicitor nodded to Johnny he should answer.

'Where did she die?'

'In the sea.'

'Where?'

'Tenerife.'

'How did she die?'

'She was hit by a water ski that was running out of control.'

'Who was the driver of that machine?'

'I was, but I was cleared at the autopsy of any involvement in her death.'

'Yes, so I believe. Did you suffer any remorse at her death, did you grieve.'

'To be truthful, I didn't. I hated her for what she did having that affair. I would have killed the bastard like Justin did if I had seen him shagging her.'

'It takes two to tango, Mr Long,' said Wendy.

Johnny didn't look so cool after his outburst.

'What were your feelings towards women of this nature who had illicit love affairs?'

'What do you mean?'

'Did you despise them? Hate them even? Wish they were dead?'

'Even if I did, I did nothing about it,' replied Johnny.

'Did you ever drive your father's white van when you came home?'

'Sometimes, why?'

'It was caught on CCTV at various times, and we have reason to believe it was seen in places near where the murders took place.'

'Quite likely, we were delivering food all over the area.'

'Does your van advertise the fact you sell food?'

'One does. The new one we bought. It doesn't prove anything. I went all over the place in the van, day and night. But I didn't do your bloody murders.'

Mitch was stumped for questions. He turned to Wendy.

'Have you any questions?'

'No, I don't think so. Oh! just one.'

'Go on,' said Mitch.

'Johnny, can you tell me the number of bar staff working there on a Friday night?' asked Wendy.

'Quite a lot, four I seem to remember.'

'Did you get to know any of them?'

'Yes.'

'Who?'

'My dad,' he laughed.

'Thank you, Mr Long,' said Wendy.

Solly touched Mitch on the shoulder and signalled for him to go outside. Wendy updated the interview tape as to what was taking place.

'Mitch, I have two squad cars going over to pick up Jerry Long. They are bringing him in for questioning and I have a warrant to search his house.'

'Do you think he did it, sir?'

'I have a hunch he did. I can't be certain but I am hoping to find evidence. Mr Long senior is coming in for questioning. We will do it as soon as he arrives. Put this one in a cell if you want to. I don't want them to talk to each other, understand. Alright go back in and close the interview.'

*

'Mr Johnny Long, we are holding you for further questioning appertaining to the murders of five women,' said Wendy.

'I didn't do it. I want to make a phone call. I know my rights.'

His solicitor looked on helplessly. There was nothing he could do. Once he was put in a cell, Mitch and Wendy got together.

'You think he's the killer?' Mitch asked Wendy.

'I think he knows more than he's telling us. I think that affair his mother got involved in really made him nasty.'

'He didn't show any remorse at the death of his mother, did he?'

'He's a most unusual man,' said Mitch, as he left Wendy, and walked into Solly's office.

'How did you get on with Johnny Long?' asked Solomon.

'He's a bit of a mystery man. He appears very self-confident and tries to ask the questions. He wasn't very helpful. He denied having anything to do with the murders without us even implying he might have.'

'So we're no nearer getting the killer.'

'No sir, I'm stumped. Wendy asked a question at the end, right out of the blue. I don't know what made her ask it.'

'What did she say?'

'She asked him how many people worked in the bar on a Friday night.'

'Ah Mitch. Women have devious clever minds. They're not like us men. Call her in for a chat.'

Wendy came when summoned, and Josh followed her in, merely curious as to what was being discussed.

*

Solly was told by the drug squad that they were interested in Justin Long. There was a raid arranged for dawn the next day on the house of Justin Long. It seems there were undisputable facts which made him a very suspect drug dealer. Solly explained that the man was also wanted for questioning regarding the murder, which he considered gave him priority in the case of interviewing him.

The drug squad agreed that Solly's crime squad could have first go at getting a murder conviction and they would interview him later. It seemed obvious that his long prison sentence for killing his mother's lover had only taught him bad habits in drug dealing. There were two vans full of police, with Solomon and Mitch in charge of the operation. The house they were raiding was a very smart six-bedroom detached, set in its own grounds in North Bristol.

There was a high wall all round and a large wrought-iron gate blocking their entrance. Two engineers with circular disc cutters soon made short work of this obstacle and the little army surged forward. When they came to the front door, four policemen went round the back of the property to block an exit that way. The front door bell was rung several times but no lights came on in the house and no one answered the bell. A large blue Jaguar car stood in the driveway, when it should really have been in its purpose-built garage.

'Break the door in,' commanded Solly.

It took a little while because like the front gate it was fortified. Metal bars ran latterly across the door and these were set in concrete. It took ten minutes to gain an entrance via the front door. The search party rushed forwards shouting as they did so an alarm: 'Police, Police.' They searched the rooms and when they burst into the main bedroom it was to find Justin Long and a young man sitting up in bed drinking tea.

'It looks like we have unwelcome company, Basil,' Justin said, putting his tea down.

Solly read him his rights, and told him the purpose of their visit.

'And who says I have been selling drugs? I have done no such thing,' said Justin, full of confidence.

'We have it on good authority from one of your pushers, who is facing a charge of possession and dealing. He named you as his supplier. Now either you show us where you keep it or we take the place apart until we find it.'

'Go ahead, there's nothing here.'

'Right, men, search the place inside and out to find incriminating evidence.'

Immediately, wardrobes and cupboards were opened and searched, everything being dumped on the bed. Justin could see the police meant business and were not going to give up.

'Alright, alright. I admit it. The drugs are in the garage, and the money in the safe.'

'Open it,' demanded Mitch.

Justin put his nylon dressing gown on and fluffy slippers and indicated they should follow him. In the dining room, hidden behind a large Rembrandt painting was the safe. Justin unlocked it and stood aside. Bundles and bundles of money were hauled out of the safe. In the garage was found two large bags of white powder which passed the taste test to show it was cocaine.

'There's a lot of money here,' said Solly.

'Yes, I was just about to buy another consignment. Now you have messed the whole deal up.'

'It's going to remain that way for a long time, I'm afraid. Read him his rights, Mitch, and put him in the car.'

Solomon turned to a uniformed officer. 'Secure the property inside and out.'

The convoy returned to base, and Justin Smith was put in a cell in the police station. He was charged with drug dealing and sent to Wandsworth prison to await his trial.

'We're getting a bit crowded in the cells, sir. All six of them are full,' said Wendy.

'It's surprising what one uncovers from crime to crime, how one crime can lead to another, isn't it sir?'

'Yes, Mitch,' said Solomon, taking his coat off. 'One needs some luck, and a lot of skill. But we are still no further in solving those five murders.'

Josh came into Solomon's office. 'Well done, Solly, that was some very good police work catching that drug dealer. Just relax. I feel sure you will find your murderer soon,' said Josh, patting him on the back.

*

The next morning Solly and Mitch continued their interviews. As they entered the police station they could hear a lot of banging on cell doors from people who wanted their freedom.

'We have brought Ronny Long in, sir,' said DI Collins.

'He's changed his name back to Jerry White after his divorce,' said Solly. 'That is his proper name. His sons are keeping the name of Long. I know it's confusing but I can't make them change.'

'I wonder why they're doing it,' said Simon.

'Perhaps it's to confuse us. Has Justin gone to prison awaiting trial?'

'Yes sir. We're still waiting for the Crown Prosecution to confirm they will try him.'

'That could take weeks. So we have Johnny Long and his father Jerry White waiting to be interviewed.'

'Yes sir. We found a lot of evidence at his house.'

'Did you get the list of his customers and their addresses?'

'Yes sir and we found a hammer head.'

'Is Jerry White in the interview room?'

'Not at the moment. He's waiting in his cell.'

'Bring him in ten minutes. We should be ready for him then.'

*

Josh met Solly in the corridor of the police station.

'How's it going?' he asked.

'Very well sir, I ...'

'You still haven't got the killer, have you, Solly.'

'No sir, but we are almost there.'

'I want results Solly, not empty promises. I can't stand the pressure from the top. Be a good chap and solve it this week because there won't be a next week,' said Josh, walking into his office.

'I want DI Collins, yourself and Sergeant Mitchell in my office directly after the interviews, said Solly to Wendy, as she entered one of the interview rooms.

'Yes sir, I will tell them,' she said.

Once they were all assembled and seated, Josh opened the meeting.

'How many suspects have we got?' asked Solly.

'Well, two definitely sir,' said Mitch

'Have they all got the same motive?'

'It seems that way.'

'And have they the opportunity?'

'Yes sir,' replied Wendy.

'So now we have to find which one it is, and the evidence to prove it.'

'Have we got the register of their food deliveries?'

'Yes sir, we have,' said Wendy.

'Please read what it says,' said Solly.

'Ah yes! Here we are. First we have the date and the customers name and address. Next is the food required and time of delivery. Then at the end a signature of who delivered it. It's all there,' said Wendy. They all agreed.

'I expect you noticed that all five of the women murdered are on their list of customers, though not on the same night they went missing,' observed DI Collins.

'Are we going to accept the fact that only one man committed the crime,' asked Mitch.

'We still have no concrete evidence as to who did it. Forensic has a bag of paper cuttings which might be of some help. Johnny lives with his father. We have yet to check Johnny's room. It is being done today. We know he hates his own mother for what she did and whether he was responsible for murdering her with that water ski in Tenerife we will never find out. He does, however, have a dislike for women who play away from home; though whether it is a strong enough hate to kill is not beyond question,' advised Solly. 'Let's see what the interviews bring forth. Collins, you and Wendy interview Jerry White. Watch him, he is a tricky character.'

Chapter 25

'WHAT THE HELL is the meaning of this?' shouted the big Scotsman to Solly, as he entered the interview room. 'I have better things to do than come here to help you solve murders. You should have done that month's ago,' he bellowed in disgust, as he was shown a seat on the opposite side of the table to the detectives.

Solly opened the interviewed. 'You are not being charged, Mr MacDonald, you are here helping us with our enquiries. I know you have the café, and you told us that you deliver hot food in the area, is that right?'

'Aye.'

'I am showing Mr MacDonald a hardback lined book as Exhibit A

'Is this the book you write all your orders in and who delivers them?'

'Aye.'

'Who does these deliveries?'

'Me of course.'

'Anyone else?'

'Aye, there's wee Johnny Long and his father helps sometimes.'

'Does he get you to do his deliveries?'

'When his van isn't working. Also he sells pizzas, which I don't, so I help him with his deliveries.'

'So there could be both of you out at night delivering.'

'That's right. I have known him hire a van when we were busy.'

'You have your van back from the Forensic department.'

'Aye, I have.'

'Have you got a hammer?'

'I have somewhere out the back. Do you want to borrow it?' he laughed. Solly ignored him.

'We found your toolbag in the van, Mr MacDonald. I am now handing Exhibit B to Mr MacDonald,' said Solly. 'Do you recognise it as yours?'

'Aye. I do. Johnny's father gave it to me when he sold his van. I hadn't got any tools.'

'I haven't got any more questions for Mr MacDonald. Have you, Sergeant Mitchell?'

'I see, thanks no further questions.'

'Yes sir, may I?'

'This tool bag – have you looked inside it to check what's in there?'

'No I haven't even opened it.'

'We would like to have a look at the contents.'

'Feel free. It's back at the café. You can pick it up when you drop me off,' laughed Big Mac.

'Thank you for your help, you are free to go,' said Solly. The tool bag was collected and taken to the Forensic Department. Solly didn't want to interview Jeremy White until the tool bag had been examined. He had asked that the tool bag be given preferential treatment because of the intended interview. The report was on Solly's desk the following morning. He read it through and handed it to Mitch, before telling Josh.

Once Big Mac had left, and the room was empty, Solly told Mitch to come with him and watch the interview in Room 2, through the two-way glass. When they arrived, Josh was already there, watching the interview by the two junior detectives. The interview was well under way when the detectives arrived.

DI Collins had the forensic report for the tool bag before he started the interview on Jerry White.

'What else do you do besides run the Wicked Elf pub?' asked DI Collins.

'I used to, I don't now,' Jerry replied. 'I sold up and left.'

'What other sideline had you?'

'Making and selling pizzas.'

'Did you deliver them?'

'Yes.'

'So you knew the names and addresses of all your customers in this book.'

'Yes.'

'What do you do now?'

'I'm retired.'

'What did you do with your van?'

'I sold it for scrap.'

'What did you do with the tool kit.'

'I gave it to Big Mac.'

'Did you clean it out carefully before doing so.' Jerry's face reddened.

'I don't know what you mean.'

'When did you give it to him?'

'About three weeks ago.'

'Yes.'

'After the death of Betty Hedges?'

'I don't remember when she died.'

'According to this ledger you were delivering a pizza to her that day.'

'Was I? I don't remember.'

'It's got cancelled written by the side of it. Is that your writing?'

'Ah yes I remember.'

'But you went out in the van anyway, didn't you?'

'I might have. I don't remember.'

'Let me remind you, Mr White. You went out, and instead of delivering a pizza, you killed this lady with a hammer, stripped her naked, cut off a lock of her hair and threw her in the river,' said DI Collins.

'Don't be ridiculous,' replied Jerry White.

'When we searched your house we found a plastic bag with shredded paper. I am holding Exhibit C up to show the witness. Do you recognise it?'

'It looks like mine, though one bag of shredded paper looks like another. I don't think you have a shred of evidence there, smiled Jerry. Some smiled, everyone else said nothing to this pun.

'It has taken the police a long time to go through that paper and find it was the shredded remains of a poem you sent Detective Chief Inspector Solomon.'

'I don't see how you can prove that,' said his attorney.

'Quite simple. I will explain: Forensic are certain that the cuttings of shredded paper are the same as a small sliver of paper found between the blades of the scissors you included in the toolkit you gave Jim MacDonald. Furthermore, Forensic found that although the tool kit bag had been cleaned out, there were minute particles of hair which match those of Fiona Walters, Brenda Marlow and Betty Hedges.'

He handed a copy of the report to Jerry's solicitor.

'That still does not prove that my client carried out the murders, Inspector,' said his attorney, rather weekly.

'It wouldn't on its own, but a thumb print of Mr White's clearly shows up on the scissors. He was careless at the very end, when cleaning the tool kit to hand to Jim MacDonald, though the particles of hair in the tool kit is the most damming evidence. He even tried to incriminate Mr Macdonald by sending poems that the murders could have been committed by him. Plus the hammer we recovered with Big Mac's DNA on. Read him his rights, Sergeant Morrison, and charge him with the murder of the three women whose hair was found in the tool kit – namely, Fiona Walters, Brenda Marlow and Betty Hedges,' said DI Collins as he left the room. Wendy did as she was told.

'Take him to his cell, Constable,' said Wendy.

In the side room watching the proceedings Solly, Josh and Mitch were over the moon to have charged the culprit. Congratulations were in order all round. DI Simon Collins was congratulated for the grand job he did in the interview. They all agreed it had been a very satisfying day.

*

'Why are you looking so glum? When you should be celebrating,' asked Josh.

'I'm not happy sir, I think we've missed something.'

'What do you mean? Got the wrong man?'

'Yes.'

'Why is that?'

'It's a gut feeling that everything went too smoothly.'

'Well, Solly, you have interviewed all three men. I thought you were satisfied.'

'No, I feel there is a cover-up, it all went too easy.'

'Well, you better be quick. We have the press and television here in two hours,' said Josh, leaving Solly deep in thought as he left his office to return to his own.

'You alright sir,' asked Mitch.

'No I'm not. I want to interview Johnny Lock again.'

'Why sir?'

'I think there is a cover-up for him.'

'But the evidence is overwhelming; remember the thumb imprint on the scissors.'

'I have taken all that into consideration. I have made my mind up. I want you, me and Johnny Long in the interview room in half an hour. Get his lawyer over here right away.'

'Yes sir,' said Mitch, going off to do just that.

In the interview room was Solly, Mitch, Johnny and his solicitor.

Once the formalities were complete, Solly started the questioning.

'Do you like poetry, Johnny?'

'No!' he replied.

'That's strange because Mr MacDonald told me that the poems framed in his café were written by you.' Johnny didn't answer.

'Do you deny that?'

'No comment,' he replied.

'We have been informed that the box of tools found in Big Mac's van belonged to you. Do you deny that?'

'No comment.'

'We have also been informed that you carried them on your van when you went out delivering,' said Solly.

Johnny didn't reply. Even when Solly produced the tool bag as evidence Johnny said nothing.

'Your refusal to answer questions isn't helping your case, Johnny. Do you realise your father is being charged with these murders. What have you to say to that? Do you want him sent to jail for crimes that you committed? It was you who committed these murders, wasn't it. You killed your mother with the water ski machine.'

'It was an accident,' he blurted out in his defence.

'Why did you cut pieces of the women's hair off when you killed them?'

'No comment.'

There was a knock on the door and Wendy looked in. She apologised and asked to speak to the Chief Inspector. Solly knew it must be relevant to the case and went outside to speak with her. On his return the interview was restarted.

'We have searched your rooms at your father's house and found your computer, Johnny. We have also found an exercise book with the hair clippings of the women you killed. On your laptop computer we found for sale items of jewellery which belonged to the ladies you murdered. We have you cold. I am charging you with the murders of the four ladies: Fiona Walters, Brenda Marlow, Mary Dagleash and Betty Hedges. Have you anything to say?'

It was most unlike the man, but he suddenly burst into tears.

'My dad didn't do them, he was covering for me.'

'Do you want to make a statement?'

He shook his head. 'They were whores just like my mother, they deserved to die.'

'We will change your father's charge to being an accessory to the murders.

'What about Big Mac? Does he get away with it scot free?'

'Yes, he is clear of any prosecution in this case .He proved conclusively he was not connected to the murders. Why do you ask?'

'Because he was the one who gave me the tip-off if any of the women who visited his café were playing away, you know what I mean – having affairs. Without his help I couldn't have done the murders. In fact, he was the one who suggested that I murdered them.'

'Did he actually get involved with the murders?'

'No, he just told me some good leads to follow up. He also helped to lead false trails for the police, by hiring vans, changing number plates and delivering food at night so I was fee to commit murders.'

'So there were three of you involved.'

'Yes.'

'Detective Sergeant Mitchell, bring Big Mac in. It looks like we have a full house,' said Solly.

Josh had been watching the proceedings through the two-way mirror. When Solly had charged Johnny Long, he was delighted. At lasts a positive result. It had been a hard task trying to solve the murders. He smiled at Solly as he exited the interview room.

'Congratulations, you did a splendid job, you and your team.'

'Thank you sir. I must admit at one stage I thought we would never solve those murders, there were many false trails.'

*

It was four weeks later that Solly called Mitch into the office.

'Did you enjoy your holiday. Mitch?'

'Yes! We both did.'

'So did I. Now, what we want is a good murder to solve,' said Solly with a grin

'I'm sorry sir. I can't see it being till our next novel.'

An answer to which they both laughed their heads off.

www.ingramcontent.com/pod-product-compliance
Lightning Source LLC
Chambersburg PA
CBHW060922180626
46817CB00004B/1359